RIVIERA

RIVIERA

Matt Raskie

Burnham Press

Burnham Press – Atlanta, Georgia

Printed in the United States of America

Library of Congress Control Number: 2015905418

ISBN-10: 0-692-42345-1
ISBN-13: 978-0-692-42345-5

BurnhamPress.com

To Rebecca and Jedediah

CHAPTER ONE

Nick Duncan finished fastening his cufflinks through his sleeves and stepped into the white light of the moon to check his watch. It was half past nine. He moved quietly to the side of the open deck and looked down into the glittering reflections in the water as he reached for a cigarette and a light in his breast pocket. The sky above was immensely clear, and the silent lights from the high hills of Monaco lay before him like an audience waiting to hear him sing. He took a deep breath and ran his fingers through his damp hair and felt the freshness and warmth of the late spring night move through him. The stars above reflected the city lights and beamed them back down onto him as he stood ready to perform.

"You look nice, Mr. Duncan," came a strong voice from behind him on the deck. Nick turned to find the captain making his final rounds before taking off for the night.

"Oh, thanks Burke," said Nick with a smile. "Didn't see you there."

"Just finishing up, sir." The captain turned to go up the stairs to the bridge deck above.

"Has the taxi been called?" Nick asked.

"It has, sir. It should be here any minute."

"Thanks," he said with a nod.

The captain paused just a moment to see if there were anything else. "Well," he said, "good night, Mr. Duncan."

"G'night, Burke."

Nick turned back to look out over the surrounding city and patted down the breast of his tuxedo as he took a breath from his cigarette. He leaned against the wooden rail and could still taste the gin from the afternoon drink in his breath even now. After another minute, the short sound of the horn from the taxi interrupted the silence and echoed in the clear night air around the harbor. Nick looked up and took a last deep breath from the cigarette, then pulled it from his lips. He tossed it into the water below with a glowing hiss.

The long dock that took him up to the waiting sedan was lined with brilliant yachts he knew very well from his many seasons here. Some were owned by good friends. Nearly all he had been aboard, but perhaps was unsure if he had ever met their owners. Yet there had been many weekends along the French and Italian coasts aboard the *Yallah* and the *Miradora*, which he passed now. The *Ouranos*, a tall sailing yacht, was owned by a man named Stavos—a silly little Greek man who Nick had just met last year. Nick had never actually seen her leave the harbor. The *Miradora* was owned by a man he had met when he had first arrived in Monaco five years before named Benicio Prado, a man whose family money had been made in the Brazilian rubber trade and who was well liked for the lively parties he threw aboard. Both yachts were slightly larger than Nick's, and quite older but very well kept. They had been purchased from fortunes amassed over many generations past. Nick, however, had had his built new in Massachusetts before crossing the Atlantic with her. He had been very particular, and he had been involved in every aspect of her design.

At the end of the dock, he climbed into the cab that would take him to the Brecards' party high up in Monte-Carlo. "*Au Casino, s'il vous plaît*," he told the driver. The man nodded without speaking and began his way up. Nick leaned over and checked his watch again in the light from the window. He didn't want to arrive too late, but he also wouldn't let himself feel rushed. He sat back comfortably and closed his eyes, still feeling the sleep he had recently left behind.

The Brecards were a young French couple with old money who had taken a brief but genuine interest in Nick the year before. Nick had met the wife Michelle at a dinner party late in the season where both had been invited as single parties. Nick had sensed they were being set up by the hostess, but it quickly became clear that he had been invited simply to fill the table when Nick caught sight of Michelle's immense engagement ring. When they found themselves neglected by the rest of the party who were all much older, they turned to each other and to the wine to make it a more enjoyable evening. Michelle was unmistakably and frantically in love with her fiancé who had just proposed before leaving for a week on family business, but she didn't allow it to consume their conversation. She asked Nick every question she could think of and discovered that he lived aboard one of the yachts in the harbor. She was fascinated by this. Upon the fiancé's return, Nick took the young couple out for a day off Cannes, but he had not seen or heard from them since that outing, until he'd found an invitation waiting for him at the Hôtel when he had arrived in Monaco earlier that afternoon.

The cab ride to the Casino was short. The car took him up winding streets in front of offices and apartments, shops and hotels, all beautifully adorned. There were few cars on the street tonight. He felt as though the whole world had forgotten about him.

The driver let him out in front of the Casino, where there were small crowds and several limousines. Before Nick was barely out of the taxi, another couple had entered, and the driver was off again with his new fare.

The Casino building stood as a beacon in the night. Immense in its brightness and beauty of design, it stood high above the sea with an elegant, commanding presence. Tonight it had attracted more people than he had seen throughout the rest of the city, and there were small groups here and there whose brightly colored clothing and shimmering jewelry played with the light from the shops and restaurants. This was where everyone in Monaco was tonight. There were handsomely dressed couples coming and going between the cars in the street from the hotels and the Casino. Nick passed a pair of young girls with a wink as he crossed toward the Hôtel de Paris. A limousine came to a sharp stop in front of him, only nudging him a little with its fender. He and the driver smiled to each other with a laughing wave, and he stepped up onto the sidewalk. He checked his watch again as he entered the Hôtel, wondering why at all he felt anxious. That afternoon he had fallen asleep while reading, and when he had awakened and seen that it was already dark, he showered and dressed quickly without eating. Now he was a bit glad he felt late. Eager was more like it. It was the perfect time to arrive.

After a brief conversation, half in English and half in French, the man at the desk called up to the room and then notified Nick that he was expected. Nick could hear the sounds of the party through the receiver. The man gave Nick the number, but he already knew it: "701," he said under his breath along with the attendant.

"*Merci*," he told the man and walked up the steps to the elevator.

The lobby of the building was dressed in marble, wood, and brass. It was almost empty now except for the man at the desk and a few other men waiting by the door, but the colors warmed him, and there was the faint, sweet scent of cognac in the wood and of perfume in the air. A young woman in a dark blue dress stood alone in front of the polished brass doors of the elevator holding a small silver purse. Nick nodded and said good evening to her in French to be polite, then faced the doors, waiting for them to open. In the golden reflection of the elevator doors he noticed that his tie was a little off, and he tried to adjust it the best he could in the dull reflected light. He also could not help admiring his own reflection for a brief moment. He filled out the tuxedo well. Being tall—well over six feet—with a broad chest and shoulders that had allowed him to compete as a swimmer in his college days, he liked the way he looked when he dressed up. Though the woman next to him might also be considered tall, she seemed minute standing next to him in the reflection.

The doors of the elevator opened. Nick turned to the girl and motioned for her to enter. He followed her in and caught a glimpse of her eyes as she turned around with a smile. She was quite stunning, he thought. Her dark hair flowed to the center of her back; her diamond earrings glittered and caught his eye from the dulled golden light in the ceiling. His eyes flashed toward her hands as he glanced downward to see if she were wearing a ring, but her white satin gloves covered her fingers.

The doors closed and he saw that the button for the seventh floor was already pressed. There was a mirrored panel in the back of the elevator, and Nick had noticed on his way in that his tie had already tilted to the left again. He turned around and tried to fix it. The young woman saw him struggling to get it straight.

"I can do it," she said timidly in English with a French accent as she reached out to hand him her small purse. She must have been able to tell from his accent that he was an American, thought Nick. Perhaps she had heard the conversation with the man at the desk.

"Thank you," he said in English, then remembered himself. "*Merci.*"

As she reached up to adjust his tie with her delicate hands, he glanced down into her large, silver-blue eyes. Flawless skin—not a single freckle. Perfectly symmetric nose. He noticed things like that. She smelled sweet from her perfume. Their eyes met for an instant and they both tried to look away but couldn't. Nick felt the rush to his face and tried not to show it. But then the elevator stopped with a jolt, and Nick looked up at the floor number. It was on four. The doors opened and an older woman carrying a small terrier stepped on in front of them. The doors closed, the woman pressed a button, and the elevator went up one floor where the doors opened again. She smiled back at them as she turned down the hall and was gone, the terrier growling softly at them from the woman's arms the entire time. Once again, the elevator continued upward.

After a silent pause, Nick turned to the girl. "How do you know the Brecards?" he asked. He knew they were both going to the same party. The Brecards' suite took up half the seventh floor.

She smiled. "I went to school with Michelle. To *le lycée*. When we were both young."

Nick nodded. "Are you meeting someone here?" he asked.

"No," the girl shrugged, "I came alone."

Nick paused for a moment. He took a breath for a quick flash of courage. "I came alone, too," he said. "Would you like to be my date, then?" he laughed uneasily. The way he had said this seemed so loud and abrasive compared with the girl's soft voice that she saw his face go red again. And she was indeed a girl, Nick thought, not yet a woman. She looked so young there, and he could see this now as his eyes remained on her. She smiled.

"I don't even know your name," she laughed shyly with her lovely accent.

"My name is Nicholas." He reached out his hand for hers. "Nick, really."

"Hello, Nee-cholas," she said. "My name is Aurelia."

He paused as if expecting her to say something more. The elevator came to an abrupt stop, and the doors opened to the seventh floor and a long, ivory-colored hall.

"Nice to meet you, Aurel..."

"Aurelia," she repeated more slowly.

"Nice to meet you, Aurelia." He said her name assuredly as if he were forming some sort of bond that would protect them as they stepped out into the rest of the world. He shook her hand for a second in an awkward exchange, then led her down the hall.

The two approached the Brecards' door in the hallway and could hear the boisterous sounds from the party inside as they walked from the elevator. Nick knocked on the door lightly, and they waited a few seconds. No one answered. Then he knocked again with a little more force, and the door opened slightly, letting out the sounds of the party. He carefully pushed it open for Aurelia to walk in, and the sounds of the party came pouring out. The girl hesitated for a second. Timidly, she took Nick's arm and slipped her own through his. She smiled up at him as they stepped into the doorway together, and Nick struggled to keep the smile from his face. It was only his first evening back in Monaco, but he knew this was the only place in the entire world he wanted to be.

The room before them was crowded with magnificently dressed couples. A woman standing near the door was adorned with diamonds on her ears and around her neck. A single large sapphire stood out against her skin at the end of a silver pendant. The man she was speaking with was evidently captivated by her and hung drunkenly on every word. Another girl beyond them wore a delicate green dress that showed her tan arms and back. Her brown hair had been lightened from days in the sun. Beyond her were several couples equally ornamented in gold and silver that shone above their brightly-colored dresses and black tuxedoes. A thin cloud of smoke hung above the room and added something to each of the senses. Nick did not immediately recognize anyone among the blurry mob, nor did he see the hosts, but a few others recognized him instantly. A man yelled his name from a corner of the room, and he turned to see the man named Stavos who owned the tall sailing yacht in the harbor. The man swam toward him through the crowd, using his upturned cigar as a guiding light.

"*Salut*, Nick!" the man said in a thick Greek accent and slapped Nick on the shoulder. Stavos shook his hand briskly but looked at once to the girl next to him.

"Hello, Stavos," said Nick. "This is Aurel…"

"Yes, we've met before," said the man, smiling with a wide grin that showed all of his teeth.

"Good evening, Mr. Stavos," said Aurelia.

"*Enchanté*," he laughed as he blew the dark smoke from his cigar between his lips high above the crowd. "Can I get you both a drink?" he asked. "Everyone is drinking champagne, of course."

"Sure," said Nick. "We'll have a glass."

"Or an *apéritif*. Which would you like?"

"I'd like champagne," answered Aurelia as she slipped off her gloves.

"I'll have one, too," said Nick.

Stavos flagged down one of the servers darting through the crowd and acquired three glasses of champagne, which he held in shaky hands. The light golden color and shiny bubbles complemented the colors of the apartment and the spirit of the people around them.

"*À votre santé!*" Stavos shouted as they raised their glasses and took a sip. The man downed his all at once.

Nick felt the drink on his tongue, and it made him smile as it tingled. But the other senses of the party were overwhelming. Before he knew it, Stavos had swum off to talk to another couple across the room in the opposite corner from which he had come. Nick and Aurelia were soon left alone in the center, surrounded by everyone there.

"I'd like to find Fabien and Michelle and say hello," he said to the girl, trying not to shout. She nodded in agreement. As they wandered through the crowd of people, Nick smiled at friends he recognized but did not stop to talk. He had forgotten all their names. The pair bumped into other couples in the packed suite, and Aurelia reached up and took Nick's hand in hers so they would not get separated. Nick looked back at her with a quick, assuring smile.

"Over there!" Aurelia pointed out to Nick across the room.

They found the Brecards just inside the open doors near the balcony that looked out over the Casino in the direction of the Plage du Larvotto. Michelle was speaking with a couple that Nick did not recognize, her husband Fabien at her side.

"*Bon soir*, Fabien," Nick said to the host as they approached. He smiled at the hostess. "Good evening, Michelle," he said and bowed his head.

"Oh, hello, Nick!" Michelle shouted and smiled. She reached up and wrapped her arms around his neck and kissed him heavily on the cheek. "I was afraid you had forgotten it was tonight. Or maybe you hadn't arrived just yet."

"I made it all right," he said. "I hope you don't think me rude by showing up so late. My nap this afternoon ran a little long."

They all laughed, and Nick blushed at his mention of it.

"Not at all," said Fabien. "You're here now, aren't you?" Nick and Fabien shook hands firmly. It had been a year, but now they remembered each other well.

Michelle looked next to Nick and saw that Aurelia was holding his arm. "And you brought me my Aurelia!" she shouted happily. The two women embraced and kissed each other on the cheeks. "I knew you would make it." She looked up at Nick. "Did you come together?"

"We met in the elevator," Aurelia answered. "Neecholas so kindly offered to accompany me."

"How sweet of him!"

"Do you know Alex and Ariane?" Fabien asked Nick as they both turned to the other couple standing before them. Nick had not met them before. They all shook hands and introduced themselves. Alex was a tall man, almost as tall as Nick, and looked sharp in his tuxedo. He was very thin. He had light hair and a handsome face. His wife was blonde and looked rather homely, but was pretty there in her burgundy dress.

"We'll catch up with you two later," the man said to Fabien in French. "Nice to meet you, Nick." The couple smiled and bowed and wandered off to fill their drinks.

"What business is he in?" Nick asked as they walked away.

"I don't know!" Fabien laughed. "Maybe he's a bum, just like all of us!"

It was not a serious question that Nick had asked him. One didn't speak about business here. It was a joke that had developed between them the year before from a discussion about American society. Americans were always so concerned about what someone did for a living. A man's business in America defined him. But that simply did not matter here. And it certainly was not talked about.

"When did you get in?" Michelle asked Nick as he and Aurelia closed the circle.

"I arrived here just this afternoon. The trip from Ibiza was nice; took a few days longer than I thought. I stopped in at Barcelona along the way—a bit of a detour, you might say."

"Of course!" laughed Fabien. "A detour for sure."

"I absolutely loved going out on your boat last summer," said Michelle. "I wish we had one of our own." She gave a sly look toward her husband that at the same time had an air of innocence. "Something small, maybe?"

Fabien laughed. "That's something I'll have to look into. But I can't swim," he winked.

"I was glad to get into port here," continued Nick. "It always feels good to tie up in Monaco."

There was a glance between Nick and Aurelia that showed she was more comfortable now. Nick also felt much more relaxed.

"What is it like to live on the ocean?" asked Fabien. "Besides getting seasick, I think it would feel like you don't have a home."

Nick laughed. "Not at all! Every place I go is my home, for a few weeks anyway. Monaco is my home now, until the season is over. You can take your home with you. I'm a vagabond, you know, a bum like everyone here," he said with a grin. With this, Nick could start to feel his first glass of champagne, and it made him beam.

"Nick is a bit of a sensation," said Michelle to Aurelia. "He's too restless to settle down in one place."

Nick laughed. "And what's so wrong with that?"

"Most people travel a few times every year," said Fabien to Aurelia. "Michelle and I are only down from Paris for a few weeks. But Nick, he never stops traveling. He's on an eternal holiday. One day he's here in Monaco, and then you never see him again for a year. He could be in Rome, or Gibraltar, or Alexandria. You never know…"

"I think it's fantastic!" interrupted Aurelia. "I would love to see more of the world. I've never even left Europe."

"Besides," continued Fabien, "you're getting older, Nick," he said jokingly with a hand on Nick's shoulder. "Isn't it time you settled down like Michelle and me?"

They all laughed at this while Nick blushed, partly from the attention on him and partly from the champagne. Fabien and Michelle were a very young couple. They were only in their early twenties and had already been married nearly a year. Nick was a few years older, but he knew they were only kidding him. Even though he felt embarrassed, part of him adored the attention.

A server came behind Aurelia and exchanged their half-empty glasses for full ones. Nick took a sip of the champagne and sensed that it was cooler and sweeter than the first glass.

"Drink as much as you like," said Michelle. "We bought too many bottles."

"You mean that *I* bought too many bottles," said Fabien. "I found a great bargain and couldn't pass it up. I bought four whole cases—the big ones, you know."

"I couldn't believe it!" cried Michelle. "We have no room for so many bottles!"

"You'll have to have another party," Aurelia smiled, "just to get rid of it all."

"Make sure you take a bottle or two, Nick," said Fabien, "when you leave, I mean. Get it from one of the waiters. I'd like to give some of it away."

"Sure," said Nick. "Thank you. Then you can come over and we'll open it on the boat."

As the conversation continued, Nick felt a pair of eyes on him from across the room. He had felt the eyes on him since he had entered the party. He did not look over, but Michelle could tell he was uneasy. Still, he tried to ignore it.

"It's Richard, isn't it?" she finally asked him as her eyes moved across the room to see the man standing there.

"It's nothing," said Nick.

"I didn't invite him tonight, Nick," she said. "Someone brought him. I didn't mean to…"

"It's fine, Michelle," interrupted Nick. "Really, it's all right." As he said this, he looked over and met Richard's eyes for the first time through the crowd and stared directly back at him. The man across the room scoffed and turned away.

"Don't mind him," said Fabien. "He thinks he's better than everyone here. Thinks he's royalty or something. Never worked a day in his life."

"I'm fine," said Nick to reassure them. "Really." He wasn't as upset as they thought he was. A few moments later, he was fine.

Nick passed the glass of champagne to his other hand and relaxed his arm by his side. He felt himself brush against Aurelia. She looked up and smiled.

"Are you going out sometime this week?" asked Michelle to change the subject. "I'd love to go swimming away from the beach where the water's cooler. I like the cooler water."

Nick thought for a moment. He had no definite plans, as he'd just arrived. "I'll take you out whenever you stop by," he replied. "I'll be your captain for the day."

"That's nice of you, Nick," said Fabien. "We'll bring lunch along."

"Great!" said Nick. "We'll make it the four of us." He turned and nodded to Aurelia. She smiled in reply.

The party was starting to get warm from the mass of people in the apartment. As Nick and the girl talked with the Brecards, elbows and shoulders bumped cheerfully into them, and he didn't really mind, as long as there was cold champagne in his glass. He felt Aurelia's body against his as people passed and as the crowd swayed with the music. The cooler air coming in from the balcony chilled the sweat forming on his forehead and gave him some relief. The party moved in one fluid mass. If one person moved one way, the others moved to balance out the displacement. It was still comfortable, but the men wrapped tightly in their tuxedoes and the women braced up in their dresses breathed heavily in the warm evening.

"I need to open more windows," said Michelle. She felt it, too, even though she had the cool breeze at her back.

"I'll go with you," said Fabien. "We'll talk again tonight, Nick. Take care of Aurelia for us. Make sure she doesn't get stuck talking to anyone tiresome."

"Do my best," he said. "It was nice seeing you again Fabien, Michelle."

"You, too, Nick," replied Michelle.

Nick and the girl waved and drifted off among the conversations with the music hanging high above the crowd, enjoying the cool drinks and brilliant people around them, never finding themselves alone. An appealing menagerie of personalities displayed itself before them—an infinite collection for them to behold. One man, a man from Morocco with a supremely French accent, dark desert skin, and long dark eyelashes, told them excitedly of thoroughbreds he was raising to race at Longchamp in the fall. His glowing laugh betrayed the solemn look he exhibited on his face between smiles, and before long they found themselves invited to the races themselves and to his home if ever they visited Tangier. French and Italian couples spoke at length of the places from which they had just returned and where they were off to next and what places were good this time of year and what places were not. A girl from Cannes with her blonde hair held high on her head and who sipped a drink that matched the color of her dress asked them if they knew so and so, but they did not recognize the name, but maybe they knew a friend of hers. Men from far off countries endeavored in both finding a common language between them and in finding common interests of which to speak while their wives showed each other how bronze their skin had become from their trips to this place or that and talked eagerly about whose parties they had been to recently. Nick watched this and perceived that with the sounds of the party and the people around him no specific language was required but that the smiles and laughs and glances conveyed all that needed to be understood.

Young couples asked them if they were married, and when they said no they were asked when they would be, and Nick could not help but laugh at this as he had only met her no more than an hour or two before. There was the sweet smell of perfume among the warm bodies pressed to one another. The rush of servers in and out of the crowd. A high laugh that rose over the others around the room and above the music. The taste of champagne and cigarettes and cocktails. But Nick did not want to be there right now, and the young girl beside him could sense this, though he acted as though every person with whom he spoke were the most interesting person there. And with the soft touch of her small hand on his, they broke away from a man who had just finished telling them a joke, and they shook his hand politely and told him they were delighted to meet him and that they must say hello to friends they had not seen since last year who had just arrived.

Nick and Aurelia found their way through the party and walked out into the cooler air of the balcony that faced in the direction of the harbor and the Palace on the plateau high above it. It was as if they had escaped someplace, and they breathed a heavy sigh once outside. Below, they could see the rows of yachts and small fishing boats lined along the docks far down on the sea. She had not left his side since they had arrived. The lights from Monte-Carlo lit up the light haze that had settled over the water and glowed against the coast. Aurelia leaned against the balcony and looked out to the horizon as Nick offered her a cigarette.

"*Merci*," she said as she slid one out of his polished silver case and he lit it for her.

For a second, Nick thought about what Michelle and Fabien had said about him settling down somewhere and laughed at this to himself. He never liked to stay in one place too long—never felt comfortable unless there were someplace else to be. He could not occupy his mind with such thoughts just now because there was so much else out there to explore. He always enjoyed seeing the young couples filled with madness and love wherever he went, but that was not something he wanted for himself anymore. There was such hope in them, such desperation for one another. He saw it in Michelle and Fabien tonight.

Nick turned to the girl next to him and looked over her as she drew in a breath and blew the smoke far out toward the water. He heard a deep bell ring and resonate from the harbor, and the sound reached him and echoed moments longer in his mind. It was the same bell that had awakened him that evening. But there was nothing that could distract him from the girl's alluring brilliance, he thought as he studied her closely. Her luminous eyes had a radiance that no one among the party that night could match.

He lit a cigarette himself and leaned on the rail next to her. The end burned brightly as he inhaled and felt the warm air against the coolness of the evening that had descended as the sun had retreated. A lone car passed below them on the way up to the Casino. Its headlights lit up the street and flashed over a couple walking with loud tapping steps down the hill. It was good to get away from the sounds of the crowd inside.

"Who was that man in there?" she asked him, breaking the calmness.

"Just a man," Nick said coolly.

"You don't like him?"

"Well…he doesn't like me," Nick answered as he continued to look out over the water. He didn't want to talk about it, and Aurelia could sense this.

"You don't have a place here?" she asked.

"Oh, no," he said. "I got into Monaco just today."

"On your boat?" she asked.

"Yes." As he said this, he knew he had arrived in Monaco later than he had wanted. He had missed much already.

"What is the name of your boat?" she asked. She smoked her cigarette casually, but he could tell she had more questions for him.

"The *Diamant*," he said.

"What does it mean?"

Nick looked at her questioningly. "*Diamant. Dee-ah-mont*," he emphasized the syllables. "You know. It's French," he paused. "Dia-mond."

"Oh!" Aurelia laughed. *"Diamant!"*

Nick blushed. "Did I say it wrong?"

"Oh, no. Not at all. Your French is so wonderful!" she smiled.

"Thanks," he laughed. Nick took a long draw on his cigarette and felt the warmth move down into his chest. The smoke came out in a cool stream into the night air. There was a long period of silence.

"I've met you once before, you know," she said to him as she turned toward him against the rail. "I just remembered where."

Nick turned and looked at her to see if she were serious. They had both had a few drinks. "I thought I knew you from somewhere," he said, playing along and feeling the champagne in his head. "Where have we met before?"

"It was last summer," she said, "in Nice. I remembered it was you when I saw you downstairs."

Just as she said it, he thought he remembered her as well.

"I remembered your face in the elevator."

Nick thought for a moment. Something flashed in his mind. "It was at a restaurant near the beach, wasn't it?"

"You remember!"

"And you wore a green dress. I remember. You were with someone."

She turned away. "I was with a man I didn't like."

"I remember. He was mean to you, wasn't he?"

"He was a friend of my father."

Nick could tell she didn't want to revisit it. "I can't believe you remember me," he said.

"Of course I do. You were afraid to talk to me."

Nick smiled to himself. He and the young girl had caught each other's eyes at a party the summer before, but Nick didn't want to approach her until someone introduced them. She had looked so young then.

"You were very shy," said Aurelia, "but you were very cute."

"Cute," Nick laughed. "I was shy because you looked so nice and I wanted to talk to you," he said, embarrassed that he had said it. "But you were with someone, so I didn't want to intrude." He took a last draw on his cigarette and blinked a few times as he looked her over. He knew it was her by the way she smiled. The girl blushed. Nick flicked his cigarette off the balcony in a burst of bright ash. They both watched it float down to the curved street below and fade out of view.

"I wish you would have come over to talk to me," she said. "I wasn't having fun that night."

"No? But tonight you are?"

She smiled.

Nick reached into his jacket for another cigarette. He offered one to the girl and reached up to light them. But at that exact moment there was a loud commotion from inside. A woman screamed, and the roar inside dulled instantly. Nick grabbed Aurelia's hand and led her inside from the balcony. Everyone looked to the other side of the room. Fabien and another man were lifting a woman from the floor near the door to the other balcony that faced the beach.

"Someone drank too much!" Aurelia laughed over the silence.

Nick looked closer. It was Michelle in her husband's arms.

"Oh, Michelle!" cried Aurelia.

The two rushed over through the gathered crowd, hand-in-hand.

"What happened?" Nick asked Fabien as he helped him lift his wife.

"She fainted," he said in French as they lowered her onto a sofa that been had cleared at the edge of the room. "She said she needed some air, and she left while I filled our glasses. She didn't make it to the balcony."

"Is she sick?" someone asked.

"She said she felt hot."

Michelle's face was flushed, but she opened her eyes and said something in a weak voice.

"I'm right here," Fabien said as he held her hand firmly. "I'm right here."

"What happened?" she asked as she looked up and saw all the people gathered around her.

"You fainted," said Nick with a smile. He knew she was all right now.

"I couldn't breathe," she said weakly.

Most of the other guests had resumed their murmur in low voices and left the woman to rest on the sofa at the side of the room with those who attended to her. In a few minutes, Michelle had cold water to drink and a wet cloth across her forehead. She held the glass with both hands like a child.

"You'll be all right," Nick said. "We should get her to her room."

Fabien lifted her in his arms from the sofa while Nick and another man cleared the path to the bedroom through the crowd. Aurelia followed them into the room with the glass of water. Fabien laid her gently on the bed, and Aurelia took off her shoes. The other man opened the window, asked if there was anything else he could do, and then went back to the party.

"Oh, she'll be fine," said Fabien. "She just got a little hot." He turned and looked to his wife. "That's enough for tonight," he said. "No more champagne."

Michelle looked up at her husband and smiled. "*Viens-ici, mon amour,*" she said. "Come here, my love."

Fabien leaned over and kissed her on her cool lips.

"*Merci,*" she said softly and closed her eyes.

"I think she just needs to rest. Thank you, Nick, for your help."

"No problem," he said. "I think that's enough for me tonight, too," he announced. He could feel the champagne strongly in his head. "Thank you for the invitation." He shook Fabien's hand and smiled over to Aurelia who was at the bed comforting Michelle, then he turned to walk out of the room. Aurelia followed and caught him softly by his arm at the bedroom door.

"I think I should stay with her for a while," she said. "I hope you do not mind."

"Of course not," Nick smiled. He could not help but smile at how lovely she was there. "She needs a friend right now. I think she's more embarrassed than anything."

"Yes, I think so, too," she said, then she paused. "I want to see you again, if you'd like."

"I would, too," said Nick. "Of course." He looked at how delicate she was, standing there before him. "Look for me down at the harbor. Tomorrow, perhaps. The *Dee-ah-mont*, remember?"

Aurelia smiled. *"Le Diamant, oui."*

"You're welcome anytime. Or ask for me downstairs here at the Hôtel. That's the only way to reach me. Someone will know how to find me, one way or another. I'm not going very far."

"All right. Good night. *Bonne nuit, Nee-cholas,*" she said and smiled so that he would always remember that smile.

He bent down and kissed her lightly on her cool cheek. *"À bientôt,"* he said. "I will see you soon."

Nick turned and started toward the door through the immense crowd. On his way, he grabbed a glass of champagne from a server's tray and downed it quickly in a few sips as he walked. He had already had enough to drink, but he liked how fresh it felt. He stopped only briefly to wave goodbye to a friend and shake his hand, and before he knew it he was alone in the elevator heading down to the lobby.

"Funny," he said aloud as he emerged onto the empty street from the Hôtel, "Only here," he said. "Only this place."

Instead of calling a cab he walked out into the cool air coming in from the sea and down the hill to the harbor. He enjoyed the walk. He enjoyed seeing the familiarity of the place, though it had been many months since he had left. It seemed so unreal that he was back here again.

That night, after he returned to the *Diamant*, he lay awake and listened to the sounds of the harbor around him, but not for long. A warm glass of Scotch put him to sleep before he could reach up to turn off the light.

CHAPTER TWO

At the Gare de Monte-Carlo, the nine thirty-five morning train from Marseille was arriving six minutes late. The engineer had been held up leaving Vidauban because of a track change and was now trying to make up time between stations by increasing speed and rushing each stop. He had already made up ten minutes.

Down from one of the first class passenger cars stepped a handsome young woman in a light yellow dress. Normally this woman would have been instantly recognizable to anyone catching sight of her, except that she now wore a large hat and oversized sunglasses so that even the porter who helped her onto the platform with her single large suitcase did not know who she was. She was an American actress, born Miriam Stockton but known to the world as Miriam Banks. Her fourth major film had just been released across Europe and the United States the week before. For several minutes after the train had rushed on, the woman stood on the platform looking as if she were expecting someone to meet her. Then, realizing she was there alone, she picked up the heavy leather suit-case and stepped through the station and outside into the bright morning sun.

A phone call had been placed early the evening before from the Gare de Lyon in Paris to the Hôtel de Paris in Monaco, and a message had been left disappointedly with the concierge on duty. It was the only way she knew to reach Nick Duncan. And as Miss Banks thought about this on the short cab ride to the harbor, it was certain that Nick had not received the message.

"He's not here at all," she said to herself in the taxi. "He's not even here."

"Pardonnez-moi, madame?" asked the driver as he changed lanes to avoid a car stopped in front of a store.

"Oh, I was just talking to myself."

"Comment?"

She did not respond. Instead, she was consumed in her own thoughts. The city and the people passed by all around her, unnoticed. Miriam doubted that Nick was in Monaco and wondered why she was even here. She only guessed he might be since they had spent many of their springs and summers here together, and it was here where she had last seen him, and where it had all fallen apart. But that was years ago, she thought. And as she turned it all over in her head, she realized she never should have come.

The driver let her off at the edge of the long docks that stretched out into the harbor and offered to help her with her bag. She declined, but as she had no inclination that she'd find what she was looking for, she gave the man an extra bill and told him to wait in the car so that if she were not back in ten minutes he could leave. When she stepped out onto the dock with the blue water and the white yachts surrounding her, she was certain that Nick wasn't there— a worry that had absorbed her mind during the sleepless night on the train.

The first dock she walked along yielded no results. She walked all the way to the end and back, stopping several times, with nothing but mounting frustration. She remembered the boat well and knew she would not miss it if it were here. When she returned to the edge of the harbor, the taxi had gone, and she felt the tears well up in her eyes. But the second dock seemed more promising, as many of the larger yachts were here, and as she was still fifty yards away her heart rose as she was sure she saw the bridge of the *Diamant* rise minutely with a passing wave. She couldn't believe it. Nick was here after all! And she quickened her step despite her heels and the bulk of her suitcase.

High up on the second deck of the *Diamant*, Nick sat at
the table with yesterday's newspaper, having just finished
breakfast, sipping on a cool glass of Ricard, cloudy and
white in his glass, to fend off the oncoming warmth of
the day. He liked the way it hit him in the morning, and
he needed it. He read the paper with little interest and
idly scanned the headlines and captions, including a short
article about the lengthy delays in train service along the
coast that had been caused by the last days of the film festival in Cannes. Before him on the table lay some checks
he wanted to take to the bank and a few letters he meant
to send sometime that day. He would take them up himself instead of sending them with one of the crew. Around
him, several of the large motor yachts were preparing to
leave the harbor for the day on the sea, and the port was
already busy with boats coming and going.

He had awakened that morning with the light of the
sun peering into his cabin from a day calling for him to
emerge. His head felt heavy from the night before, and the
dry taste of cocktails and cigarettes lingered in his mouth.
It was the way he liked to feel in the morning, when he
knew he had not overdone it or overstayed his welcome.
He knew from the sun that the day would be bright and
warm. A hot shower perked his body as if he were ready to
jump into the ring with a heavyweight; his senses picked up
every sound, every movement around him, and he turned
quickly in the mirror as if ready to strike. There was the air
of anticipation around him, now that he had arrived, and

he felt alive today more than he had felt in a long time. His skin was starting to get dark. The weeks on the beaches of the Spanish coast and along the Mediterranean were tanning his body, and his hair had been lightened by the sun. He saw it in the mirror. His arms were thick, and his broad chest stood out firmly. He felt healthy here—far different from New York and the world he had left behind him many years ago, one to which he knew he no longer belonged.

He had eaten the breakfast that Elena the cook had prepared for him. As he ate, he had begun to scribble out a note for Aurelia in pencil that he would send to her hotel. He began it in English, then caught himself and crumpled it in his hands. On another piece, he started over in French, trying his best at the accent marks. When he had finished, he had gone below to find a pen, some better paper, and an envelope.

Some of the crew had been up early and were nearly finished washing the massive white hull of the *Diamant*. The bump of the buckets against the wood and steel, mixed with the sound and smell of spray from the hoses and soap running along the deck, made him feel happy. He heard the water run off into the harbor and churn in the water below.

Down in his cabin he had found the three checks in an envelope from New York that he had meant to deposit the day before, or the day before that, or even back in Spain. The envelope had been with him for weeks since

Barcelona, but he always neglected the mail. There was stationery in a drawer, and on the table next to his bed he had found a book he had been meaning to finish. He went up and sat back down at the table on deck and rewrote the note to Aurelia, and then he'd sent it up right away with one of the deckhands to Aurelia's hotel so that she might join him for lunch one day. Then he'd picked up the book and tried to read, but his mind was distracted. He had stayed a few extra weeks in Barcelona. April there had been warm and dry. There had been a liveliness there that he had not felt there before, and it had been hard to leave. In the evenings in Barcelona, he would venture into town and along the quay and meet friends for dinner and drinks or have guests aboard the *Diamant*. Each day played out the same, but it was as though he were trying to repeat a perfect day over and over. It was all one fluid dream to him—the beaches and the water, the city and her people. One day ran into the next, weeks melded together, and before long he had spent two months in Spain.

But it was always toward May that he felt drawn toward Monaco. The people who knew and loved this place best always arrived around this time. It was not the high season. Summer was the time that bathing beauties and expensive cars filled this place. But those who really knew came early for the season before the season—a time for the best weather and the absence of the crowds. He had learned early on here that this was the best time to truly enjoy this place. And so he came back year after year, sometimes staying on a few weeks into the summer after many of his friends had left.

Some of the same friends from Barcelona would be here now in Monaco. This is where the party had moved. He was one of the last to leave Barcelona, but he was glad he had stayed on as long as he had. His memory of the weeks in Spain was already fixed in his mind. It was a single complete moment that had been repeated many times over while he was there. The coarse sand against his skin; the sweet sting of the salt air; seagulls hovering silently above the boats; a young girl hopping by, holding her mother's hand as she counted the stones she stepped on. Mid-afternoon, he sat at a café along the row of tables that ran the edge of the Port Vell marina—empty tables set with the restaurant staff waiting for customers in their white uniforms. All the places had matching beige umbrellas and equally matching drinks and service, but the Emperador was the one where he and his friends spent most of their days. Once, he was humming along with a song on the radio when the waiter came up behind him humming the same song in time. Nick stopped and laughed at the boy who was embarrassed and served their drinks in silence. For their short duet, Nick left an extra tip for the boy who smiled and politely refused to accept it. But Nick left it on the table anyway and went away with his friends to walk along the beach with a bottle of wine.

The marina in Barcelona was lined with yachts and small fishing boats that swayed as small waves came through from the sea. From where Nick had sat at the café he could see the *Diamant* among the other boats. The moment in his memory was always disturbed by friends he sat with who were often deep in discussion, or by a couple he was with that was fighting insignificantly, only to make up once again when the wine had worn off; but still he had enjoyed being there, and it felt good to remember the place. Barcelona had always been a good place for him. He had been there at the beginning of every year for five years before moving along the coast to France. It was always a place he thought he might want to live, if he ever wanted to live somewhere. But he also loved to leave it so that he might come back to it again. Monaco was his home now, at least for the next few weeks until the end of the season here. And if there were any place he loved more than the Spanish coast, it was this place.

Nick lay down the newspaper he had been staring at for the last twenty minutes. He realized that he had absently read the same lines over and over and had not turned one page. He tried reading again, but was drawn back to the cool glass of pastis and took a long sip. As he did this, he heard a soft voice call up to him.

"Nick?" the voice came with a hint of despair.

He wasn't sure he had heard anything at first. He perked up his ears.

"Nick, darling? Are you there?"

Nick stood up slowly and went to the edge near the stern and looked down. He didn't immediately recognize the girl standing there. He raised his hand against the sun and squinted his eyes to make her out. With the hat and glasses, he thought it might be Aurelia from the night before, and he waved and called out hello to her. But as the girl crossed the gangway and climbed the ladder up to him, he suddenly realized who it was.

"I'll be damned," he said under his breath. As he heard her coming up the stairs to him, he took a long, slow sip from his glass.

"Starting early, I see," said Miriam with a laugh when she reached the deck with a pant, relieved to see Nick standing before her.

Nick looked at her without a word. His face was absent of expression.

"You don't recognize me?" She took off the hat and glasses and shook out her hair.

"Oh, of course I recognized you, Miriam. But I'm so used to seeing you on the screen now."

She laughed unamusedly and set the hat on the table. "Nick, you could always be so mean. You were good for that."

"No, I meant…," he began. He hadn't meant it that way.

Miriam moved over to the edge of the boat and looked around below. It all looked so familiar to her again.

"It's Miriam Banks now, I hear," said Nick behind her. "You married then?"

"Oh, of course not!" she laughed. "It's for the films. Everyone changes their names in Hollywood."

Nick stood for a moment. He wasn't sure of anything. He wasn't sure if this were real. He didn't even want to breathe. "How did you know I'd be here?" he asked, taking another sip from his glass.

"I didn't. I guessed."

"Well, you guessed right. Didn't know I was that predictable."

Miriam walked over to him and faced him with a smile. Nick didn't move. She was pretty there in the sun, the way he had always remembered her. She hadn't changed a bit. Then, with a rush, she reached up and threw her arms around his neck and kissed him, half on the lips and half on the cheek. "I'm so glad you're here," she said softly, almost at a whisper. "I knew you'd be here."

Nick held her there for a moment and felt her against him and smelled her familiar smell. It brought everything back to him all at once. He had not held her for two years.

"Your hair's so long," he said after she had taken a step back. He didn't know what else to say. "I've never seen it so long and so dark. It looks almost red! Or maybe it's the sun."

"No, it is a little red. It's for the movie," Miriam laughed.

"Well, how long have you been here?" he asked. He had moved to set his drink down on the table.

"I just got in this morning," she said. "Just now."

"Just now?"

"Uh huh."

"And where are you staying? Do you have a room up at the Hôtel?"

"No, not yet," she said. "I was thinking of getting a place there, but it might be booked up." At that, she remembered her suitcase she had left on the dock at the foot of the gangway. She had not even thought of where she might stay or what she might do if she had not found Nick here.

"No chance," said Nick. "You're staying here, of course. Besides, the Hôtel is all booked up for the race next week. All the decent hotels are. The teams have the rooms rented."

"But I wouldn't want to make you feel…," she began, but a look from Nick told her not to be ridiculous.

"You're here alone?" Nick asked. "I thought you were engaged to some bigwig Hollywood director." He winced at himself. He hadn't meant to say it that way. But he had seen the headlines.

"We called things off. I'm too busy with everything. We're shooting the new film up in Paris right now. But I wanted to get away to the sun. There isn't enough sun up there."

Nick nodded. Whatever it was that had brought Miriam to him again, he was glad for it. "And how long are you here?"

"Don't know. Maybe a few weeks anyway." She sat down at the table and took her hat again and threw it in the chair next to her. Nick found another glass at the bar and poured her a drink, watching the clear liquid become cloudy in the ice, and set the bottle back on the table next to him. But Miriam had found his glass and had taken half of what was left down right away. "If you want me to stay here," she said, "maybe I should get my things from below."

"Stay there and have your drink," Nick said as he took a sip of the one he'd just poured before setting it in front of her. "I'll take care of it." A minute later, Nick had brought her suitcase onto the deck below and had given it to one of the crew to make her up a room.

"You don't mind me being here, do you?" she asked. "Really, Nick?"

"No. No, of course. Not at all. You belong here." As he said it, she looked at him and smiled pitifully. It was as if the last two years had passed in an instant, but there would be things that would remain unsaid.

The two sat there and had their drinks in the sun. It was warm and they sat in silence, looking between one another and out to the scene around them. A biplane flew high above them where they could not see it in the light haze so high, and the sound of the engine seemed very distant. The ice in the glasses melted quickly and had to be replenished. Nick took a cigarette from a pack and lit it but only smoked half of it before putting it out.

"You're upset I came," said Miriam as she lit a cigarette for herself. "I can tell. You're so quiet."

"No, not at all," said Nick. He hadn't been thinking that at all. "No, of course not."

"You're glad to see me then? You're awfully quiet. But you always were, I guess."

Nick smiled without a word, and Miriam was glad that she had decided to come to him. She knew she could come to Nick.

The sound of distant footsteps from a couple on the dock came near, and then passed toward the edge of the harbor. There was silence again.

"Nick, you don't mind if I lie down for a bit, do you?" Miriam asked. "You wouldn't mind?"

Nick looked at his watch for no reason at all.

"I couldn't sleep at all on the train. Not a wink. I'm so incredibly tired."

"Of course," said Nick. "The place is yours. Completely yours. They're making a room for you below. I'm sure it's made up by now."

"Thank you," said Miriam. "I'll be more social once I've had a little sleep. I promise. I'm just a little tired is all."

"You're fine," said Nick. "The place is yours, really. Sleep all day if you'd like."

After another small drink, they went below into the cabin that had been made up for her. It was good to be out of the sun. Miriam ran her hand slowly and deliberately along the familiar wood of the walls below, down the hall and to her cabin, remembering this place.

"Turn around while I change," she said to him once they were in the cabin and Nick had helped her lay out her clothes on her berth.

"Yes, ma'am," he laughed and turned away. As she slipped off her yellow dress in front of the mirror, he turned halfway back around and leaned on a dresser to look at her without even attempting to hide it. He continued to watch her as she slipped everything off down to her underwear. Her arms reached high above her head and flowed down to her shoulders and around to her back. Her smooth skin ran down to her long legs and to the floor.

"I know you're watching me, Nick," she said without looking at him and without making a fuss.

"I know," he said. He finally turned away and played with something on the dresser as she sorted through some clothes to put on. "You don't mind?"

"I never did."

Nick looked at her again in a mirror and caught her eyes as she pulled a blouse over her head. She smiled and laughed to herself. She finished changing and began to run a brush through her hair.

"I'll leave you if you're tired." He looked at his watch. It was almost noon. "Will you want lunch when you wake up? Elena can make something."

"Sure. I don't know how long I'll sleep, but I am a little hungry."

"Do you want something now?"

"No. I'm too tired to be hungry now."

"All right. I'll go back up and leave you." He moved the rest of the things from the bed to a chair to make room for her. "Just don't sleep too long," he said. "Benicio is having a party tonight, and I'm sure he'd love to see you again."

"Oh! Benicio is here?" she asked excitedly.

"Of course he is. Nothing's changed since you left."

Miriam responded with a forced smile. She knew what he meant, even if he hadn't really meant it, and she was sorry for it.

Nick shut the door softly once she was lying down, and he left her below and went back up to finish his paper to keep himself occupied. But his mind was all over the place. To see Miriam here, after all that had happened, and after so long. He couldn't figure it all out, and he forced himself not to try—to just let it all be. But, of course, his mind wouldn't just let it be. This was Miriam, and she was back aboard the yacht with him. He couldn't understand any of it. His mind jumped in every direction, searching eagerly for an explanation. But, he forced himself to think, why question it?

Around two o'clock, after two hours of restless thought and several glasses of pastis, he considered making the trip up to the bank and to the Hôtel to exchange his mail. Anything to distract himself. But he was afraid to leave the *Diamant*. He was afraid that, somehow, when he came back, Miriam might not still be there. He wanted to make sure this was all real. Part of him wanted to peek into the room below to see if she were truly sleeping there. Maybe he had imagined her arrival for some reason. But he did not go below. Instead of venturing out, he mixed himself another drink and sat up on the top deck in the afternoon sun. The captain had come up to see if there were any instructions for Elena or for the crew before he released them until the next morning.

"Nothing for the crew, Burke," he said, then caught himself before the captain left to go below. "Burke," he said, "Miriam came in this morning. I had the crew make up a cabin, and I had Elena make up a plate of food to keep cold."

The captain nodded. "Yes, Mister Duncan," he said with what Nick perceived to be the slightest hint of a pleased grin, though Burke would never let his expression betray him. "I know, sir."

"She'll be staying with us again. I'm not sure how long."

"Of course, sir." The captain nodded again and left him and went below.

So it was real then. Miriam was here. It was not all in his mind and not part of some daydream. It was not because of the drinks. Not this time.

Once alone again, Nick smiled to himself and took another long sip from his glass. He leaned back in his chair and felt the yacht sway beneath him at the dock and embraced the warmth of the sun that shone down on him.

CHAPTER THREE

The afternoon came and nearly went in the warm Riviera sun. The only thing that kept it cool enough to endure was the soft wind blowing with a low whistle through the masts of the harbor, and the ice in Nick's empty glass that he drank as it melted. The tide had risen to its peak and was putting a strain on the mooring lines of all the boats, the ropes creaking with each passing wave. Everything was still around the city in the warmth of the day. High up near the Palace and up in the hills, and all along the coast, the streets were empty. Everyone was down along the beach or out on the water in beautiful white boats to stay cool. At about five o'clock, with beads of sweat inching down his skin, Nick heard a soft voice calling to him and smiled as he looked up from his book, expecting to see Miriam coming up from her nap below.

"Nicholas?" he heard the voice again. It was coming from the dock below him.

"Oh, hello, Aurelia," he called from the edge of the deck as he went down to greet her. He knew it was her by the way she said "Nee-cholas."

"*Salut*, Nicholas!" she waved up to him. *"Bonjour!"*

In a few moments, all that had happened the night before at the Brecards' party played itself out again in his mind. The Hôtel, the crowded suite, the bottles of champagne, the fascinating guests, the soft, inviting smile of the girl. He had nearly forgotten about her when Miriam had arrived that morning. Aurelia looked so different there in the sun from last night. Still wonderful, still astonishingly wonderful, but different. Even younger, if she could look younger. She wore a bright orange patterned sun dress and dark sunglasses. Her hair was tied in a single long braid down her back. Nick was glad to see her standing there, but at the same time he wasn't sure that any of what he remembered from the night before was really as he remembered it.

"You got my note then?" he asked her.

As she stepped down from the gangway to the deck, he offered his hand and set her down gently on board.

"Oh, I didn't get a note," she said. "Did you send me a note?"

"I sent one up to your hotel. Earlier this morning. Just inviting you here, because I wanted to see you again. And, well, now you're here."

"Yes," she said, "now I am here."

They embraced and kissed each other on the cheeks.

"I wanted to come by to let you know that I will be leaving for a few days," she said.

"Oh, really?" said Nick. He was surprised by this.

"I asked for you at the Hôtel like you said. *Le Diamant*, I remembered. They said you'd be here on the second dock."

"They were right," said Nick. "Would you like something to drink?" He looked at his watch, having no idea of the time. He had been fully absorbed between staring though the words of his book and thinking of Miriam below and was still coming back to reality, surprised to see Aurelia there. Last night didn't even seem real now.

"Yes, thank you," she replied. "I can't stay very long, but I wanted to stop by and say hello to you."

"Oh. Well how long can you stay?"

"Just a few minutes," she said. "The car will wait for me to take me to the airport in Nice. I spent the morning packing. Throwing things into my suitcase."

"You weren't expecting to go then?"

"No. But it's only for a few days."

"All right," said Nick, "we'll have a drink then. If that's all right."

She smiled and nodded. *"Bien."*

Nick took her up the stairs to the deck where the table was set with the bottle of Ricard that was nearly empty, his sweating glass of ice, the newspaper, and his book. He cleared the table into a chair and pulled out two fresh glasses and ice.

"Something to eat?" asked Nick over his shoulder. He had idly picked at his own lunch at noontime, but he knew there would be a plate of something below. Elena always had something ready.

"I won't have anything to eat," said Aurelia as she moved her sunglasses from her head back to her eyes in the bright sun, "but I will have a drink. Something cool. It was so hot riding down from the hotel. It is very hot today for May."

"Yes. A gin and tonic then?" asked Nick.

"Sure. That sounds nice."

"And one for me."

There was a pleasant silence as she watched him while he poured the glasses and cut the lime. After a sip, the two sat there quietly, listening to the sounds of Monaco's harbor. The light breeze whistled higher through the masts and the lines of the sailboats around them. The few sounds of the motors from the boats entering and leaving the harbor became a muddled hum in the background against the hills of the city that enveloped them. Nick looked at the girl as she smiled and looked around her in the brightness of the day. She was fascinating to look at.

"I like this very much," she said finally to break the quiet. "This is your home on the sea."

He did not respond but only pondered this to himself.

"You are the captain?" she asked.

"No," he laughed. "I wouldn't know what I was doing. I have a captain and a small crew. The captain has the rest of the day off. The other crew have taken off as well."

There was more silence as the two sat contently sipping their drinks, not needing to speak. It was comfortable. Nick felt the sun on him and the cool breeze on the sweat of his body.

"It is so strange to see you last night," said Aurelia. "I knew I had seen you before. It was a whole year ago. Do you come here from time to time? For the summers?"

"For a few weeks anyway. All along the coast, really. I bounce around." Nick thought back to last night and the way he had left her. He was sorry that he had left so abruptly, but he knew he'd had much to drink. "How is Michelle, by the way? Did she feel better after I left?"

"Oh, she is fine," the girl answered. "She slept right away. But the party went on for a long time after. I fell asleep in one of the rooms. This morning, when I awoke, there were three other people in the bed with me! Can you imagine?" She was blushing with astonishment.

Nick shook his head and laughed. He was all too familiar with parties that ended that way.

"Everyone had their clothes on, of course. Even their shoes. I left before anyone else was up. I just didn't want to leave Michelle."

"And how did you feel this morning?" asked Nick.

The girl made a face. "Awful! I had far too much to drink. The waiter kept bringing me champagne. I could not resist. I can never turn down champagne!"

"I have the same problem," said Nick. "Especially when it's good champagne."

She laughed and took a sip from her glass.

"This drink will make you feel better," said Nick. "It always does when you've had too much the night before. I made them strong."

The two sat for a short time and finished their drinks. Aurelia looked at her watch and moved in her chair for a second, then sat back.

"You have to go?"

"Soon, but I am not rushed."

Nick got up and poured them each another small drink as Aurelia made herself more comfortable. He was starting to feel the gin from the first one, and knew she was, too.

"Feel a little better?" he asked.

"Yes," she said. "I really do. This is good medicine. Thank you."

"When you have more time," said Nick, "I'll have to show you the rest of the boat. There's more to it than just this table."

"That would be nice. It looks so beautiful from what I can see of it. It looks very nice from the dock as well."

"Thank you," said Nick. "Where are you off to, if you don't mind?"

"Of course not," Aurelia smiled. "I am flying to Geneva. My father's business. He always takes me with him."

"That's nice."

"Not really!" she laughed. "I think it's so boring. He wants me to learn his business because he doesn't trust anyone else. He doesn't want me to manage it, but he wants me to know all about it, just in case."

"What does he do?" Nick tried to stop himself from asking that, but it was just a reflex. In an attempt at conversation, it seemed to him that he was prying. But she didn't seem to mind.

"He has several banks. One in Geneva, two in Paris, and one here in Monte-Carlo. He wants me to be more involved with the one in Geneva, because that was his first one."

"That sounds interesting."

"Ha!" she cried. "That is the last thing I want to do!"

Nick decided to change the conversation away from business a bit. He tried to recall what they had talked about with all the other guests last night. "I thought you were on vacation. Are you enjoying yourself here, or is it all work?"

"Oh, of course!" she said. "There is always something to do here. I love the beaches, especially in Cannes. We come here at all times of the year, even when it's very quiet."

"Have you been up to the Casino yet this time?"

"Yes. I went for a drink the other day with Michelle. She has been invited to the Palace as well, for a dinner, and she wants to take me along. Fabien says he doesn't want to go."

Nick laughed to himself as he listened to her soft voice. He adored her accent.

"What is it?" she asked.

"I feel bad," he said. "Your English is so good. I feel like I should be speaking to you in French, but my French is atrocious."

"No! I think it is wonderful! You can speak French to me if you'd like to practice, but I don't mind speaking English. I like it. I need to practice, myself."

"You're sure?"

"Of course."

"Well, I'll try to say the words I know, anyway."

"All right," she smiled. "I'll help you."

The two spoke of the party the night before and laughed about all the people they had met. They spoke of Michelle and Fabien and of the other couples they knew, and they found that they had many more friends in common than they had known. It was a small crowd that moved along the coast throughout the year. In reality, everyone knew everyone else somehow. And by the end of a season, it was assured that you had met nearly everyone at this friend's party or that. But the crowd was growing each year. There was always a new face at a party, a new house built in the hills, a new yacht in the harbor. By now, through persistence over several years, Nick had nearly become an established figure, though there were some of the crowd who fiercely rejected newcomers. All it took was time.

As the conversation continued, Aurelia laughed when Nick mispronounced easy words, and Nick laughed at himself, too. He was doing it on purpose because he liked to see her smile.

After they had a cigarette, he led her back down to the lower deck and took her hand and helped her onto the dock. On the last step, she stumbled with a short gasp, and he caught her from falling.

"Merci!" she said, and with that he hated to let go of her hand.

"Will you be around again soon?" asked Nick.

"I'll just be gone for the next few days," said Aurelia. "My father left this morning. I will come and see you when I return. I promise."

"I'd like that." Nick walked her down the dock to the waiting car and kissed her on the cheek goodbye. She waved to him out of the window as the car pulled away. He took out another cigarette and lit it as he went back up on deck. He smiled to himself, and he sat down and resolved, despite his far-wandering mind, to finally muscle through the last nine pages of his book that had followed him from Spain.

CHAPTER FOUR

The sounds of the party reached Nick sitting at the bow of the *Diamant* in his tuxedo before Miriam had come up from her cabin. The evening was clear, and the sounds of the couples and groups arriving and talking excitedly rang out through the harbor. The party began just as the sun finished setting.

Nick sat on his yacht further down the dock from the party sipping a cool glass of Ricard as he watched the light from the sun fade over the high hills above him. He wondered what this scene would look like tomorrow with the new day and the new warmth that came with the morning. Every evening that came to the Mediterranean gave a sense of all the possibilities ahead as the twinkling of lights on the hillsides and the sounds of laughter overcame the exhaustion from the heat of the day. There was something before him there that he wanted to grasp in his hands; and yet he knew he could never hold onto it and that he could only taste it and be a part of it as it slipped away from him.

Miriam emerged on the deck in Nick's oversized bathrobe, drying her dark hair with a towel. He had not heard her wake or take a shower. As she approached, her figure was amplified by the light from the hills and the aura of the remaining sunlight that shone amber against her body.

"The problem with long hair is that it takes so long to dry," she said as she walked up toward the bow where Nick was finishing his glass.

"That's something I'll never have to worry about," he laughed.

Miriam reached over with the wet towel and messed up his hair.

"Hey! Not fair!" shouted Nick as he fixed it by running his fingers back through it. "Not fair at all."

Miriam giggled at him. "Are we going to have dinner? I came up because I smelled food cooking."

"Dinner's ready, I'm sure. Do you want to go and change first?"

Without a word, Miriam handed him the towel and untied the front of her robe. In a moment she was standing there before him with the robe at her feet, elegantly dressed for the evening.

"Ah ha, you sneaky girl!" Nick laughed. "You're a trick-ster, aren't you?"

"It's a habit I can't break."

"Don't break it," he smiled. "It would be such a shame."

The two walked back to where Elena had laid out dinner on the small table at the stern. A bottle of champagne sat in ice between two tall glasses.

"I still have to brush my hair before we go," said Miriam. "I can't leave it wet like this."

"You'll have time," said Nick. "They won't be leaving for another half hour or so. When you hear the horn sound, that's when we have to rush."

Nick flipped on the lights of the deck and sat down to open the familiar bottle with its familiar yellow label.

"Veuve?" asked Miriam. "You're addicted to that stuff, aren't you?"

"Well, at least I'm predictable."

As he popped the cork and filled the glasses, a couple wandered past the *Miradora* and down to where Nick's boat was docked. A voice called up to them as they raised their glasses.

"Nick Duncan! Are you joining us tonight?" the voice called.

Nick and Miriam stood up and walked to the stern where they saw a young couple standing below them on the dock.

"Hello there!" called Nick. He recognized the man but did not remember his name. "We'll be along shortly. Just sitting down to dinner."

"Hi, Nick!" called the woman as she waved. "Is that Miriam up there with you?" Then to the man: "Is that Miriam?"

"Oh, hello, Alice," called Miriam. "Yes, it's me!"

"I knew it was you. I can't wait to hear what you've been up to."

"Let's not disturb them," Nick heard the man say to the woman.

"It's no problem," said Nick. "We'll see you in a few minutes then. Tell Benicio we'll be along in a bit. Don't leave without us!" He and Miriam waved to the couple as they watched them walk back towards the party. The voices from the boat had grown louder and were calling to the young couples of the Riviera to join them.

"You remember them?" asked Nick. "I recognized the face, but I didn't know his name."

"I remembered Alice," said Miriam. "Gregory's his name, I think. Or Gary. Or something like that."

They sat back down at the table.

"Who was that you were talking to this afternoon?" Miriam asked Nick.

"Who's that?"

"I heard someone on board. This afternoon. I heard some voices up above here."

"Oh," said Nick. "It was just a friend I'd met again at the Casino last night."

"Anyone I'd know?"

"Maybe." He left it at that. "Oh," he said, "and maybe Burke. I was talking with Burke about something."

"Oh, Burke! I miss him so much. Do you think he missed me?"

Nick laughed. "Sure. He's glad you're here, too."

Nick and Miriam turned to their dinner and found themselves eating quickly without speaking. They were anxious to join their friends and the growing crowd. Nick watched Miriam eat and was glad to see her there before him. It had been a long time since they had smiled and laughed together.

"Don't worry, they won't leave without us," he said as he watched her shove a large forkful of food into her mouth. "Especially now that they know *you're* coming."

Miriam laughed as she covered her mouth. "I don't mean to be rude," she said after she swallowed and took a sip of champagne. "It's just that I've been stuck in Paris for this shoot for the last few weeks and I haven't had a chance to get out. All work. Just work."

Nick leaned back in his chair and filled his glass again. There was still most of his food on his plate, but he was done eating. He wanted the champagne instead.

"What's the name of the film? Something I would know about?"

"It doesn't have a title yet, but you'd like it. It's about a girl who robs a bank."

"How fitting."

"That's the big sell, because of the name thing. She never gets caught though."

"And who do you play?"

"The lead, of course!" she laughed.

Nick laughed, too. "I mean, what's the character like?"

"Her name is Penny. She doesn't get caught because she's the mistress of the chief of police, and she would ruin him if he arrested her. You'd like her. She's a real piece of work."

"How does it end? She gets away with it?"

"I don't really know. They haven't written the end just yet. They change the script so often, I stopped reading my lines until we're ready for the scene. But we're about half-way through shooting."

Nick had known Miriam ever since she had been doing small roles on stage back in New York, when she was barely seventeen. Just two years before, she had received her first on-screen role as a minor character in a Hollywood film and had been boosted quickly to command leading roles ever since. The fame had hit her all at once. It's what she had always wanted.

Miriam finished eating and set her fork across her plate. She mirrored Nick as she leaned back and sipped from her glass and lit a cigarette as the last remaining light from the sun faded from the sky. She set her glass down on the table, holding the cigarette away from her and blowing smoke above her so that it caught the wind and rose above them. Nick enjoyed watching her there. It was exactly where she belonged.

"I think I should go fix my hair," Miriam said. "The party's going to leave without us."

Nick smiled. "No," he said, "I think you're fine for a…"

But just as he said this, one long blast came from the horn of the *Miradora* and filled the harbor. Nick dropped his glass on the table, spilling champagne, and stood up sharply.

"Hurry!" he said. "We've got to run!" He grabbed her arm in one hand and the bottle of champagne in the other and started for the stairs down to the dock.

"But what about my hair!" Miriam exclaimed.

"No time!" Nick knew the *Miradora* would leave immediately. There was no time to waste. The party was leaving earlier than he had expected.

As they reached the stairs, Miriam stopped. "My purse!" she yelled, and she jerked her arm free long enough to leap back and grab it off the chair. When she turned back, Nick was already down the stairs and waiting on the dock. "I look horrible!" she said as he helped her off the boat.

"You look fine," he said calmly. "Everyone will just be glad you're there."

"I look like I just took a shower!"

Nick laughed. "You just did!"

The two ran hand-in-hand down the dock toward the *Miradora*. Running toward them were two other couples that had just been dropped off where the dock met the land. They all couldn't help but laugh as they ran.

"Nick!" called out one of the men with an Australian accent running toward them in his tuxedo. "Don't let them leave without us!"

"Hello, Warren!" Nick called back as he raised up the bottle of champagne in salute. "Hurry up!"

Nick reached the *Miradora* with Miriam trailing by her arm just as the lines were being thrown aboard and the gangway was being brought in. He handed her off to the other men at the stern who helped her aboard. Then he jumped aboard after her and was caught by several pairs of arms.

"We made it!" he shouted to Miriam. He turned back to the two other couples who were running down the dock and helped them aboard just as the boat was pulling away.

"Warren!" Nick laughed as he caught his friend. "Glad you could make it!"

"Always on time, mate, you know me." He was panting and holding his chest, but laughing nonetheless.

As the engines came up and the boat pulled away from the dock, Nick reached up and helped the last man onto the boat as his legs remained on the dock. In one last leap, the man jumped on top of the others with outstretched hands, toppling a few of them onto the deck. Everyone laughed loudly. Nick landed under the man, and a drink spilled across his chest. Eventually, everyone scrambled up, and he brushed the drink off and laughed. The half-bottle of champagne in his hand remained intact. Not a drop had spilled.

The stern of the boat was now crowded with young men and women, and in a moment he found Miriam standing among the crowd.

"That was a little too exciting!" she laughed.

"It's always fun to watch," said Nick. "But I never wanted to be part of it."

He took her hand and led her up the stairs to a second deck that was a little less crowded to get a little room.

"I need to go fix my hair," she announced as she pulled a brush from her purse. "I came prepared."

Nick held her hand a moment longer and looked back to the dock. A car had pulled up and was blaring its horn. Everyone aboard watched with laughter as two couples emerged and sprinted down to where the *Miradora* had departed.

"Looks like they'll miss the boat," Nick laughed as he watched the men run ahead. The entire stern of the boat laughed and pointed as they watched the latecomers panic. One of the girls tripped over her dress as she ran and fell onto the dock. The girl behind her who was watching the boat pull away tripped over the first girl and landed on top of her. With this, the *Miradora* roared up in laughter.

"Oh, no!" Miriam gasped.

"Oh, she'll be fine," someone beside her said.

The two men in tuxedoes ran ahead of the girls to where the boat had pulled away and shouted their pleas in Italian for the boat to stop with arms and bottles of wine raised high in the air. One of the men gave up, but the other continued on running. As he reached the edge of the dock where the boat had been, he made a full-speed wild leap towards the stern, sending the bottle of wine in his hand in one direction and his two glasses in the other. The entire party watched with a single breath as the man seemed to pause in the air before crashing into the water behind them, a full ten feet short of the stern. At that precise moment, the entire party burst into laughter before the man's head even bobbed back to the top of the water. A few seconds later, the man was being helped back onto the dock, and the scene drifted out of sight as the *Miradora* pulled out into the harbor.

"I'm glad we made it," said Miriam. "Thanks for pulling me along."

Nick winked at her.

The men at the stern discussed among themselves and quickly decided that if he'd launched himself just a second earlier he might very well have made it to the boat.

A waiter came up the stairs, and Nick pulled two fresh glasses from his tray and poured them full of champagne from the bottle he still held in his hand.

"Just a minute," said Miriam when he offered her a glass. "I'm going to find a mirror and brush my hair. I have to."

Nick took a sip of the champagne to cool himself and realized he had left his tie back on the boat. Miriam saw him reach up around his neck in disappointment.

"You'll be fine," she said. "You look wonderful. Can't say the same here." She turned to walk away with her brush in her hand.

"I'll wait right here," he called to her as she went.

Nick was alone now on the top deck with everyone else below where the party was. He leaned over the side and saw his friend Warren drinking and talking below amongst the crowd. He had not seen Warren since he had arrived, and he didn't recognize the girl with him. Then again, he thought, Warren always had a new plaything by his side. Nick watched as the lights of Monte-Carlo spread out before him and shimmered in the cooling air of the evening. There was hardly any wind, and he knew the sounds from the party would carry up to the city until the boat was far out to sea.

He heard footsteps from the stairs behind him and turned, expecting to see Miriam coming back.

"Nick Duncan," came a man's voice. "It is very good to see you, Nick Duncan."

For a second, he thought it was Warren, but the accent told him it was the host of the party, Benicio. He turned and shook the man's hand.

"Good to be back," said Nick. "I've been away too long—almost a year."

Benicio was a rough but handsome man. Skin dark and worn by the sun. His short white hair and beard made him look distinguished rather than aged. Nick knew that he could only hope to look that good when he was older.

"I saw you docked there," said Benicio, "but I haven't seen you around. I wanted to come say hello, but I never got the chance. You received my invitation from the Hôtel, I see."

"Yes, thank you," said Nick. "You know I couldn't miss this. You give the best parties."

"Almost didn't make it!" Benicio laughed. "I saw you run up with your girl."

"Oh, she's not my girl," said Nick. "But you remember Miriam?"

"Oh, Miriam? I didn't recognize her from above. I can't believe she's such a big star now. We can say we knew her when, eh?" he began nostalgically as Miriam emerged and joined them. Her hair was finely combed and held tightly around her head until it came to a knot in the back.

"Miriam, you remember Benicio?" Nick asked as she approached.

"Of course! Hello, Benicio. Hello."

"*Ciao*, Miss Stockton, or is it Miss Banks, I hear?" He took her hand and kissed it gently. "Nick and I were just talking about how you had become such a big film star."

"Really?" she smirked at Nick. "What were you saying about me?"

"That's all we got to," replied Nick, "before you came."

Miriam reached in her purse and pulled out two diamond earrings. She handed one to Nick. "Do you mind helping me?" she asked.

"Allow me," said Benicio as he took it from Nick's hand. "Nick here isn't the only one with an affinity for *les diamants*." He paused for a second to make sure the two perceived the reference to Nick's boat. They both did, and they smiled politely at the man's simplicity.

"Did you know the man who jumped in the water?" Miriam asked as he helped her put on the earring.

"No," he laughed. "I do not know half of the people aboard tonight."

"You're joking!" she gasped.

"No. You two are probably my oldest friends here." He put his hands in his pockets as a waiter passed by and offered them more champagne.

Nick looked around the deck and saw that others had started to join them from below.

"I guess I should go around and introduce myself to everyone—those I didn't invite, anyway." Benicio laughed as he walked off and left Nick and Miriam by themselves. "Enjoy yourselves!" he shouted back, then was gone among the crowd.

"Lovely little man," said Miriam.

"He's always good for a laugh. Very nice."

"I know. I miss being here. I missed Benicio. I missed everything."

The party had spread from the stern to the rest of the boat. Couples began to scatter across the decks and the bow, drinking and laughing amongst themselves. It seemed as though the number of people had suddenly multiplied, and the boat became crowded in all directions.

Nick caught himself looking at Miriam as she looked out over the water.

"What?" she asked, thinking there was something wrong.

"You look very nice tonight," said Nick. "I didn't tell you that before." He knew it was an understatement and that he could do better. "You look *astounding*," he winked.

She smiled. "You do, too." She reached up and pulled on the bottom of his ear.

"Dare I interrupt the adoring couple?" came a voice from behind Miriam.

Nick turned and saw Warren approach alone. Immediately, Warren saw that it was Miriam.

"Miriam!" he exclaimed. "I didn't know it was you. I couldn't recognize you with long hair."

The two kissed on the cheek, and Nick offered to fill Warren's glass from the bottle he had in his hand. He tilted the bottle until it was empty and had just filled the glass.

"It's for the new film," she replied. "Do you like it?"

"Oh, I love it!" he said emphatically. "You look great." Nick could tell Warren was full of energy tonight. Warren was always full of energy.

"Thank you," she said.

"What are you doing with an old dirty scoundrel like Nicky Duncan again, Miriam? You know he's an old jailbird and all."

Nick laughed. "Good to see you, too, Warren. Miriam just got into town this morning. She's staying with me for a few days."

"How long are you here?" he asked her.

"I'm actually here for a few weeks, but I have to leave on Friday for a wedding in Rome."

"Oh really?" said Nick. "You didn't tell me that."

"It's a family friend. The Colonel is making me go."

"The Colonel!" said Warren. "How is the old man?"

"He's good," said Miriam. "Still kicking. Still giving orders." The Colonel was Miriam's father; and though Warren had never met the man, he knew all about him from Miriam's wild stories.

"What about Cannes?" asked Warren. "Did you make an appearance at the festival this year?"

"Oh, yes," said Miriam. "Of course. But just for a single day. Publicity, you know. Then right back up to Paris the next morning for more filming. The production schedule has us tight on time. But of course the studio flew me down to do a quick photo shoot on the beach. I had to at least show my face. I certainly would have stayed down longer if I could have."

Nick turned to Warren. "Who are you here with? I didn't recognize her when you were running on the dock."

"Her name's Marie," he said. "Not much to look at, but she's got family in the right places. Absolutely gushing with money."

"That's horrible!" said Miriam. "You shouldn't say such things, Warren. Take it back."

Nick laughed. He knew Warren well.

"Oh, come on," Warren continued. "She's actually very pretty. I was just kidding, Miriam."

"I know."

Warren, like Nick, was not old money like the money that surrounded them. But unlike Nick, Warren only pretended to have money. It was a game he played as he bounced from heiress to heiress. And the girls fell willingly into his hands.

"I'll introduce you to her if I see her," he said. He looked around the place uninterestedly but did not see her right away. "She must still be below."

"Nick's taking me out tomorrow to go swimming, Warren," Miriam said with a nudge to Nick. "You'll join us of course?"

"Oh! Is that all right with you, buddy?" he asked without listening for a response. His eyes were wandering elsewhere, looking for other playthings.

"Sure," said Nick. "I should bring along a few other people I promised I'd take out."

"Can't it be just us tomorrow?" asked Miriam. "Just us three?"

"Oh, ok. That's fine," said Nick. "We'll keep the party small."

"Nick," Warren interrupted with a pat on his shoulder, "I've got to go speak to someone. But I'll come and find you two later."

"Sure, you'll be able to find us. We're not going far."

"But before I go, I want to give you one of these…" He reached into his breast pocket and pulled out two long cigars. "I picked these up in Paris. Hard to get good ones like this. They're from Venezuela or someplace." He handed one to Nick. "We'll smoke these tomorrow on the boat. I'll bring more if I can. I've got a whole box of 'em."

"Thanks," said Nick. He put the cigar carefully inside his jacket.

"Don't forget it tomorrow."

"I won't."

"I'll see you later then," said Warren as he turned away.

"Make sure to bring Marie with you when you come back," Miriam called to him as he left, but he was already gone.

"Something's gotten into him," Nick smiled. "I've never seen him strung so tightly. Must be some new girl."

"You know how he gets sometimes." Miriam laughed. "I missed Warren. I missed everybody!"

"Good," said Nick. "I'm glad you're here. I'm going to head to the bow for a bit if you'd like to join."

"Too crowded?"

"Just a little."

"I'll come with you."

At that moment, a couple Nick did not recognize came up to Miriam.

"Miriam!" shouted the girl. She was a short, squatty girl in a light blue dress. The man next to her was in a dark suit and did not speak. He only smiled and nodded to Nick. Nick thought he might be a driver for the Grand Prix. He looked like a driver. The race was coming up in a week. They had not held the race here the last two years, so it was going to be a big event.

"Oh, hello," Miriam replied. Nick knew she did not remember the girl's name.

"How have you been?" asked the girl excitedly. She started pulling Miriam with her toward the stern.

"I'm going to go up to the bow," interrupted Nick over the girl. He knew he was being a little rude, but he didn't feel like talking to people just now.

"All right," said Miriam. "I…"

"It's ok. You have too many adoring fans who want to talk with you." He winked at her. "You don't know how many new friends you have now that you're back. Go on down." Nick motioned to the deck below. The girl was pulling her that way, and he knew Miriam wanted to go. She loved the attention. A few minutes before, he had begun to notice all the eyes on them ever since they had gotten underway. But he didn't want to spend the evening being interviewed by all the other guests aboard. It exhausted him, but he knew Miriam needed it.

"All right," said Miriam. "Wish me luck!"

"You'll do fine," he said. "Smile. Pretend it's a role."

He watched her walk away with the other couple, down the stairs to the deck below. The volume from below raised up with her appearance. "Good luck!" he laughed under his breath.

Nick left the rail against which he had been leaning and went to find the bar. He was done drinking champagne for now and wanted something a little stronger to warm him against the wind passing over the boat. The day had been warm, but the air coming from the sea was cool.

On the port side he watched as silhouettes of the high cliffs shone against the last glow of the sky. A thin evening haze was starting to descend upon the coast and was now illuminated from the stars in the clear sky above. The low-lying outline of lights from Monaco reflected in the sea behind the *Miradora* and scattered in her wake. As he made his way to the bow, Nick passed some couples and bumped into others. Some he knew, but he simply waved and smiled and didn't stop to talk. When Miriam was by his side, he felt as if they were the only two people in the entire world. But now that he was alone, he sensed the presence of everyone else aboard and wished only to be by himself.

"Where's the bar?" he asked a white-haired waiter as the man passed hurriedly by. He knew where it was, but he wanted to know the quickest way to get there.

"What would you like, sir? I can bring it to you."

"A glass of Scotch then, please," he said. He held his fingers out to show the man how much he wanted.

"Of course," said the waiter.

"I'll be up near the bow." Before he said this, the waiter was gone, and he knew he might never see his drink. Still, he continued on toward the front of the boat to escape the crowd that continued to grow around him.

By the time he made it to the bow, he was nearly alone. A solitary couple stood at the bowsprit and leaned out over the edge toward the oncoming waves. He felt the boat rise and fall in the water. The wind rushed over them and blew the girl's hair and dress back. Nick gave them some space and sat down against the rail along the starboard side. He was glad to be alone here, and he knew the cool wind would keep the rest of the party near the stern. And as the dust settled on the day, he saw the lights of the small towns of the coast there before him, all around him, as he had never really seen them before. And it was glowing and magnificent.

He looked over his shoulder as the small waves rushed by below. The cool air sent a shiver down his back, and he hoped his drink would arrive soon to keep him warm. He wished he had a cigarette with him, then remembered the cigar in his pocket.

"Better save that for tomorrow," he said to himself in a low voice. "Promised Warren."

As he said this, his warm breath swirled around his face and fought back the cool wind. He smiled at how it felt and blew out again slowly to feel the warm air against his cheek. It made him laugh.

He looked up again in a minute and the couple had gone from the bow without him noticing. He stood up slowly and began to walk to the front.

"Sir," a voice called from behind him. It was the white-haired waiter with his drink. "Here you are, sir."

The man offered the glass up on a tray, and Nick took it in his hand. It was cold, but he knew its contents would warm him quickly.

"Thank you," he said, and he turned to walk forward.

"Should I bring another in a few minutes?" the waiter asked.

Nick thought for a second. "Yes," he said. "That would be fine."

Now fully alone, he walked to the bow and leaned over the edge where the couple had been. He felt his damp hair rise up in the wind that streamed over the bow. He ran his fingers through it and took a long sip of the drink. He felt it on his tongue and felt it move down and burn in his chest. It felt good against the wind.

"You can't have me yet," he whispered to the wind. "I have my friend with me." He tapped the glass before him and looked at the amber-colored liquid in the dim light reflected off the water. As he did this, he realized that he was not totally alone, but that the captain of the boat could see him from the bridge high up behind him. He turned slowly and gestured in salutation with the drink, but he could see no one through the dark glass, and no one gestured back.

His hands were growing cold in the wind, so he took the glass with the other hand and put the colder one inside his pocket. Another long sip from the glass made him feel better.

The sea was calm except for the small waves created by the light wind, and he looked out past the bow to the northeast. In the distance he saw the glow from the Italian coastline where Ventimiglia and, much further on, Sanremo spread out before him along the sea. Two eddies of light among the hills and capes. His watch read nine thirty, and in another hour the boat would slow imperceptibly and begin its wide arc as it turned back toward Monaco.

Nick knew that the party would not end when they returned to the dock. There would be several dozen couples waiting at the dock who had spent the evening in the Casino or at other events. Then the party would begin again. He knew there would be no sleep tonight, even if he went back to the *Diamant*. The party would go on into the night and would spread to several other yachts close to the *Miradora*—anyplace that would open its doors. And he knew he wouldn't turn anyone away if they wanted a drink.

A soft hand touched him on the shoulder and startled him. He had not heard any footsteps over the wind.

"How did I know you'd be here?" asked a warm voice. It was Miriam.

"Because you know me too well." He turned and looked into her soft blue eyes, the same eyes that had made the world fall in love with her on the screen.

"You always slip away at parties. I remember, in Valencia. You used to even then."

"I'm always trying to get away from the crowd."

Miriam wrapped her arms around herself. "It's a bit chilly, don't you think, up here with the wind?"

"Here," said Nick. He took off his jacket and placed it around her. "Stay with me for a minute longer."

Miriam reached over and took his drink in her hand. She took a long sip and nearly finished the glass of Scotch. Nick was surprised she could take it so well. Then she coughed, as he knew she would.

"It's a bit harsh," he said.

"I know. But I still like it."

He took the glass from her and lifted it back to get the last few drops. Then he reached to set it down on the deck behind them. In turning, he saw the white-haired waiter coming with a new glass and exchanged it for the empty one.

"Should I bring another?" the man asked.

Nick smiled. "No, thank you. We'll be coming back in a minute." He turned back to Miriam and put his body against hers to stay warm.

"I love it here," she said as the boat continued along in sight of the coast. "I wish I could stay here for the summer."

After a few minutes of silence, Nick remembered why Miriam had left him alone.

"What was the crowd like?" he asked. "Were they nice?"

"Oh, everyone wanted to know about the new film that just came out. Everyone asked about Hollywood, about who I knew out there. 'Do you know Marlon Brando? Do you know Audrey Hepburn? Do you know Frank Sinatra?' A man even asked if I knew Errol Flynn."

"What did you tell him?"

"That he was a good dancer!" she laughed. It was actually true. The two had met Errol Flynn aboard his sailing schooner *Zaca* in Cannes several summers before, before Miriam had left for Hollywood. He was, in fact, a very good dancer. "It's all so tiresome," she said, a bit insincerely. She knew it was what Nick wanted to hear.

"It's because you're such a famous star now, and people adore you."

Miriam stared out into the distance and was silent. "I'm always afraid it won't last," she said. "They have younger girls coming out all the time. Prettier than me. There are so many of them there, just waiting to take my spot. And they're all so much prettier than I am."

"Not true," said Nick, holding her tighter. "I don't think you're going anywhere just yet. You've only just begun."

"I know," she sighed. She was silent for a minute as they continued on. Nick felt her hair brushing against him in the wind.

"Well," he said, "I won't make you repeat any of it. I know you get bored with the same questions all the time."

Miriam continued to stare out over the bow. "A little."

The ride back along the coast had the air of anticipation as the lights from Monaco guided the way before them. It was still early, and there would be a constant stream of people coming down from the Casino. Nick and Miriam returned to the party together, and Nick watched happily as she perked up again and excitedly answered all the questions from old friends that came with her newfound fame.

"Who have you met in Hollywood?" one woman asked.

"What are you going to be in next?"

"Won't you join us this weekend for lunch?"

"What are you doing Saturday?"

By the end of the evening, Miriam had a packed social calendar for the rest of the month. Nick, by his proximity to the young starlet, had been swept in and invited as well.

"I think everyone assumes we're a couple," laughed Nick as the *Miradora* neared the harbor.

"Well, we used to be." Miriam reached up and touched his face with her cold hands. "I've never had so many friends," she said with a half-smile. "This gets a little tiring."

"You know you love it, Miriam. Just watch out for the ones that seem a little too friendly."

As the boat neared the dock, Nick spotted Warren with the young girl he had brought.

"Warren!" he called and motioned them over.

Warren took the girl's hand and pushed his way through the crowded deck to join his friend.

"There you are," said Warren. "I brought Marie this time. Nick, Miriam, this is Marie."

Nick looked at the girl who couldn't have been more than sixteen. She was thin and immensely attractive with big eyes and long eyelashes. In a few years, he thought, she would be a real woman. But it would be several years yet. Warren had gotten to her before she had learned how commanding she might be. She was not yet aware of herself. And then, thought Nick, she may never fully realize what power she might hold over men.

Miriam was the first to speak. "Nice to meet you," she said. "I've heard nice things." They all greeted each other quickly as the engines groaned to stop the boat and the crew threw out the lines to the crowd of tuxedoes and dresses waiting on the dock. The group who had missed the yacht as it pulled away was noticeably absent. Some of the party began to disembark right away.

"Are you staying?" asked Warren.

"I'm not going far," said Nick. "Join us back at the boat for a bit if you like. I'm not going to stay up too late, and Miriam's been traveling all day."

"We'll come and have a drink then," Warren said to his girl.

"That's nice," said Marie with glassy eyes. She was leaning heavily against Warren.

The deck began to clear as couples dispersed to the decks of the surrounding boats, and some headed up to the Casino and other parties around the city. A line of taxis and chauffeured cars was waiting.

"I'm going to say goodbye to Benicio," said Nick.

"We'll see you in a few minutes then," said Warren. He was already halfway on the dock in search of another bottle of wine.

After a few minutes of searching, Nick and Miriam found Benicio alone near the bow. He was leaning against the railing as a thin puff of gray smoke rose up from his cigarette. Benicio Prado was older than most of his guests that night. He threw parties often to surround himself with youth again. But at the end of the night, he could always be found alone.

"Benicio," Nick said in a soft, low voice.

The man seemed to awake from his pensive stare out over the water and return to his party demeanor, as if putting on a mask.

"Mister Duncan!" he said excitedly. Then he saw Miriam was behind him. "...and Miss Banks."

Miriam smiled with a wave but remained a few feet away.

"I just wanted to thank you for the evening," said Nick. "I didn't mean to interrupt you."

"Oh no," said the man. He seemed to slip back into his thoughts. He faced back to the water and took a draw on his cigarette. Nick joined him on the rail.

"You know," began Benicio in a whisper, "I throw these parties, but she never comes."

"Who's that?" asked Nick, thinking that it was someone he might know.

"My lady," the man went on. "I don't know where she is, but my lady is out there." He pointed with his glowing cigarette to the hills above them.

Nick was silent. He, too, looked out over the water. The wind had died, and the sea was solemnly calm. It made him feel warm again.

"Every night I go looking for her, the lady that might love an old man like me," Benicio laughed. "But of course she never comes."

Nick wanted to say something to make the man feel better. He knew there was nothing he could say, and he knew that the sight of Miriam there made him feel even worse. Benicio had had a few drinks, and Nick knew from over the years that he could get a bit emotional after a few drinks.

Benicio laughed hard again. "I don't want to spoil your evening!" he said to Nick. He turned to shake his hand. "You're young and alive. Go and enjoy yourself this evening!" He said with a wide, forced smile.

"Sure you won't join us for a drink?" asked Nick. "We'd love to have you aboard."

"No, no, no. You go and enjoy yourself, Nick." Benicio already felt better with Nick's presence there.

Nick looked his friend in the eyes and smiled back. "She'll come, Benicio," he said assuredly. "Don't worry. You'll find her at your next party. You just wait. I have a good feeling."

Benicio smiled and laughed to himself.

Nick shook the man's hand firmly and walked back to the stern with Miriam.

"He was sad," whispered Miriam. "I could tell."

"It's nothing," laughed Nick. "You know Benicio. He'll be fine. He'll be just fine."

CHAPTER FIVE

Nick and Miriam stepped back onto the dock and walked down toward the *Diamant* where Warren and his girl would be waiting for them. They passed several groups heading to other parties in a night filled with eager talk and laughter and music blaring from radios around the harbor. Car horns from the city sounded out as taxis spread the party up into the hills. Miriam took Nick's arm and held herself close to stay warm in the night that had cooled quickly.

Warren and the girl were already aboard, and Warren had found glasses and a few bottles and was pouring drinks chaotically. Two other couples unfamiliar to Nick sat with them.

"Glad you could join us!" said Warren jokingly. "Come and see my new boat!"

"This is your boat?" asked Warren's girl Marie.

"Sure!" said Warren.

The girl laughed loudly as if she were still at the party. She was slung in the chair with one leg over the arm and her shoes on the table. Her dress had slid up her leg.

"Who are your friends?" asked Nick as he extended his hand to one of the unfamiliar men.

"This is Hank and Elise Thompson," Warren answered without getting up as he sloppily poured a drink. "They're from Chicago. The others...," he paused and looked at them as if seeing for the first time, "...never met."

"Nice to meet you," said Elise in a forced, fake English accent. But Nick knew she was just as American as he was. People did that here.

Miriam recognized the other girl as someone she had played tennis with once several years before. "Lucia!" she said, "so good to see you." Nick handed the girl a glass of wine in a tall glass.

"You know the best way to make friends?" asked Warren.

"How's that?" asked Nick, knowing a bad joke was coming.

"Find strangers, and give them lots of booze!" He thrust a glass into Nick's hand.

Nick smiled to himself, and Warren alone laughed aloud. Then, a few seconds later, Marie let out a delayed laugh, too, even louder than Warren.

"How long are you in town?" the man asked Nick. Now he knew he had met him before. There were only a handful of Americans he regularly met along the coast. They seemed drawn to one another.

"Until the season is over, I suppose," he answered. "Or until it gets too crowded with the summer flock. I'll be the last to leave. Always am. I just got in from Spain yesterday."

"Oh, I was in Seville last month," said the man. "Seville, then Madrid."

"Seville's nice. I spent most my time near the beach. Valencia and Barcelona this time."

"It shows," said Warren. They all saw how dark Nick was.

Warren pulled out his cigar and asked Nick for his lighter. Nick tossed it to him across the table.

"It's out of juice, mate!" said Warren as he flipped it open and tried to get it to light. There were sparks from the flint, but no flame. He turned to Miriam. "Miriam, hand me your purse."

"Why?" she asked.

"Wait, Warren. I'll get some matches," said Nick. He was already up and reaching in a drawer for them.

"No worries," said Warren. "Miriam, hand me your purse."

"Why, Warren?" she asked again.

"Just let me see it, damn it!" Warren was always a little rough. He didn't mean anything by it. Miriam just laughed. She knew how Warren could be.

Warren reached into her purse and pulled out a bottle of perfume. He shook it and sprayed a little on his wrist and rubbed his wrists together and smelled it. Then he took the lighter and sprayed it on the wick and tried it again. On his third try, the sparks caught, and he had a flame. He brought up his cigar and methodically lit it until he had a glowing end before the flame ran out. The task mesmerized everyone until a thick stream of blue smoke rose from the cigar. The lighter went out, and he passed around the cigar until those who had cigarettes had lit theirs from the end.

Nick lit a cigarette and then paused. "I thought you were saving that for tomorrow," he said.

Warren just smiled. Nick handed his cigarette to Miriam and then pulled out his cigar from his breast pocket and lit it, too, and puffed on it strongly until it was fully lit.

"I've got a whole box full of 'em," said Warren when he had his cigar back. "Whole box." He handed the purse back to Miriam.

"Warren's always full of tricks," she said. "I'd never have thought of that."

Warren winked at her. "Just makes it taste a little funny, that's all." Then he turned to the man at the table. "Sorry, Hank," he said. "I don't have one for you."

"That's all right," said the man. "Not much of a smoker myself." He reached into his pocket and pulled out a cigarette that he lit with his own match. Marie watched him and laughed loudly again. She had slumped even further down in her chair.

At that moment, a group of five or six people who had come from Benicio's party, who had apparently been up at the bow of the *Diamant* without anyone knowing, walked back along the lower deck and spilled from the yacht drunkenly onto the dock. Nick walked over to the edge when he heard them and looked down at them and laughed aloud. The party had spread all around, and he himself had been known to wander as they had. No one could be turned away. He raised his glass to them and called out, and one of the men raised an empty bottle back.

"*Salut!*" the man called up to them.

Nick raised his glass cheerfully and took a sip.

"Do you know them?" asked Miriam.

"Nope," said Nick, and then a second later, "probably."

The night faded gradually as the parties seemed to migrate from boat to boat and back up toward the Casino. For a very long time, a constant stream of cars honked their horns as couples called out in reply and left the harbor for the various hotels.

"The party's dying," said Nick after they had been there an hour or two talking over the music on the radio. The two other couples had just left, and there were several bottles of wine that had been finished off lying on the table.

"Just moving on," said Warren. "Everyone's tired from all the parties this week. Not me though."

Nick finished a cigarette he had been smoking with one last puff and threw the butt over the side with a flash and a hiss in the water below. Warren did the same.

"Stay here, if you'd like," said Nick. He looked at his watch and blinked a few times to see clearly from the wine. It was nearly three in the morning. He was amazed at how quickly the time had gone.

"Are you sure?" Warren asked. "Is there enough room?"

"I think we can manage," said Nick with a laugh.

"I haven't really even unpacked, Warren. You can have my cabin," offered Miriam.

"Don't want to be any trouble!"

"No trouble," said Nick. "Please. We want you to stay."

"Great," said Warren. There was no reply from Marie. She was asleep in the chair with a glass of wine spilled in her lap. Miriam reached up and pulled the girl's dress, which was sitting up around her waist, down over her legs.

Nick went below with Miriam to move her things into his cabin.

"Sorry it's such a mess," he said, picking up a shirt from his floor.

Miriam laughed. "Much neater than I expected," she smiled. She walked over to the wall and fixed a photograph that was hanging crookedly. It was a picture of her and Nick from somewhere. "You just need a woman to keep things nice for. You're such a mess without me."

As Miriam undressed, Nick and Warren carried the girl down from her chair into the other cabin and said good night.

"We're still on for tomorrow then?" asked Warren.

"Sure," said Nick. "We'll go along the coast and have some lunch."

"Sounds great." Warren winked to Nick as he shut the door.

Nick laughed his way back to his room. He was pleased to see Warren again, even if he was strung a bit tight tonight.

"All set, sir," said the captain as he passed Nick on the way back to his room. "We've got three-quarters fuel for the morning."

"Thanks, Burke," said Nick. "I didn't know you were up."

The man just nodded to him.

"Good night then," said Nick.

"Good night, Mister Duncan." The captain tipped his white cap and went back to his own room.

Nick opened the door to the cabin slowly and found Miriam already in bed. There was music coming softly from the record player so that he could barely hear it.

"I hope you don't mind," she said as she pulled the covers close up around her. "You have the most comfortable bed I've ever slept in!"

"And the music?"

"I saw the record you had on," she said. "I like that one."

Nick smiled and took off his jacket. The tie for his tuxedo was lying across the arm of the chair next to the dresser. He picked it up and looked at it as if to put it on. The alcohol from the evening had gotten to him pretty hard, but he still felt good and could taste the cigar on his lips. He flipped off the light for the room and waited for his eyes to adjust to the darkness.

"Did you have fun tonight?" he asked from the sink as he washed his face in the mirror and the dull light coming through the window.

"I did," she said from the bed. "I can't believe how many old friends wanted to talk to me."

Nick laughed aloud as he rinsed his mouth. He walked back into the dark room and felt his way clumsily to the bed.

"I hope they're all just as friendly the next time you see them...," he began, but there was no response. She was lying quietly, half asleep.

He moved silently to a window and cracked it slightly so that the cool air of the night could enter the cabin, and so that just the slightest bit of light would let him know when the day had come. He found his way back to the bed and moved under the covers to lie beside the sleeping girl. As he lay there, he felt the cool skin of her body next to him.

"Good night," he whispered and laid his head into the pillow. He felt Miriam's arm move against him. As he waited for sleep to come, he stared up at the ceiling and listened over the soft sound from the record as the last of the couples left the dock, headed for the last stretch of another party. Miriam rolled to her side and reached up around Nick's neck in her sleep and kissed him softly on his cheek. He was glad to have Miriam lying next to him again. It was the only thing he had ever really wanted since she had left.

CHAPTER SIX

In the far reaches of his mind, Nick had lived this all before. In his dreams that night, his thoughts and bright flashes from the day welled up and whirled around him. It was there before him within grasp; but like a vapor when he reached for it, it swirled around him and coalesced in another space. The figure of the girl, Miriam, was there— her body surrounded by the glittering sparkles, lights from the hills of places like Monaco and Barcelona and Marseilles behind her. He reached out to touch them, and it shattered and fell like diamonds from his hands. It was the memory of summers past—of a thousand days lying in the sun and evenings of champagne and cigarettes; of eluding reality into the marvel of daydreams. He had felt it

with her before, years before when they had been insepa-
rable. Those were the nights Nick sought endlessly. It had
escaped him until now, and all he could do now was take
in every moment with supreme contentment.

It had been two years since Miriam had gone. It was
something she had needed that had called her away.
Everything she had ever wanted for herself, Nick gave
to her glowingly; but there was always something more.
Something he could not give her. Something money and
passion could not buy. Was it fame? Nick had thought that
for a long time, ever since he had known her as a young
stage actress in New York. Was it freedom? She had both
now. Was that why she had come back to him? The image
of her in his mind faded and reformed, each time coming
back to the image he saw of her tonight. He had never let
it go. Just as Benicio looked out longingly for his lady each
night, Nick, too, had waited and searched for her, though
never truly allowing himself to go find her again in someone else. Miriam had left for her own reasons, and there
was nothing he could have done to bring her back. And so
he had let her go; and so he had thrown himself into this
world and into a void that no amount of drunken gratifica-
tion and no number of women could ever fill. He chased it
each night with music and drinks and cigarettes anywhere
the land met the sea, always searching for something final,
something fleeting, always finding instead the taste of alcohol and ashes and a ruthless headache in the morning.
During the day, he sought it all again in the sun with a

stiff, cool drink that helped him fight away reality. If he could keep reality at bay, perhaps he might float through time with some distorted sense of contentment. Anything to ease that pain inside him.

But the appearance of Miriam now brought everything back to him. It had stayed with him all these years. He had brought her into this world so that she would know it and embrace it. She became part of it, and it would never leave her. And now she was back. He felt something now that he had not felt in a very long time, and he knew that it was only because of her. To know that she was not gone from his life gave him something. It was small, but it was something, and he would grasp onto that as long as he could hold on.

Somewhere in the night, in the middle of his thoughts, as his mind faded between sleep and reality, Nick awoke in the darkness of the room and lay for a moment to determine where he was in both time and space. He felt around him and touched the warm skin of the girl there in the cool sheets and pushed her hair back away from her face and saw that it was indeed Miriam and not some other girl as it always had been. He heard her deep, familiar breathing and smiled as he knew it was real and not dream. The wind blew lightly through the room. He didn't feel it, but he knew it from the way he saw the air move before him, as if he really could see it. He lay awake for a long time thinking his thoughts and feeling the sway of the boat under him as low waves moved through the harbor. The blue darkness of the room surrounded him, and finally he rose in the cool night and slipped on a shirt and walked out onto the empty deck.

The night was silent except for the creaking of the boats against their ropes and the steady, dry wind that blew through the taught lines. His body ached in the coolness, and he leaned over the side and looked out to the water below and closed his eyes and listened and felt everything around him. In the far distance he could see the first new light of the coming day reaching to the edges of the sky among the black and the stars and wondered if it were real or if his eyes put the morning light there.

A sound from high up on the hill near the Casino caught his attention, and he looked up to see a small drunken group coming down the street from one of the hotels. Apart from them, the city was sleeping. They called out madly in the early dawn air, laughing at themselves as they stumbled their way home.

Nick stood for a while not moving and just watching and listening and absorbing all he sensed, and it was fresh to him as it had never been. He stayed there until he knew for certain that the light he saw in the sky was indeed the new coming day. And when he longed for the warmth of the bed, and for Miriam's body against his, he turned and walked back down to the room and lay next to her, listening to her soft breathing until he fell asleep once more.

CHAPTER SEVEN

Nick awoke to hear Warren talking with the captain. He listened from his state of half-sleep but could not make out what either was saying. Miriam lay asleep across his chest with her head tucked under his chin. His fingers ran back and forth softly over the bare skin of her arm, but he did not dare wake her. He knew that Warren's girl from the night before had already been sent home.

"Hope I didn't wake ya, mate," said Warren as Nick emerged after his shower. He had left Miriam in bed to sleep. "I was pretty hungry when I got up. You've got a damn good cook there."

"Not at all," said Nick. "You didn't wake me. And Marie?"

"Gone back home," said Warren. "Got her in a cab pretty early. I didn't want mommy and daddy to worry."

"How considerate." They both laughed. "How old is she anyway?" asked Nick. He had told himself he wouldn't ask, but he wasn't able to catch it before it slipped out.

"Didn't really get into that," said Warren. "Old enough, anyway." He slapped Nick on the shoulder and laughed to himself.

The captain and some of the crew were up getting the boat ready for the day. It was Saturday, and the new stock of food and cases of wine had arrived at the end of the dock for the week. The two deckhands were bringing it to the *Diamant* in two large carts.

"It looks like we're going on a trip around the world," said Warren. "Who eats all this stuff?"

"Just me." Nick stuck out his chest and patted his stomach. "And any stragglers like you who happen along."

Warren picked up his plate of eggs and bacon from the table and continued to eat with the plate in his hand. Nick felt the emptiness left by the alcohol in his stomach and couldn't wait to have breakfast.

"Is there any left?" he asked.

"She's making some more eggs and toast for you as we speak," answered Warren. "I told her to make extra. Told her we'd be real hungry."

Nick could almost taste the food already. The drinks from the night before made him hungry, though his head did not hurt as much as he thought it would. That would come later.

"Tell her I'll take it up here," he said to Warren as he went back below deck.

"Aye aye, captain!"

Miriam was still asleep in his bed when he entered the cabin, but she woke when she heard the door open. She sat up heavily and yawned with the blanket wrapped around her body.

"G'morning," said Nick in a strong but low voice. "You slept well."

"I know," she said. "You shouldn't have let me stay here so long. What time is it?" She saw the sun had been up for several hours. Then she remembered Warren was aboard. "Is Warren up yet?" she asked.

"He's already had breakfast."

She let out a groan and fell hard on her side back onto the bed. "I can't even think about food!" She took in a deep breath and held it for a second. "I don't want to get up yet," she whimpered.

Nick laughed and shook his head. "You're a pitiful sight."

From the bed, a pillow came flying at his head. He dodged it and let it hit the wall.

"Play nice!" he laughed harder and tossed the pillow back onto the bed.

Miriam lay there motionless with her eyes closed.

"I'll tell you what," said Nick. "You stay here. I'll wake you up once we're underway."

"It's a deal," said Miriam without opening her eyes. She remained lying sideways across the bed and didn't move.

Nick walked over and kissed her hard on the cheek and left her there, shutting the door behind him.

"Taking it pretty hard, is she?" said Warren as Nick emerged from the cabin alone.

"I don't think she knew how much she was drinking. It was probably all the champagne and the wine. She'll be fine in a bit."

The day ahead was sunny and warm. Nick felt the breeze pick up and enter the harbor from the Mediterranean. The wind had come to the Côte d'Azur, but it was not blowing hard. The wind made the skies clear during the day and cooled off the evenings so that they were more bearable.

"Fantastic day!" said Warren. "I wish I had remembered my swim trunks."

"No worries," said Nick. "I have a few extra pairs down below. I'll get them later so you can see if one fits you."

Warren was a tall man; almost as tall as Nick. But he didn't have Nick's thickness.

"I think they'll fall right off me," said Warren.

"Just make sure you cinch them up tight," Nick laughed as he looked over his friend in his button-down shirt and black slacks from the night before. Warren had even gone to the trouble of putting on his suspenders, though his shirt was still untucked. He had the girl's makeup smeared over his face. "They'll fit you fine. Go and take a shower, and I'll get you some different clothes to put on."

It was a half hour after they had gotten underway towards Nice when Miriam emerged on her own.

"There she is!" announced Warren. He watched as she approached from the stairs, drying her hair with a small towel. He raised his hands and gave her applause without taking the cigarette from his mouth.

"Morning, kiddo," said Nick. "How was your shower?"

Miriam looked a little sad as if she were on the verge of tears. "I got a little sick," she whined. "The boat was moving. I'm sorry."

Nick put his arm around her waist as she stood next to him. "You feel better now, though, don't you?" he asked.

Miriam smiled. "Yes, I do," she sniffed and put the towel to her nose.

"Hungry?"

"Oh no, not yet, but I will be." She gave Nick a kiss on the cheek and then walked over and sat on Warren's lap and gave him a kiss, too.

"Whoa!" he cried.

"You don't mind, Warren?" she asked him.

"Ha! Not at all."

"I'm not too heavy?"

"Hardly." Warren bounced her up and down on his leg.

She reached over to the table and took a sip from his glass. "Ugh! How can you drink this stuff in the morning?" she asked.

"It's good for ya. Take the headache right away!"

Miriam coughed and then forced herself to take another big sip.

Nick left them for a moment and climbed up to the bridge where the captain was steering around a bend where a hill came down and entered the sea. From higher up, he could see the clear blue water surrounding the boat until it turned light where the waves broke near the shore.

"Take us to that hidden beach in the cliffs," he told Burke. "There's a cove. It's another twenty minutes or so."

The captain knew exactly where he meant, and he nodded that he understood.

Nick went below to fix himself an early drink. His watch showed that it was just eleven o'clock, but the day had already begun strongly, and he was sweating from the heat. He knew the only way to fend off his headache was with another drink. As he put ice in the glass, he remembered Warren's empty one up above and set another tall glass on the bar for him. "Warren's back to himself this morning," he said aloud to himself. "Not as strung up as he was last night. Maybe it just took a little to get used to him. I haven't seen him in almost a year."

He poured two strong gin and tonics and left the other half of the lime in the ice to stay cool. When he returned to the deck, Miriam was sitting in his chair sipping a glass of pineapple juice.

"That stuff's hard to come by," he joked as he handed Warren his drink. "They don't grow on trees, you know."

Warren shook his head at Nick's failed attempt at a joke. "Oh, man, you've got to stop reading the book where you get those from," he smirked.

"Aw. I'll try harder."

"I think the problem is that you're already trying hard enough."

"Well," Miriam chimed in, "I like his jokes. They're not funny, of course, but I like them."

"Thank you for your confidence...I think," laughed Nick. "I'm glad I have at least some appeal."

Nick nodded to Miriam's glass. "Would you like some rum in that? I've got some below."

Miriam held up her hand and shook her head. "No alcohol for me!" she exclaimed. "I'm done, at least not until tonight."

"Hungry yet?" he asked.

"Getting there. Is there something ready?"

"We'll have an early lunch when we stop. It should only be a few more minutes."

Nick left them again and lay down in a chair on the lower deck alone near the stern. He held the cold drink in one hand on the table and laid the other arm across his eyes to block out the sun. He was already in his swim shorts, and he wore a white button-down shirt identical to the one he had given Warren. As he let himself drift near sleep in the morning sun, he listened to the groan of the engines as they churned the water behind him, and he smelled the exhaust mixing with the salty water.

Back up above, Warren was finished with his drink and was chewing noisily on his ice.

"I've never seen Nick look better," Miriam said to Warren.

"I know," said Warren between crunching. "It sickens me."

"He's so relaxed, so fit."

"Ha! Don't flatter him too much. You might give him ideas."

"I guess being on the water does something to him." She paused. "Warren, that's bad for your teeth!"

"I know. It's my one vice—well, the one for today, anyway."

"I could never do that." She ran her finger across her lower teeth. "The director would kill me! I'd be afraid to chip a tooth and wouldn't be able to finish a shoot."

"I'm glad I don't have to worry about my appearances," Warren said securely. "I've never cared what I looked like. Ever."

"That's because you already have every girl in the world swimming at you!"

"Not true," Warren returned with a smile. "Besides, I think Nick has you cornered there."

Miriam smiled. "Oh, it's been a few years. I don't know."

Warren nodded.

"I haven't seen him in so long. I always hated myself for leaving, but it was what I had to do."

"You're still close. Look at you two. Only a day back together and you're like old pals."

"He was the only one I knew who'd be here. I knew I could run to him."

"Run?" asked Warren. "What are you running from?"

Miriam hesitated. "No, I'm not running *from* anything. I just had to get out of Paris and knew he'd be here and we could start back like when things were still good between us."

"Nick's good like that," said Warren. "He's genuine. Never changes. You can always count on him."

"That's why I love him. That's exactly what he is. Genuine."

"Nick's that way with everybody. Ever since I've known him."

The engines slowed, and Nick was startled from his half-sleep in the sun. When he looked up, Warren and Miriam were leaning over the rail looking down at him. He could only make out their dark outlines in the harsh sun that was already high above them.

Warren whistled loudly with his fingers. "Looking good, Nicky!" he shouted down. Still in a daze, Nick attempted a smile. "Can I bum some swim shorts off you then?"

Nick took a quick last sip of his melting drink and brought himself back. "In my cabin. Second drawer. There should be a pair that'll fit you. The red ones."

Miriam called down to him. "I don't have a suit, Nick. Do you have anything I can wear? It's hot."

"There's a bottom drawer with some of your old stuff in it," he called up to her. "I'm sure there's a suit in it. Go down with Warren."

When he said this, Miriam felt empty about everything that had happened between them, and humbled that Nick had kept her things for so long.

The captain brought the boat to a stop and threw the engines in reverse as the two deckhands lowered and set the anchor. Nick was alone on the deck and looked up in amazement to see how close they were to the high brown and gray cliffs that seemed to surround the boat. The water was shallow and clear, and there was a smooth sandy beach nestled up among the beige rocks.

"Perfect spot," said Nick to the captain.

"Just as you wanted, sir." The captain smiled.

"No one else around? No other boats yet?"

"Except for a fishing boat about a quarter mile out. And I'm sure there will be more boats along as the day gets on."

"It's perfect," said Nick. The one thing Nick always wanted was to have things perfect for his guests, especially for Miriam and Warren. He wanted today, if any day, to be perfect.

Nick threw his shirt over a chair and dove in off the port stern, and when Warren and Miriam returned in their bathing suits, he had already swum halfway to the empty beach.

"Wait for us!" Miriam shouted and dove in head first. Warren followed with more of a flop and a splash than a dive. But it got him into the water.

As the pair swam to catch up with Nick, they heard splashes behind them and looked back. It was the two deckhands. Nick had let the crew enjoy the day, too, but knew they would stay closer to the boat and leave the beach to them.

"What about Burke?" asked Miriam when she had caught up to Nick a few yards from the beach. The captain was standing alone on the bridge.

"He's afraid of the water," Nick answered. "Can't swim."

"You're joking!" she cried.

Nick smiled and was proud of himself. "Of course I am."

"Not funny!" said Warren. "You had me for a second, too. Damn you, Nicky!"

The three reached the beach in a mad sprint to see who could get there first. Nick took the lead but was dragged down by Miriam. In the end, Warren won by default.

"We let you win, Warren," Miriam laughed. "We felt sorry for you."

"Likely story." Warren still had his arms raised in triumph on the sand, but he was panting the hardest. "I'm all out of shape."

Nick paused for a moment to look back at the *Diamant*—its white hull reflected the light coming off the water. She was a good boat, he thought. One hundred and one feet of steel, wood, and brass, with two decks and all the amenities he required for his travels. With the high cliffs framing the scene on either side, it was the picture he had always dreamed of having as his own.

"She's a beauty, Nick," said Warren. "What a sight! Wish she were mine."

"She is yours, remember? Your new boat, you said so last night." Nick slapped Warren on his back and ran ahead on the beach, trailing a spray of coarse sand. Warren and Miriam let out and chased him until he ran back into the water where they both tackled him. Nick held Warren under for a second, then picked him up and threw him into the air with a splash. Miriam was scrambling to get away, but he caught her by the foot and dragged her back into his arms.

"Let me go!" she cried. "Warren! Help! Save me!"

Warren stood in the waist-deep water and laughed with his arms folded. "You're on your own, I'm afraid."

Nick threw his legs out and landed in the water with the girl in his arms. Then he pulled Miriam up as she coughed out the water in her mouth.

"You play too rough, Nick!"

"I'm sorry." He set her back down on her feet. "You're not hurt, are you?"

Miriam did not answer. Instead, she held his hands in front of him while Warren snuck up and jumped onto his back.

"Not fair!" shouted Nick. He realized she had tricked him.

The two finally subdued Nick in the water when he gave in and sank below.

"You win!" he cried. "I can't beat both of you."

Laughing and coughing, the three made it back to the beach and lay in the rough sand that clung to their bodies. It took a while for their panting to stop and for them to catch their breaths before any of them spoke. Nick looked up at the sky and watched the clouds slide high over the cliffs. He couldn't have asked for a better day. He felt the sun warm his skin from the cool water. The only thing off was the pounding in his head from the drinks last night and his heart beating so strongly.

"I hurt my foot," said Miriam. She was sitting up holding it in her lap.

"Let me take a look," said Nick. He sat up and held her foot in his hands. He ran his hands over her tight legs and down to her heel. He loved to feel her skin. "It's just a little red. From a rock. You might have a bruise there tomorrow."

"It hurts," she said with a whimper.

With this, he knew she was no longer a worldly starlet, only a vulnerable child as he had always known her to be. Nick rubbed his hand over her foot for a few minutes until she said it felt better. Then they lay back on the sand and looked up at the sky, her wet hair over his shoulder.

The few clouds that passed hung high above them against the wisps of the midday sky. Sun trickled down and teased their eyelashes that beaded water from the sea. The warmth absorbed them and embraced them and consoled them until several minutes later they resisted no longer and welcomed it to them.

Many minutes later, from their long, deep intoxication from the sun, Miriam sat up and looked out to the boat. She picked up a handful of sand and sprinkled it delicately over Nick's hand. "I'm hungry," she declared, bringing them all back to reality.

Warren sat up and chimed in. "I'm thirsty."

"Aw, listen to you two!" laughed Nick as he lay and squinted in the sun. "You two sound like a couple of babies."

"Well I didn't have breakfast," said Miriam. She reached over and threw her sandy arm around Nick's neck. It startled him from his daze.

"I did," said Warren, "but I could go for a drink. We should have brought some things with us."

"The boat's yours," said Nick. "Have whatever you like. Elena can make anything."

Miriam and Warren stood up and wiped the rough sand off their legs and backs. "Are you coming, too?" she asked.

"I'm going to stay for a bit. I'll have lunch later." He lay back and listened to their splashing as they made their way back to the boat. It felt comfortable to be alone there on the sand.

At the boat, Warren helped Miriam up as she grabbed the captain's hand above the swim ladder.

"There are some sandwiches ready if you want them," he said, handing them each a towel.

"Thank you," said Warren. He made his way up the ladder onto the deck. "I'll mix myself a drink. You want anything, Miriam?"

"Just a soda water, please," she said as she dried off and threw the towel around her waist. She went up the ladder to the upper deck and found the plate of sandwiches in the center of the table covered on a large silver platter.

"If you don't find something you like, I can make something else," Elena explained. She was still in her apron and lifted the cover off the platter.

"Oh, thank you, Elena," said Miriam. "I haven't seen you since I arrived. It's so good to see you again."

"You, too, Miss Miriam," said Elena. "We're all happy to see you back."

"These will be perfect," said Miriam. "I could eat anything right now!"

"Well, enjoy." The woman caught herself before she walked away. "Miss Miriam?"

"Uh huh?" She had already taken a big bite.

"Where is Mister Duncan?" she asked.

"Oh, he'll be along soon," she answered. "He stayed on the beach for a bit."

"All right," she said. "I don't want him to eat too late and spoil dinner. He always does that. Let me know if you need anything else."

"Thank you, Elena. I will."

Elena was an older, chubby, Spanish lady that had joined the crew from the beginning. She was a bit motherly to Nick, and she kept him in line. Over the last year, she had prayed on Sundays for Nick and for his happiness. And when she had first heard that Miriam had returned, she kneeled and said of prayer of thanks, gripping tightly the small cross that hung around her neck.

Nick lay there alone in the sand for a few minutes until he felt rested in the sun. The coarse sand felt cool against his back, and he listened to the soft waves rising in low tones against the rock walls. As he sat up to brush the sand away, he saw that the beach was untouched except for the scattered footprints the three had made along the water-line to where he lay now. There was a mound of heavier gravel higher up above him where the waves only reached during the highest tides.

He was happy to have Miriam with him. Warren, too. He had spent a long time without seeing his friends. Too long. He knew many people all along the whole coast, but these were the two he cared about the most. All the others were just a blur to him. Warren was a bit to handle some-times, but he was a good man altogether. Always knew when to take your side, when to step in. And it had been Miriam all along and Miriam alone that could make him happy. And with Warren there, too, it was as if nothing had ever changed. It was the perfect day he had always remembered.

Miriam was still a girl in Nick's eyes. When she had left him for California, he knew she was just naïve, looking for something that she had right there before her. He told her he would take care of her, that she would never have to worry about anything. It was all they had ever talked about back in New York. But that was not enough for her. Somehow, even then, he'd known she had to find it on her own.

That was a long time ago, Nick thought to himself. Things were different now. They were both different. She had grown up. She was not such a little girl anymore. And he knew he had to stop thinking of her that way. It wasn't doing him any good.

Nick rose and walked along the high cliffs and passed from the deep sand to the rocks along their base. It hurt his feet at first to walk along the jagged stones, but he knew there was a deep cut around the corner that ran all the way to the top. When he reached the bottom of the crevice, he sat on a large rock out of the sun and watched the scattered clouds pass high overhead. In a minute, he would head back to the boat. But for now, this was his and his alone.

"Should we save some for Nick?" Miriam asked Warren. "Do you think he'll be hungry?"

"We probably should," he replied. "We shouldn't eat all his food."

"Oh, he won't mind," laughed Miriam. She left two small sandwiches on the platter and covered them. She was still hungry, but she would settle with what she had eaten. She didn't want to trouble Elena.

"I'm going to lie in the sun," she said, "up at the bow."

"Suit yourself," said Warren. "It's too hot for the sun after I just ate."

Miriam grabbed a fresh towel and found her sunglasses inside her bag in a chair.

"Come wake me before I turn red," she smiled. Warren winked at her in reply. She made her way up to the forward deck and followed the rail along to the open bow. There was a large space above the cabin where she could lie out in the direct sunlight. She spread her towel and took a deep breath as she prepared for the full force of the sun.

"She wants to get as dark as Nick," Warren said to the captain when Burke was making his way from the bridge to the stern. "I'm afraid she's going to burn."

"We'll keep an eye on her," said the captain. "She'll burn quicker than she knows."

Warren put on his sunglasses and sat down at the table with another drink. He lifted the platter cover and saw the two sandwiches there. Better leave 'em for Nick, he thought. He'll be hungry when he gets back.

It was a hot May day off the coast, and the wind from the day before failed to make an appearance. Nick was happy sitting on the rock back on the beach, but he knew he wanted to join Miriam and Warren back at the boat. He needed to be close to them. Without a thought, he ran along the water and dove straight into the clear blue shallows before him. The water felt chilly as it slid over his body. It made his lungs grasp for air, but he held them tight and burst out onto the surface. The boat was still fifty yards away. He turned on his back and swam with his head above the water, watching the clouds swirl and transform above him as he kicked with his legs. Nothing else occupied his mind except for the beauty of the day. The only other emotion he felt was the hunger pulling on his stomach as he swam.

When he reached the boat, he climbed the ladder and stepped onto an empty deck. There was no one around. He dried off quickly, found his shirt, and climbed the stairs to the table where lunch awaited him. Warren was asleep in the chair with his sunglasses over his eyes.

"Anything left for me," asked Nick, waking Warren with a start. Nick lifted the platter and saw the sandwiches that were left for him. There was no response from Warren, who smacked his lips together against the warm sun, then lay his head back again in the chair.

Nick ate in silence. He wasn't sure where Miriam was, but the rest of the crew was silent. No one moving about. It was the middle of the day, and they were all tired from the night before. As Nick ate, he looked over his friend sitting there and thought a bit to himself. He had known Warren for many years now, the first Australian he had ever met. He had learned from friends that Warren had played the violin at one point in his life and had once been a world-renowned performer of some notoriety, but Nick had never heard him play himself, and Warren never spoke of it. Nick never asked. All he knew was that Warren lived between London and Paris, and the Riviera in the springs and summers, venturing back to Australia once every few years. Except for this, he actually knew very little of his friend, including his last name.

The captain came down from the bridge and saw Nick finishing his lunch.

"Do you want to move further down the coast, Mister Duncan?" he asked.

"Burke," he said, "call me Nick, for God's sake."

"Of course, sir." Burke, in his thick English accent, always said 'of course, sir' but still he always called Nick 'Mister Duncan.'

"This is a good spot, Burke. We'll stay here for a bit longer. Maybe move in an hour or so."

The captain nodded. "Miss Banks went below for a nap. I got her out of the sun before she started to burn. She wants you to wake her when you're done with lunch."

"Thanks. I'll let her rest for a little while longer."

The captain left him, and he was again alone. Nick looked at Warren lying back asleep in the chair. Warren's drink was melting and had a pool of water around the base of the glass. The bar being too far away, Nick picked up the glass and took a sip. It felt cool and helped wash down the sandwiches.

Warren heard him put down the glass and awoke. "Hey! Get your own!" he laughed. "Or get me another one."

"Yes, sir," smiled Nick. He got up and went to the bar and filled two new glasses with large chunks of ice. He poured in a little gin and stirred it with tonic water and a lime. His mouth watered for the fresh, cool drink. He sat back down next to Warren who was awake now looking out over the water.

"We didn't see where you went," said Warren. "Does it cut back there behind the rocks?"

"There's a small rocky beach around the corner. You remember. I just went back there for a minute. It's quiet back there. Can barely hear the waves."

"You know all the best places," said Warren. "I wish I knew the coast like you."

"You spend too much time in the cities."

"I know. But that's where all the fun is."

"Are you going swimming again?" asked Nick. "It would feel good right now."

"I'll wait 'til everyone wants to go. Miriam's asleep I take it?"

"Yeah. She wants me to wake her up now."

"Is she in the sun?"

"No. Down below."

"She's been sleeping ever since she showed up!"

"She's a tired girl," said Nick. "She works hard. I'm sure she doesn't get much sleep with her busy life. It's not the life of leisure like you and me, bumming around from place to place."

"Hard life, I'm sure," Warren said jokingly.

"You do have to give her some credit. She does work harder than you or I do."

"I guess you're right. You don't work at all. But I do work hard—hard at enjoying myself. This life doesn't come easy. It takes talent and persistence." He winked behind his sunglasses. For Warren, his business was the pursuit of leisure. In his mind, there was no more noble pursuit.

Nick finished his glass and stood up. "I'll see if she's up."

Warren was silent but raised his glass in gesture.

Nick stepped lightly down the stairs as he entered the cabin. If Miriam wasn't awake, he would let her sleep; but the door creaked slightly when he opened it, and she turned her head and opened her eyes. He stood still.

"I didn't mean to wake you," he said when he saw that she was getting up.

"I wanted you to," she said. "Did you eat?"

"Just finished." Nick came through the doorway and sat down on the bed.

"I was dreaming about Spain."

"It's easy to do that. It was beautiful this spring."

"I haven't been there since we went together. That must have been more than two years ago."

"I think it is."

"Promise you'll take me back."

Nick placed his hand on her forehead and stroked her hair back over her ear. "Just say the word."

"Where's Warren?" she asked.

"Warren and I are going swimming again in a bit. Do you want to come, or stay here?"

"I'll go with you. I just have to put on my suit again."

Miriam pulled back the covers and sat up in one of Nick's shirts and a pair of his shorts.

"A little big for you, I think," Nick laughed.

"My suit was wet. I found them in the closet. I think they look good on me. What do you think?"

"Can't argue with that."

He watched as she stood and walked into his bathroom and emerged a few seconds later in her bathing suit with a towel around her neck.

"Leave that one here," said Nick. "We'll get you a new one."

The two climbed the stairs and reemerged onto the deck and saw no one. The crew was still resting, but they didn't see Warren either.

"He must have gone already," said Nick. "I left him here at the table."

Miriam looked out toward the water and scanned the beach. "I don't see him."

At that moment, the two saw something move above them near the side of the boat and heard a loud splash in the water below. When they looked down over the edge, Warren rose laughing in a pool of white bubbles, treading water next to the hull.

"Where did you come from?" Miriam asked.

Warren pointed. "Up there!"

She looked up and saw the small ledge on the side of the top deck from where he had jumped.

"It's easy if you hold onto the side." He was still gasping for air.

Before Nick knew it, Miriam was making her way to the top deck.

"Be careful," he called up to her. "Don't break yourself!"

"I'll be fine."

Warren climbed the swim ladder at the stern and joined Nick as he watched Miriam climb to the top of the boat.

"Watch me, Warren!" she shouted. "I can do better." With her arms raised high, she bent her legs and pushed herself out away from the boat. In the air, she arched as she fell and slid effortlessly into the clear blue water with the smallest splash. When she reappeared, fixing the top of her bathing suit in her circle of tiny bubbles, Nick and Warren gave her an ovation.

"Well done," said Warren. "I give it a nine point five."

"Nine point seven five here," said Nick.

"I can't do that anymore," she said. "My top almost came off." She made her way to the back of the boat and climbed the ladder to where they were.

"I guess it's my turn," said Nick. "I've got this. I'll give you a ten."

Nick took off his shirt and climbed the stairs to the top. He climbed over the edge and held onto the side while he looked over and judged how far it was to the water; maybe fifteen feet down. He knew he should jump a little out to clear the boat. He had done this dozens of times. The other two watched intently. He arched his back and leapt out, touching his legs in the air and extending out until his fingertips reached the water. It was a clean, deep dive. His splash was bigger than Miriam's, but only because of his size.

Under the water, he held his breath and felt the bubbles rise all around him and bounce off his skin. The water was cool and clear. He could see the blurry rocks a few more feet below him. It felt cooler now against his warm body being so deep. He kept himself down until only a few bubbles remained, and then he followed them back up to the surface. When he broke through to the air, Miriam and Warren were high above him ready to jump again.

"Watch out!" Miriam shouted as she jumped out past him, legs first.

There was a giant splash followed by Warren as he jumped in on the other side of Nick. Nick felt the bubbles rise up all around him. In another moment, the two emerged coughing and laughing.

"I win!" said Miriam as she climbed onto Nick's back.

"Why's that?"

"Because I do, that's why."

Nick felt pleased inside. He didn't want today to end. Even in Barcelona where he had been happiest there was something missing. He had felt it and had known he wanted something more, but he could not grasp it yet, not perceive what it might be. He knew now that he had found it, and he did not want to let it go.

They spent the rest of the day in the water and headed back to the harbor just before sunset. That evening, they ate a nice dinner Elena prepared aboard the *Diamant* before Warren left them and headed to the Casino to catch some of his friends who he knew were down from Paris. He showered aboard and changed into his freshly ironed tuxedo that Elena had prepared for him so that he wouldn't even have to go back to his hotel to change. Miriam said she would leave for Rome in the morning for the wedding so that she wouldn't be rushed in getting there, since it was yet a few days away, and all that Nick had felt today would be gone. He was already anxious for her return.

As they said good night to each other, Nick kissed her on the lips and they held each other close. Now that she was settled into Nick's cabin, there was no reason to go back to the other one, she said.

"Thank you for today," said Miriam. "I feel like I'm home here. I didn't think I'd feel this way."

"It was like it used to be," said Nick. He kissed her strongly and pulled her body to his. A moment later, their lips moved together, and then their bodies moved together; and, long afterwards, as he lay running his fingers along her back as she fell asleep tangled with him, he knew that it was exactly the way it used to be.

CHAPTER EIGHT

Miriam left for Rome early the next morning just after the sun had come up. Nick awoke with her and brought her down a light breakfast and helped her pack. Then he carried her bags to the taxi waiting at the end of the dock. She now had two suitcases—the one she had brought from Paris, and another filled with a few dresses and some things of hers that Nick had kept aboard the *Diamant*. He had insisted on riding up with her to the train station, but she said it was not necessary and that she was all right riding alone. She kissed him strongly and said she would be back in a few short days.

Nick was glad to climb back into his cool bed with the scent of her perfume on the pillows. It was with thoughts of her in the bright sun from the day before that his mind faded and finally wandered off into dreams. He awoke again just before lunch, refreshed and yet a bit sluggish, unwilling to emerge back into reality. At one o'clock he headed up to the Café de Paris across from the Casino to meet Warren for lunch, and it was as if he could not remember a moment when he was away from Monaco, as if all the springs and summers flowed into one and to this day and to this single point in time. Warren was exactly the way he remembered him—brash and energetic, severe yet harmless. He had missed these people and this place. When he arrived at the Café, Warren was sitting with a French couple he recognized, but their names did not immediately come to him.

"Nick, good to see you," said the man in English with a strong French accent. "Warren said you would be coming. We saved you a place." They were speaking English because, though Warren spent many months of the year in France, he spoke very little French. And, Nick thought, though he was often seen with Italian girls, he spoke even far less Italian.

"You don't mind?" asked Nick.

"*Pas du tout,*" said the woman. "Not at all. Come join us. We have drinks coming, but we are about to order."

Nick shook the man's hand and bent over to give the woman a kiss on the cheek, then sat down as the waiter came up to take their order. As he glanced quickly over the menu he knew well, he heard them all order in French except for Warren who ordered in his piercing Australian English and had the woman translate. Nick knew that English of any accent sounded harsh amongst the more pleasing languages of the Mediterranean coast. As he ordered, he did his best to suppress the American in his voice.

After a few minutes of buoyant conversation spurred on by the woman asking Warren all sorts of questions, Warren sensed that Nick did not remember the couple's names. Nick had been mostly quiet since he arrived.

"Max and Christine spent the last few weeks in Russia," Warren went on. "Rubbin' elbows with the Reds."

The woman turned to Nick. "Warren was just telling us about your excursion yesterday," she said. "How lovely!"

"I also heard you had Miriam Banks aboard," added the husband. "I haven't seen her since she started acting in the films. She's a big star now, you know."

"Yeah, she's a good kid," said Nick. "I knew her when she was young. I knew her family, too."

"Yes she is. We've seen all of her films," said Christine. "Every single one."

A round of drinks arrived from the bar.

"Got you a Negroni," said Warren. "Wasn't sure what you wanted. And if you don't want it, I'll have two."

"That's fine," said Nick. "Thanks." He turned to the couple. "Did you just arrive then?" Their familiarity had come back to him now.

"We just got in last night," said Christine, "on a train all the way from Moscow. It was a long trip, but we were able to stop for a day in Vienna."

"So you missed Benicio's party the other night," said Warren.

"Yes, we did," said Max. "But of course he's sure to have another one soon."

"Of course."

"And apparently we missed the Brecards' party a few nights ago, too," said Christine. "I wish we would have made it. I kept telling Max we were missing our friends here and we should come."

"It was nice," said Nick, remembering it as if weeks had already passed since then, though it had only been a few days. "I didn't stay very late, but I had a good time."

"I heard the news from my friend Chloe this morning!" she said excitedly.

"What news is that?" asked Nick as he tried to think if he knew anyone named Chloe.

The woman looked at him with surprise. "That Michelle's pregnant, of course!"

Nick looked around the table and shook his head. "Who'd you hear that from?"

"Chloe! She was at the party. She is in Marseilles today, but I spoke with her on the phone from the hotel this morning."

"Really?" asked Nick, not feeling the need to act as surprised or excited as the woman.

"You're the last to know," said Warren, chomping his ice. "I heard from a few people. And I don't even know the Brecards."

Nick thought back to the party and how Michelle had fainted. He had just thought it was the heat and the drinks.

"They should have been more careful," said Warren.

"Oh, that's a horrible thing to say!" Christine laughed. "Michelle wanted a child. And I'll want one, too, in a few years."

"So did Fabien," said Max. "Just not yet."

Nick took a sip of his drink and brought himself back to the conversation. "They're young," he said. "That's good news."

"They're too young," added Max.

"Not that young at all," said Nick. "Twenty, twenty-two maybe. I didn't know she was pregnant. But they're good together. They'll make a good family."

"I guess we're next," laughed Max to his wife. "We're the oldest married couple left. We're too old to be having this much fun."

"Oh, you don't stop having fun just because you're married," Christine scorned with a laugh. "It's just a different kind of fun. I love being married. I love having Max to take care of me."

Warren, who had ordered another cocktail for himself, spoke up after a long sip that took the glass halfway down. "My problem is I can't choose just one girl," he threw in crudely. "There's just too damn many of them."

"You're just young," smiled Christine. "You'll grow out of it when you find the right one."

"Oh, God!" Warren laughed. "Marriage would just kill me!" He picked up a knife from the table and held it to his heart with a twist. Christine laughed hysterically.

"Well," said Max, slapping Warren on the shoulder, "we're married, and it hasn't killed either of us. Not yet, anyway!"

Nick looked around the table uneasily and took a sip from his glass. Anytime marriage came up in conversation, Warren tried to rope him in and badger him for still being unmarried in his late thirties. Warren was still young in his twenties. He did it for no other reason than the few laughs he could get from teasing Nick and flustering him in front of others. Nick was glad when lunch arrived at the table, and the four ate in relative silence among the buzz of the crowd with only a few words between Christine and Warren. He was glad to get off the topic. Nick and Miriam had been engaged when she had left him. Warren brought this up every chance he got.

They sipped coffee after their meal. Nick was now feeling a little more social than he had when he'd first arrived. "I should have you both over sometime," he said. "On the boat I mean."

"Absolutely," said Christine. "We'd love to come. I'd love to see the boat again."

"You're welcome to come over anytime." Nick did not remember having them out on the boat, but they were sure to have been there for drinks once or twice. It was a constant flow of friends and acquaintances aboard when she was docked in the harbor.

"I'll bring some wine," Max said. "I'll find a good bottle for us."

"Sure. When can you make it?"

"Well," said Christine, "we are going to Cannes later this afternoon, but maybe in a day or so."

"You want to come, too, Warren?" asked Nick. "It'll be the four of us."

Warren, who had been distracted looking at all the people around them, came back now to the conversation. "I'd love to, Nicky, but I think I'm booked up every night this week. You'll have to find another date."

Max laughed at this. Nick smiled, but he didn't really find it that funny.

"We'll see," said Nick. "I think we can get along all right without you."

Christine smiled. "Of course Warren will be busy. Every girl on the coast is in love with him." She made him blush as she ran her hand through his hair. "And most of them already have husbands!"

Warren turned red as they all laughed at him, and he laughed at himself. Nick knew he loved the attention.

Christine turned to Nick. "And what about you, Nick? Have you and..."

"*Putain!*" said Max at that same moment. He looked down at his watch. "I knew we would stay too long. We have to be at the train station in a half hour. I have to go and change."

Nick and Warren both looked down at their watches. It was already two thirty. Warren tapped his watch and then remembered that it had stopped working weeks ago, no matter how much he wound it. He would have to take it in and have it fixed, if he could get some cash. But he still wore it anyway.

"You'll have to excuse me," said Max. "I have to get going. Christine, you can stay a little longer if you'd like, and then meet me at the station."

"I should go back, too," she said. "I have some telephone calls I need to make before we go."

Max stood and helped his wife up. "We're sorry, gentlemen. We'll have to hear about Nick's love life another time then. Let me leave some money for the lunch," he said as he pulled some bills out of his wallet.

"It's all right," said Nick. "I'll get lunch this time."

"Don't be silly," said Christine. She reached up and took the entire stack of bills from her husband's hand and gave them to Nick. "Will this be enough?"

Nick looked at the bills and saw that it was far more than enough. He handed her back all the bills but two. "That's more than enough. Warren and I will get the rest."

"Are you sure?" asked Max. Christine handed her husband back his money.

"Of course."

"We hate to run, but I am sure we'll see you soon."

"I'm sure," said Nick. "Be sure to come down and have drinks when you're free. Anytime is fine."

"We will," answered Christine. "*Merci.* I'll send you a note when we can make it."

The couple left with a wave, and Nick and Warren finished sipping their coffees and ordered some grappa from the hurried waiter.

"So what about you?" smiled Warren with his big smile and a wink, repeating Christine's question. "Have you and Miriam…"

Nick ignored him, though he knew Warren wanted to know all about it. They both took a drink from their glasses.

"I need to find a good girl," said Warren, after seeing that he wasn't going to get anything out of Nick. "One who's beautiful and absolutely loaded."

Nick looked at him amused. "You're with a different one of those every night."

"Yeah," he said, "but I need one I can stand for more than just one night. These girls, these pretty little things, they all start philosophizing after just one drink. Especially the ones who talk and talk about wanting to be models or actresses. So overdone. Just because they have a pretty face and a little allowance from daddy, they think the world owes it to them." He laughed and gave Nick another wink. "Not everyone can be Miriam Banks, princess of Hollywood."

Nick smiled at this. There was a long silence while they drank their grappa after lunch and slipped back into their own minds. A blur of faces walked by them on their way to the hotels and shops around the plaza in front of the Casino. A few cars drove by and circled the fountain on their way down toward the beaches. All the other tables along the sidewalk were filled with groups and couples having cocktails to cool themselves in the early afternoon sun. The faint smell of cigarettes rose from the tables and reached Nick's senses with a pleasant sigh. He felt the grappa burn his tongue and enjoyed it thoroughly. Warren could tell there was something on Nick's mind, but he didn't interrupt. He could see his eyes moving as he thought something over.

Warren sat back and lit up a cigarette. He let the smoke curl around his face before a warm wind came and whisked it away. He sat there and listened to the other conversations around him, not for what was being said, but just to the voices and the sounds of the people coming and going. A young girl in a green dress stepped from the sidewalk into the street and hurried across the road toward them to avoid a limousine that came fast up the hill, turned around the fountain, and pulled up to the Hôtel de Paris. Everyone watched to see who stepped out of the car without turning their heads. Warren instead watched the faces of the people as they looked to see. When he came to the end of his cigarette he pulled out another and lit it from the one he had been smoking. He held the case out to his friend.

"Cigarette?"

Nick looked at him and blinked his eyes. He had been deep in his own thoughts.

Warren put the silver case on the table before him. His eyes were still on the girl in green who was now talking to a man next to another table further down. Warren continued to stare as he, himself, was now distracted. "I've got to know her name," he said under his breath.

Nick came out of his own mind and looked around until he came to where his friend's eyes rested. "Ha!" he said. "She's just a kid, Warren. Leave her alone. That's probably her father."

Warren simply repeated himself. "I've got to know her name." He watched as the girl kissed the man she was speaking with on the cheeks and turned to walk away with him. As Nick opened his mouth to say something, Warren rose from the table and went off toward the girl. Nick watched as Warren quickened his step and called to her. But then the silver case on the table caught his eye, and he reached down and took a cigarette and asked the man at the table next to him for a light. When he turned back, Warren was sliding back into his seat at the table.

"Nice girl?" said Nick.

"Her name is Anne Marie."

"Ha!" Nick laughed. "Every girl's name is Marie something or other around here, isn't it? It's becoming an epidemic. They should pass a law."

Warren picked up the cigarette case and turned it over pensively in his hands. He stopped once or twice and then continued turning it over. "I'll see her around, I'm sure."

"Is that all you did was ask her name?"

Warren didn't answer.

They both sat back and breathed in the smoke from their cigarettes. After another few minutes of watching the people around them, and another glass of grappa, the afternoon was getting long, and Nick adjusted his collar and wiped his forehead. He asked the waiter for a glass of ice water.

"*Mais oui*," said the man. He brought out two glasses with ice and a carafe of water.

Warren turned to his friend. "Hey Nicky, I've been meaning to ask you something."

Nick smiled. He had heard this tone before, and he knew what was coming. It was the only time Warren was ever serious. The forced smile on Warren's face told him he was right.

"I was wondering if you could lend me some money."

Nick looked at his friend's eyes and flicked the end of his cigarette into the ashtray.

"What you need it for?"

"Look, Nicky, I know I borrowed money from you last summer, but I paid you back."

"I know. What do you need it for?"

"I paid you back, remember?"

"Of course, Warren," Nick laughed. "What do you need it for?"

Warren paused for a moment as if he were thinking up an answer. "Um, I'm buying a car from a friend. I just need a few thousand francs to get him the rest of the money. You know I'll pay you back."

"Of course," said Nick. "I know you will. How much do you need?" Nick didn't mind helping his friend. Warren always borrowed money from him and almost always paid him back. Nick never kept tabs on how much he owed him. It never bothered him that much.

"Why not make it four...no, five thousand. That way I can pay you back in a few weeks."

"Sure thing. Whatever you need."

"Well," said Warren, "would you be able to make it an even ten then? I, um, I might need them to make a repair or two. Make sure it's running right. You know."

Nick smiled and shook his head to himself. "Sure. I'll have a check waiting for you at the bank later. Around five o'clock. You can pick it up whenever you need it."

"Thanks, Nicky. I really appreciate it, mate. You know I'll pay you back."

"I know."

"Of course I'll pay you back in a few weeks."

"I know, Warren. It's fine."

Warren nodded. He wanted to change the subject quickly. He didn't want Nick to change his mind. "Say, what are you doing tonight?" he asked. "You want to go with me to this party I'm going to?"

Nick leaned his head back and hesitated. He wasn't really up for a party tonight. "Where?"

"I don't know yet, but it's at a friend's house. I can pick you up at the dock on the way."

Nick didn't have any plans for the evening, and with Miriam out of town he didn't really feel like sitting aboard the *Diamant* alone. He thought he might go to the Casino instead to distract himself. "Well, I might just…"

"Come on," interrupted Warren. "I'll make sure you have a good time."

Nick didn't put up any resistance. He knew Warren would ultimately win out through persistence. That was his way. There was no point in trying to back out. "All right," he said as he paid the bill the waiter had brought. Warren had reached for his wallet, but Nick waved him off. He knew Warren didn't have any money in his wallet.

"I'll swing by the dock at nine."

The two rose from the table.

"I'll see you tonight then," said Nick. "Nine."

Warren nodded in confirmation. They both turned to head in opposite directions.

"Nick," called Warren as Nick stepped off the sidewalk into the street. "You sure I can pick up that check later?"

"Sure," he said. He had almost forgotten about it already. "Anytime after five." He would stop by the bank on the way back down to the harbor after making a few other stops in town along the way.

CHAPTER NINE

The party that night was up at a high, open villa in the French hills above Monte-Carlo, from which one could see much of the city sprawling out below. It was the house of a man Nick had surely met before, but he did not recognize the man's name or face when Warren pointed him out darting among the crowd.

Nick had put on his suit apathetically, expecting at any moment that he would send a message up to Warren's hotel to back out of the affair. But he never brought himself to do it. Well after nine thirty, as Nick walked back and forth restlessly on a wall at the edge of the harbor smoking cigarette after cigarette, about to give up on his friend's arrival, Warren appeared in a cab with two cackling girls.

It was clear the three of them had already spent much of the evening drinking together.

The two girls talked excitedly between each other in the car on the way up; but then once seated at a table in the garden at the villa, they sat silently with Nick there as they waited for Warren to return with drinks. Nick watched as their eyes wandered among the crowd, looking at the excitement all around them. One of the girls was the one with Warren at the party aboard the *Miradora*. Marie was her name, Nick remembered. She looked even younger tonight than she had then. Her makeup was heavy around her eyes and swelled lips, and her hair was pulled back tight, causing Nick to see her as a pitiable clown among the more elegant and refined women there. But he also felt sorry for her for knowing this crowd so young. It was partly Warren's fault, and partly her own. The other girl, Nick placed as a young singer whose face he had seen on posters in Spain and all along the coast, but he couldn't be certain. He had no interest in asking her. Though she wore her long blonde hair up in a slightly more pleasing manner, she still looked foolish there more than anything.

They had arrived at the height of the party. The sounds of the cheerful guests swelled forcefully over the quick, melodic band music playing for the dancing couples from a record player and large speakers. Nick was feeling the first drink. It seemed to make everything louder. The two girls had downed their drinks quickly, and their eyes were already glassy. Nick shook his head at them. He didn't want to be around later to pick them up off the floor. Finally, one of the girls spoke to the other so that he couldn't hear her over the noise, and he felt alone but content at the table until Warren returned, grinning wide as he always was.

"I'll drink this one more slowly," Nick said as he took the glass.

"Don't hold onto it too long, mate. I told a waiter to bring a few more in a minute. What'd I miss?"

"Nothing here. Just sitting here watching everyone."

"Didn't talk to the girls?"

The two girls looked up for a second at them, then continued between themselves.

"Couldn't remember their names."

Warren laughed. He pointed to the blonde singer and then to the dark-haired one. "That's Emily, that's Stephanie."

Nick paused for a moment as he was lifting his glass. "I thought her name was Marie," he said.

"Marie? No, it's Stephanie." Warren tossed his drink back.

"No," said Nick, shaking his head. "She's the one from the other night. Benicio's party. Marie, remember?"

Warren looked over at the girls. "No, sir, Nicky. Stephanie and Emily. I swear."

The girls paid no attention to them.

Nick looked at the girl again. He squinted his eyes at her. "Maybe," he said. "But she looks so much like..." But the longer he looked at her, the more he realized he couldn't remember what Marie had actually looked like. "Oh, sure," said Nick, "I guess you're right." He took a long sip from his drink and brushed away the whole matter from his thoughts with a wave of his hand. None of it mattered anyway. His mind was on other things.

"You all right, mate?" Warren asked over the blare of the music.

Nick nodded without smiling or a single word.

There was a long silence for Nick as he looked out over the stone patio where the couples danced and moved in front of a live band that had now begun to play. The trumpeter and the man on the saxophone stood out boldly and controlled the bodies as they swayed. Then, after only several minutes, the sounds of the evening seemed to fade from their heightened tone, and there was a moment when Nick sensed fully where he was and all that was around him. He looked out distractedly over the lawn and the people dancing in the garden among the warm lights from the glowing candles that surrounded the place.

"Have you been up to Paris lately, Nicky?" Warren asked, breaking Nick's separation from the table. "If you have, you never rang me." Nick knew Warren had just come down from Paris a few weeks before, just as this season was starting here. At one time, Nick had been a steady figure in Paris. But no longer. He never liked to stray too far from the *Diamant* anymore. He liked to be on the water.

"Not for a year or so," said Nick. "Just before last summer, I guess."

"Why not, man? You've still got friends there. Everyone always asks about you."

"Like who?"

"Like…like everybody." Warren was overly energetic as usual.

"Eh," Nick sighed, "I've got enough friends here. Big cities take so much out of me."

Warren's eyes were dancing among the crowd as his interest had already faded. His body swayed in the chair to the music, and he tapped his drink with his finger in time. Nick saw this and dropped any endeavor at further conversation. He didn't feel like talking anyway.

One of the young girls, the one with the dark hair, stood up and sat down heavily in Warren's lap with her drink. She wrapped her arms around his neck and whispered something in his ear with a giddy laugh. Warren laughed, too, and then they whispered back and forth for a few minutes, a bit of an annoyance to Nick.

"Why don't you and Emily go dance?" Warren asked. "This is good music." The band was playing over the talking, and the beat was moving the crowd. But Nick wasn't feeling any of it.

The girl next to Nick flashed a forced smile of irritation and stood to take his hand. Her golden hair flickered in the light as she turned to him. Nick stood slowly and heavily, downed his drink, and then made his way to the floor with the girl leading him. He positioned them in the middle of several couples where he would feel more comfortable.

Nick had never been very fond of dancing. His height had always made him feel awkward and too self-conscious to enjoy himself. A decade of dancing lessons early on, insisted upon by his socially-conscious mother, had done nothing except to force Nick into seeing it as a chore. And yet tonight, as the music and the crowd moved him, and as the drinks took their effect, he began to relax and quickly found the beat. It took him a minute, but he remembered that he really did not hate to dance at all. It simply required the right music, crowd, and drinks to get him going.

Emily, the young girl opposite him, thought she was a very good dancer, but she was not. But this fact did nothing to stop her. Nick looked around and felt embarrassed as the girl flailed her arms wildly and bumped into others. He did his best to tame her movements with the motion of his own body and to make her seem a little less awkward, but his efforts had little effect. She had no rhythm or control. The two danced in the warm evening air among the growing crowd. Nick tried to enjoy himself. His second drink was working on him now, and he tried to forget that he didn't want to be there. After a few songs, he caught the girl's eyes for a moment, and she looked at him sternly.

"What are you doing?" she asked. She spoke in the same sham English accent he had heard so often from Americans on the Continent. She was probably from Philadelphia, Nick guessed, or maybe Cincinnati. It was the first time he'd noticed it in her voice. He knew then that she was not the singer on the posters he had seen.

"What do you mean?" he said, annoyed.

"Why are you looking at me that way?"

"What way?" The conversation already bored him. He knew she was trying to make something out of nothing. He didn't want to get roped in.

"The way you're staring at me," she said. "Look, don't fall in love with me, all right? I'm not your type."

Nick thought for a moment. He didn't like playing ridiculous games with young girls. He decided to have a little fun with her instead. "It's your makeup," he said with a serious face. "You have a dark smudge on your cheek."

"Oh!" said the girl. She stood for a moment frantically among the dancing couples wiping her face. Nick laughed to himself with great satisfaction.

After a few moments of watching her squirm, he decided to end his little joke. "Oh, you got it," he said. "You're fine now. It's gone."

"Let's go sit down," said the girl irritably, still wiping her face with the palm of her hand.

Nick led her through the frenzied crowd to their table. When they arrived, Warren and the other girl were no longer there.

"Must be out dancing," said Nick.

"What?" asked the girl.

"Um, let's order some drinks," he said, and at that moment he anxiously flagged down a passing waiter. He decided he was going to drink himself into having a better time.

"What would you like?" Nick asked her.

"Something with vodka," she said rudely.

"Two martinis," he told the waiter. "One vodka, one gin." The waiter nodded and was off a moment later, lost among the crowd.

"Let's go dance again," insisted the girl. "I love this song."

Nick hesitated. "We just got here. Let's wait for a minute until the drinks come."

"All right," she replied roughly, "but I love to dance."

Nick looked distractedly around the party, either for Warren or for the waiter, but he saw neither. Then, a few minutes later, the waiter finally returned with their drinks. Nick took the drinks in his hands, and then the girl grabbed one right away and took a big drink before he even had his own in front of him.

"Ugh!" she cried, coughing. "This is awful!"

Nick took the girl's drink and tasted it. She had grabbed the one with gin.

"Here," he said, laughing to himself. "This is yours."

The girl took a cautious sip from the glass of vodka, and then a bigger one. Nick sat back and drank his with a smile. He was enjoying himself a bit more now that he had decided to have some fun with this girl. He was taking great pleasure in her frustration.

The girl reached into her purse that had been lying on the table and pulled out a flip mirror and looked at her cheek. It was red from where she had been rubbing it. Nick watched her as she examined it carefully, turning her face from side to side in the dull light, running her fingers over it.

"I'm going to find a better mirror," she said, and before Nick knew it he had watched her walk away upset and was alone at the table. He was glad she had gone. He sat for a few minutes longer and enjoyed his drink slowly. But then the other girl Stephanie came to the table and sat across from him. She did not look at him. Her face looked flushed, and she was sweating. He concluded it was from the drinks and from dancing. They sat in uncomfortable silence looking past each other for a few minutes before Nick made an attempt to be sociable.

"Where's Warren?" he asked.

"Quoi?" she shouted over the music. Nick was startled by her loud voice so close, and he could tell she was startled as well. "What?" she repeated, lower this time, in English. Nick could see that she was French.

"Where's Warren?" he asked in French.

"I don't know."

He could see the girl didn't feel like talking.

"How long have you known him?" he asked her. She had been playing with the ice in an empty glass. Her wrists flashed with inexpensive glass jewelry as she turned the glass in her hands.

"Huh?"

"How long have you known Warren?"

"Oh, last year," she said. "He promised he would take me to a party this year. He called me up the other day."

"And here you are." Nick laughed to himself. "And you live close?" he asked. "Near here?"

"I'm in Menton," she said. "My father has a place there on the water."

"And where do you live other times?" He felt like he was interrogating her, but he had no one else to talk to, and he felt like talking to somebody now instead of just sitting silently.

"Lyon," she said. "But I want to live in Paris. I love Paris. I'm going to be a model."

Nick sighed and looked over her face as he spoke with her. She had a young face, not very pretty. He could see through her makeup that she wasn't very pretty.

"You're in school?" he asked.

She put down the glass, and Nick perceived that she was annoyed. Her attention was elsewhere, watching the couples dance.

"One more year," she said. "I don't like it. It doesn't fit me at all."

Nick laughed to himself. This girl wasn't even out of high school yet. "What do you want to do then?" he asked.

"Be a model," she said. "I already told you that."

"Oh. And…," said Nick with a pause, "what if that doesn't work out?"

She looked at him confused. "I don't know, but I think Warren's in love with me. I want to marry him next year."

"Ha!" Nick laughed. Then, looking at her face, he saw she was serious. "Aren't you a little young to be thinking about that?"

The girl looked at him even more confused. "No. I don't think so. He told me he loved me. It only makes sense. I love him, too."

Nick finally grasped the girl's sincerity. He had seen this with other girls Warren associated with. Warren told them anything they wanted to hear.

"You're serious?" Nick asked without realizing what he was saying.

"Of course," said the girl. She smiled a forced smile. Nick sensed she was totally unaware that she was just a toy to Warren. She had no idea what she was dealing with, and he pitied her even more for it. And yet, he had learned over years that these people were simply inconsequential to him. He could not invest himself too much in them. These girls, all the people he met along the coast, even fine couples like the Brecards. They were just names and faces that floated by on the wind. He was pleasant with them, for sure, but he knew they mattered very little. It was people like Miriam and Warren that really mattered to him. People like Benicio. The genuine ones. The others, he simply used them for entertainment. Once, many years ago, Miriam had equated them to extras in films, simply background and mirrors to the leads. Nick now thought it very fitting.

Warren came back to the table a moment later with fresh drinks in each hand and a waiter with a tray following him with two more. Warren's face was flushed as well, and there was lipstick on his collar and his cheek. His hair was in disarray and had been pushed back. Nick looked again at the face of the girl he had been talking with for the last few minutes and understood only then where they had been and what they had been doing. At first, Nick said nothing and thought nothing of it. It was just Warren being Warren. Then, for some unknown reason, a sense of irritation arose within him. He looked over, aggravated at his friend.

Warren was talking with Stephanie when the blonde girl arrived back at the table and sat close next to Nick. Her cheek was even redder from rubbing it, but she had put makeup over it. Nick could tell she had been drinking with another group at the party because she had been gone for several minutes and looked even drunker when she returned. Her eyes were watery and she had an even blanker stare. She hiccupped as she sat down. Nick took a glass and touched it to his lips. Then he looked at the girl Emily for a second and caught her eye again by accident.

"I know what you're trying to do," she said without looking at him.

"Oh, yeah?" Nick asked, surprised. "What's that?"

She turned to him severely. "Don't think you can just fall in love with me!" she said. "Everyone always tries to fall in love with me. It gets so boring. I'm not your type."

Nick did not know how to react. Part of him wanted to slap the girl right there. She deserved it. He looked at her and hesitated, then downed the rest of his martini in one gulp.

"Every guy thinks he's in love with me," she went on, looking away. "I hate it!"

Nick just stared at her blankly and said nothing. For a very long time he said nothing at all.

Finally, the girl looked at him again and spoke. "I'm going to go dance," she said, and was off again before he knew it. He watched her stumble into the crowd.

Nick sat at the table and thought to himself. "Well, that's that, I guess." He had tried to be nice to her, for Warren's sake, but now he just didn't care. He took another drink—Emily's that was left on the table. He looked at Warren and Stephanie talking across the table but did not hear them. He took the glass and downed half the drink quickly.

Nick glanced around the place and stood up, leaving Warren and the girl. In his mind, he could not differentiate this night from any other night as he moved about. It was the same people, dressed differently perhaps than another night, but the same people nonetheless. The faces all ran together since he did not really care who was there. The names all ran together, too. He might have met everyone there, at some time or another, either this season or in seasons past; or he might know no one. Yet, at all times he pretended to recognize old friends and accepted invitations for drinks or dinners with the same forced smile that he always wore at parties. Miriam had taught him years before that to do otherwise would be rude.

At a table in the garden, one man sat forward in his chair and leaned into a conversation while he smoked his cigarette. It was a motion, a simple act, that Nick had seen hundreds of times, and he always wondered if the man were legitimately interested in the conversation or just pretending, as Nick often did. Nick left that table and found some couples he recognized from a party a few weeks ago in Barcelona. They said hello to him and asked him questions, and he answered distractedly. He watched as another man across the party lay against the back of his chair and sipped his drink as he laughed, surrounded by a group of young women. Then the man blurred in his mind. It was all too much for him, and he felt he couldn't breathe. He needed to get out of there.

As he stood to leave, a flash of light caught his eye as his gaze traveled from table to table. The light came from a yellow dress that shone between two men in dark suits. At first he thought it was Emily and let the thought pass, but then he focused in to see if he recognized the girl. He did not. She seemed to be alone at the table. He watched her sit back and stare blankly at the drink before her. She was Persian. He knew it from her eyes. Those dark, inviting eyes. And her hair. Glorious, incessant wavy black hair. He had known Persian women before, and he saw her and could not take his eyes away. She was the type of girl who commanded you toward her.

But he looked around her and saw that she was in fact not alone. A bulky man in a dark suit that was too small for him sat next to her, discussing something intently with another man. He watched her for a few minutes as everything else blurred around her. He wondered why he had not noticed her there before. She was not far from the table he had been sitting at with Warren. He looked at her more closely—around her neck she wore a diamond choker necklace that drew attention from its reflected light; her long earrings did the same. The girl sat there not paying attention to the conversation of the two men or to the party as a whole. She twirled a diamond bracelet around her wrist as her only enter-tainment. The man she was with had his arm halfway around her waist as if he were afraid she might slip away, though his attention was on the man with whom he was speaking.

"What's got your eye, Nick?" asked a man that had been speaking to him.

Nick was silent for a moment until he stepped away without a word and left the man. The drinks were hitting him more forcefully now, and as he made his way across the ground, he kept his eyes fixed on the girl and did not look away when she saw him approach.

"Do you mind?" he asked as he motioned to an empty chair behind her.

The girl froze. "Um…," she said as she made a motion to the man next to her. Nick sat down anyway. Neither the man she was with nor the large man he was talking to ac-knowledged his presence.

"You're bored," he said forwardly—loud enough so that the other men might have heard if they were listening. "I saw you from across the way."

Her face had no emotion, and she looked back down at her bracelet and continued to turn it around her wrist. She was nearly ignoring him.

"I wanted to come over and ask your name." When he said this, he felt foolish, but he could not take it back. He thought of Warren earlier at lunch by the Casino.

The girl did not look up, but she stopped playing with her bracelet. "Lelah," she said.

"My name's Nick," he said. It was as if his actions were unable to be controlled by his own body. He knew the alcohol was helping with that. "Do you want to have a drink at the bar?" he asked.

She smiled but did not look at him. "Thank you for the invitation, but…," she began. She motioned with her head again toward the man who had his arm around her.

"I don't think he'll even notice," said Nick. He looked at the two men deep in exasperated conversation. "Just slip away and meet me at the bar," he said, "if you want to, of course." Before she could answer, he got up and turned and walked away. He smiled to himself. If she came, she came; if she didn't, he didn't care. He headed to the bar to grab a drink. If she didn't come, he would leave and head back down to the boat. He didn't want to be there anymore.

"Something strong," he told the bartender in English. The man looked at him. "Whisky, please."

He stood there at the bar for a few minutes. The girl did not come, and he could not see where she was sitting now. The dancing couples blocked the view.

"Damn it!" he said aloud. The couple next to him moved away. He was not angry. He just didn't want to be there.

In a few minutes, before he had finished his glass, he saw the same flash that he had noticed when he'd first seen her. Nick caught the girl's eye through the crowd and motioned for her to come over to him.

"How did you get away?" he asked as she approached.

"I slipped out of his arm and left it on the chair. I said I would be right back, but I do not think he noticed." Her accent was strong but elegant.

"What will you have?" asked Nick.

"What are you drinking?"

"Whisky."

"I think I will have some champagne."

"Good choice."

Nick gave the order to the bartender. The man opened a fresh bottle. A dozen other corks lined the bar.

"Thank you for coming over," she said to him as she leaned against the bar but kept a little distance between them. She was pretending not to talk to him. "I was bored. You were right."

Nick felt a surge of momentum. "Do you want to get out of here?" he asked. "Just go somewhere else?"

The girl looked at him and smiled. He was being very forward. "No. I think I should stay here," she said. "I am sort of on loan to that man."

"What do you mean?" asked Nick, confused more by the way she had said it than what she had said.

"My brother is doing some business with him," she said. "He told me to be nice with him. He seems to think I am his for the night."

"And you are?" Nick asked.

The girl laughed softly. "Hardly. I am his for this party, not for the night. I have to go back to my brother and tell him what I have heard. They are supposed to sign a contract next week. I am here to help that along. He just seems a little preoccupied at the moment. He will sign it."

"What business?" Nick didn't know why he asked this. He just didn't know what else to say.

"Shipping." She said this bluntly, and Nick hesitated for a moment. He simply nodded. The glass of champagne arrived and Nick invited her to sit down.

"No, I should not," she said, nodding back to her table.

"That's fine," said Nick. It was a little awkward, but they stood away from the bar near the edge of the dance floor and sipped their drinks, pretending not to be together.

Nick looked out over the dance floor and caught a glimpse of the girl he had been dancing with before. She was dancing close with another man a little older than Nick. When she turned his way, Nick winked at her, more to upset her than anything. Emily saw this and sent a bad look in Nick's direction. The girl he was with now saw the look as well.

"Do you know that girl?" Lelah asked.

Nick laughed. "She's supposed to be my date tonight, I guess."

"She is very beautiful," said the girl. "She looks very young."

"Do I really look that old?" he asked as he glanced at her. The girl didn't know what to say. "She is," laughed Nick. "It wasn't my idea."

Then, Nick watched as the girl stopped dancing and stood there in front of the other man. She yelled something Nick did not understand and stormed off with a look towards Nick as she passed. The man she was dancing with and the few couples around him stopped dancing for a moment. Then the man walked toward where the girl had gone and slipped through the crowd.

"It looks like she is upset with you," said the girl next to him. "I must go." She turned to leave.

Nick touched her on the arm to stop her. "It's all right," he said. "Stay for a minute. I wanted her to leave."

The girl stopped and faced him but kept her distance. "I really should get back to my table." She had a sorrowful look on her face. "I do not want to, but I must. You know this."

Nick reached up and took her glass. "Can I have just one dance with you?" he asked. He could tell the girl felt uncomfortable. Nick was drunk, and he tried not to show it.

"No. I should not. I really should get back."

The song that was being played had come to an end, and another fast song started to play. Nick put the glasses on a waiter's passing tray and took the girl's hand and pulled her into the middle of the dance floor as she let out a soft yelp. When they found their place hidden in the crowd, Nick turned and saw that the girl was laughing.

"What's so funny?" he smiled.

"I have not been dancing in a long time."

"Why not?" asked Nick as he began to move his body. The drinks were making him bolder. "I'm sure you go to parties all the time."

"Always business," said the girl. She was watching Nick's body and quickly found the beat to move with him. But she continued to keep some distance between them and kept her body fairly rigid. "I never have time to dance."

The two picked up the music and moved in rhythm. Nick reached down and touched her hand. She didn't pull away but looked at him and moved her body just slightly toward him.

"This is fun," said Nick. "I hate to dance, but this is fun."

The two moved in and out of the couples dancing around them, and the girl started to loosen up. Nick got a few stares because the girl he was dancing with commanded so much attention. Nick just smiled. He felt the alcohol pretty well now and he let go of anything he was holding back.

"Can I have a kiss?" he said without thinking. He wondered if he had said it or if he had just thought it, but the look of surprise on the girl's face confirmed the former.

"What?!" she smiled.

Nick pondered whether or not he should repeat himself or simply let it go. He felt himself blush a little, then repeated what he had said.

"I asked if I could have a kiss."

The girl looked at him and smiled. Nick could tell she was having fun dancing. She was having more fun now than she had been having all night. He knew he was, too.

Nick waited, but there was no response, and no kiss. He thought it better just to let it all pass. He smiled back at her.

In the next moment, the girl moved close to him and reached up as if she were going to kiss him on the cheek. Nick felt a rush through his body and almost tripped over himself. At the last second, the girl brought her finger to her lips and kissed it, then brushed Nick's cheek with her finger. Her hand felt cool on his warm cheek. All he could do was smile.

"That's it?" he laughed as he continued to move his body with hers. Again, it was mostly the drinks speaking, but he was finally having a good time. The girl just kept dancing a foot or two away from him.

Nick could tell the song was coming to an end. Their few moments of fun had made his night. He might never see her again, but he was glad to know there were girls like her here, instead of girls like Emily.

"Are you around Monaco much?" he asked. The song had nearly stopped. He hoped she wouldn't leave.

"Not often," she replied.

"Do you want to keep dancing?" asked Nick. Another song had immediately started to play, and the two had not stopped their movements.

"I did not realize the song had ended."

"Sure did," he said. "A few seconds ago. It's a new song now."

"Then we will dance for a minute longer. Let me know when a minute is up."

Nick pretended to look at his watch. He would just wait until the end of the song.

In the next moment, Nick saw out of the corner of his eye a large rush of momentum in his direction. One of the men the girl had been sitting with came up and grabbed her by the arm. He yelled something in Russian.

Nick and a few of the other couples stopped dancing. He was more startled than anything.

The man turned and gave him a look. As he did this, the girl wrestled her arm free and shouted something back to the man.

The girl turned to Nick. "Thank you," she said, then rubbed her arm and walked away. The Russian man followed her out toward the door.

Nick stood there alone on the dance floor for a moment, several pairs of eyes on him. The music had faded, but it started again and the couples began to dance around him. He felt awkward, and there was a resounding tone in his ear. Slowly, he walked over to where a balcony at the edge of the garden overlooked the street down in front of the villa, and he pulled a cigarette from his pocket. Below him, he saw the girl walk out briskly in a flash of yellow and light and get into a black car that was waiting out front. The man followed behind her and got into the back of the car with her. Another man followed and climbed into the front.

Nick pitied her. She was not happy, but she didn't seem to be in any trouble. He saw by the way she threw the man's hand off her and the way she moved to the car that she could handle herself.

Now, he was left alone in the night air. He looked up at the stars and out over the sea far off in the distance. He felt very alone. He pulled out his lighter and lit his cigarette as the car squealed away.

Back on the stone patio, Nick sat down at the table with Warren and the young girl he was with.

"Where's Stephanie?" he asked, not that he cared.

"You mean Emily," said the girl. "I'm Stephanie."

Nick looked at her confused. He had to think for a minute, repeating what she had said, before he realized the mistake.

"She's dancing with someone," said the girl. "You left her alone and she got upset."

Nick looked out over the dance floor and did not see that she had come back. "I think she's left now," he said. "I saw her run out of here."

"I think you made her mad," laughed Warren. He had the girl in his lap again. "She told us you said you were in love with her."

Nick took a deep breath to defend himself but then caught himself and let out the breath with a sigh. He could feel the alcohol in his breath. He didn't have enough energy just now, and it wasn't even worth the effort. "I didn't say that," he said under his breath as he let out the sigh.

Warren heard what he had said. "I didn't believe you would say such a thing," he said. "I knew she made it up. You know these girls."

Nick smiled at his friend. He was glad Warren was there.

"What is that red mark on your cheek?" asked Stephanie.

Nick wondered what she could be talking about, then rubbed his cheek and looked at his hand in confusion.

"It looks like lipstick," said the girl.

Nick laughed and wiped his hands on the tablecloth. "It is," he said. Warren gave him a wink. Immediately, Nick felt better.

"I didn't mean to upset her," he said to the girl. He lied.

"She'll be fine," said Warren. "What do you say to another drink?"

"If you insist." Nick smiled at his friend.

The rest of the evening passed as the table was replenished with glasses as new drinks came and empty glasses were picked up. It was an hour before Nick knew he had had more than enough. He stared out before him in the blur of people that surrounded him at other tables and danced wildly before him. There was the perception that he wasn't really there, that this was only an idea that had manifested itself as a party before him. These weren't people around him, they were apparitions, creations of his own mind, just as the girl he had danced with earlier was only a manifestation before him for a few moments. It was more of a blur than reality. All of this was. It was no different tonight than any other night here, or in Lisbon or Toulon or Barcelona or Portofino, or anywhere else, and the people around him were only images that played over and over in his mind.

He looked at the glass before him and saw it was empty. He stared at it for a few seconds and wondered if it would fill itself as it seemed to do over and over. Instead, he listened to the banging in his ears and felt the whirl in his head and decided he had had enough. He didn't want to stop drinking, but he wanted instead to be back in the harbor. If he could only snap his fingers.

"No more for me," he said aloud, expecting Warren to answer him. No one spoke to him, and he sat there for a few minutes staring blankly out at the party. There was no way to tell how much time had passed.

Nick looked up when he realized again where he was and sensed the other people at the table for the first time. The alcohol had started to wear off a bit from its peak, or at least he didn't feel as good as he had. An older man was sitting across from him, and it was as if he were seeing him for the first time, even though he had been staring at him for several minutes.

"Where is the girl with the glasses?" asked the man.

Nick looked around for a moment. Warren was gone. He was alone at the table with the man, but there was a couple sitting in chairs nearby. He was confused by the man's question. Was it the waitress the man wanted? Did a girl pass by? He looked around and scanned the faces of everyone he saw. There was no girl wearing glasses.

"I don't know," said Nick. "I don't know where she went."

The man did not hear him. He was listening to the conversation of the couple nearby.

Nick repeated himself. "I don't know where she is," he said loudly.

The man turned and looked at him with surprise. "Who?" the man asked.

"The girl with the glasses."

There was a pause. "Who?" repeated the man with a confused look on his face.

Nick wondered what he was saying. He looked around the place and didn't recognize anyone.

"Never mind," he said. He stood up heavily and left the man at the table, nearly knocking over a chair as he headed toward the door. He only stopped for a drink at the bar that he downed quickly before hitting the door.

There was a voice behind him calling his name. Nick turned and saw Warren standing there with Stephanie, but even their faces were a little blurry.

"I thought you left," said Nick. "Where the hell did you go?"

Warren laughed. "We just took Emily to get a cab home. She came back for her purse."

Nick remembered vaguely the girl he had last seen storm off the dance floor.

"I didn't like her," said Nick bluntly. "I'm glad she's gone." He looked at Stephanie's face to see her reaction, but she was watching the party and was very drunk.

"I don't think anybody likes her," said Warren. "But she seems to think everyone does."

"I didn't like being seen with her tonight."

"Why not?" asked Warren.

Nick just looked at him; the message was conveyed with his eyes.

"I'm sorry," said Warren. He looked at Stephanie and knew that his girl was even younger than Emily. "She's a good girl." There was a pause as he watched her looking out over the tables and the people before them.

Nick pulled Warren to the side and left the girl standing there. He had had a lot to drink, but there was something he wanted to say to his friend.

"Be careful with her," he said. "With Stephanie. Be careful with her." Nick felt that he was doing someone a favor.

Warren looked at him with a confused face.

"She doesn't know this place," Nick continued, drunkenly. "She's not a toy."

Warren's face had changed to a look of frustration. No one liked to be judged. He knew Nick was drunk. Nick looked into his eyes and said nothing.

"I want to get out of here," said Nick.

Warren handed him the fresh drink he held in his hand. "Rub some whisky on it, Nicky," he said. "Whisky'll make it better."

"I don't want any more."

"Just have one more with us, mate," said Warren. "Then I promise we'll go."

Nick looked at him for a moment, but he did not want to stay. He could tell Warren wanted to stay with the girl and continue the party.

"I think I'll head out on my own," said Nick. "I just need some air tonight."

The two stepped back and rejoined Stephanie who was watching the last of the dancers intently.

"Have a good night, Stephanie," said Nick. "It was nice to meet you." He said nothing of the other girl but held out his hand to shake hers. She took it drunkenly yet politely, and he felt how fragile and soft her skin was.

"I'll see you soon, Warren." Nick smiled at his friend. He tried to wink but blinked both eyes instead. The alcohol was still having its effect, and he felt good that he was leaving. If he could have snapped his fingers and been back in his bed, he would have paid anything at all for that.

Nick left the party and caught a cab outside from the villa to head back to the harbor. There was a line of taxis and cars coming up the street on the hillside as people left. Extravagant sedans and limousines. Coupes and convertibles. In the cab, he pulled out a tiny metal flask from his jacket pocket that he had forgotten about and took a big swig from it; then he watched out the window as the hillside became the city once again in a blur of lights. But when the driver stopped at the edge of the harbor to let him out, he hesitated.

"Take me up to the Casino," he called loudly to the driver.

"Where?" asked the man.

"To the Casino," said Nick. "I don't want to end the night like this."

CHAPTER TEN

The Casino of Monte-Carlo stands high on a sprawl-ing swell of land rising out of the sea between the harbor and the beaches of Larvotto on the Mediterranean coast. In the day, she sits quietly above the water, watching over all of Monaco as the center of the jewel where the sea rises into a city the color of sand. Surrounding her, palm trees that remain tranquil even in the summer wind, high cliffs shining above her in the sunlight, and a perpetu-ally azure sky. But at night, she is alive and flowing with extravagance. A proud and stoic building, the Casino is a beacon to visitors along the coast who gather here to mingle among other people of brilliance. Her façade is graceful yet simple, modest in fact, but her interior bears dazzling paintings, faultless marble floors, and elaborate gilded detail that attests to her eminence. On hot summer nights, during the height of the season, the famed and the wealthy alike meet here in lively pleasure, millions of francs flowing across the tables, with millions more displayed on wrists and necklines. Champagne flows in crystal glasses, charming fragrances fill the cool air, and warm lights invite eager guests to play. It is where some nights begin, and where others reach their culmination.

Nick walked into the Casino with the satisfied air of triumph and a confidence only an evening of profound drinking can muster. It was a feeling tinged with anger, as he had not enjoyed himself with the girls at the party. But he was going to change that. The marble entrance hall flourished with stylish couples engulfed in the pulsating air, an energy that struck him instantly and drew him with a force that could not be refused. Blurred faces passed that he sensed might be familiar but did not stop to address; he wore a smile, but it was not a smile for them, it was a smile that welled up from within him and surrounded him for his own pleasure. A great crowd passed fluidly between the brass gates of the entryway where they checked his passport that he had luckily slipped in his pocket while getting dressed. It was the crowd of opulence, a canvas streaked brilliant with luster. Echoes from his heels through the hall absorbed among the voices that spread into the high open room that held the green felt tables and the clack of the colored chips that called to him. He passed from the hall to this room and sat down at a table between two transparent men and pulled several bills from his wallet.

"Ten thousand francs," he said in French as he counted out the bills.

The dealer took the bills without looking up. "Ten thousand," he said. "In thousands?"

"Sure," answered Nick. It didn't matter.

When the dealer had counted out the chips, he waited for the manager's approval, then slid the stack across to Nick and placed the bills into the slot at the corner of the table. Nick looked up at the small sign to the side of the dealer that showed the maximum bet was five thousand francs. The first empty seat he had found was at a low-limit table. He divided his stack in two and slid half his chips out to play, his fingers passing over the familiar green felt. The dealer looked up at him for the first time, but his face did not show any surprise. Nick smiled inwardly and watched the first cards come out. The others beside him received face cards; he got a nine. The dealer pulled a seven and dealt around again, giving the first man an ace. Nick watched with contentment as the dealer slid a face card to him. Nineteen. That was all he needed to beat the seventeen the dealer was showing. The man to his left received an eight.

The dealer paid out the blackjack and, as expected, pulled out a face card for himself. It was an easy hand. Everyone beat the dealer when there were good cards on the table. Nick looked at the men beside him who only had small bets out. He smiled as he took back his original stack and a rectangular five-thousand-franc chip. The ceramic chips felt solid and heavy in his hand. Good start, he thought. He tossed the dealer a thousand-franc chip to make change for when a waiter might stop by with drinks.

He looked up at the dealer and studied his stoic, pockmarked face as he dealt the next hand. Nick had only placed a thousand on the table this time. As he predicted, he lost the hand with a seventeen against the dealer's twenty. He only lost a thousand. It was the price of waiting for better cards. He no longer paid attention to the bets the other men placed. He only cared about their cards.

Nick leaned back in his chair and looked around him after throwing out a small bet that he won on a weak hand. His attention turned from the table to the vibrant people moving around the Casino. He really hadn't noticed them when he had walked in. The drinks were still wearing on him. There was a group of striking girls standing across from him watching the roulette wheel spin. Only one of them was betting. Nick wanted to go talk to them, just to feel the attention on him again. A man walked by with a hand full of chips and dropped several of them when another man bumped into him. No one stopped to help him pick them up. Champagne was making its way around the room on a silver waiter's tray. Before the waiter could make it halfway across the room, the tray was empty and he returned to get some more.

"*Monsieur*," said the dealer.

"Huh?" said Nick.

"*Monsieur*, would you like to place a bet?"

Nick looked around him and snapped back to the table. "Oh, yeah." He grabbed a handful of chips and placed five thousand francs in front of him. The dealer dealt Nick a twenty and a blackjack to himself and immediately took the chips up from around the table. Nick didn't react, but only took another stack of chips and placed his bet.

"That was stupid," he said under his breath as the dealer laid the cards. "I wasn't paying attention." One of the men at the table had left, and it was now only him and a dark-skinned man to his right who had two girls standing uninterestedly behind him. He looked at the man's chips next to him and saw that he had more than twenty thousand in front of him, but he was making small bets of a few hundred at a time. Nick paused, and the dealer looked at him. He had to think for a second about what he was doing. The dealer showed an eight. He had fifteen. He had to hit. A ten came out and he went bust.

"Damn it!" he said aloud. The outburst was lost among the crowd. The coolness with which Nick had entered just moments before had been taken by the dealer. Now, frustration swarmed him. And he was only a few hands in.

"It's just money," he told himself. "Just money." Still, he hated to lose.

Without thinking, he threw out the rest of the chips and went bust against the dealer showing twenty. His eyes watched the chips go to the dealer and also the flash of a woman with a diamond necklace float by. He turned but could not follow her. In the same motion, he pulled out a few more bills and put out another bet for five thousand.

"You shouldn't have done that," he told himself as he saw his chips lying in front of him on the table. He watched the dealer give him fourteen and pull a six for himself. It wasn't a great hand, but compared to the dealer, he had a chance of winning. The man next to him only had a three and a five showing, giving him a winning hand with a decent hit. The man doubled his three-hundred-franc bet and pulled a seven, giving him fifteen. Tough luck, though Nick, but he still might win if the dealer went bust. Nick waved off any additional cards and focused on the dealer's hand. His only hope was that the dealer might go bust. The dealer turned over his hidden card and showed a three, giving him nine. Nick's heart sank. Then the dealer pulled out a ten in rapid succession. He had beaten the table, and the dealer pulled in the chips from the man next to him and the five thousand Nick had placed out.

Nick knew he had forgotten about the cards. He was very distracted. The fog in his head clouded him, and he had let himself get caught up in losing and had raised his bet for no reason. He had lost three in a row and knew he couldn't lose four. Again, he pulled out another five thousand from his wallet and placed it on the table. The dealer exchanged the money for chips and slid the stack over to Nick who immediately slid the stack back into the betting position. He received a discerning look from the man next to him and gave an annoyed look back. He knew what he was doing.

"If I lose this," he said to himself, "I'll walk away." That would put him twenty thousand down if he lost, or just ten thousand down if he won. He knew it wasn't good to bet so much without really paying attention. That took the fun out of it. The money itself didn't matter to Nick. He had plenty of that. But it still hurt to lose.

Nick's jaw dropped when he watched the dealer pull another quick blackjack. His heart sank and he felt a sudden rush of blood to his face. He looked down at his cards and had a king and a jack face up. On any other hand, he probably would have won. He couldn't believe what had just happened.

With a dejected look on his face, Nick stood up and reached into his wallet one last time. All he had left was ten thousand francs. The other man sitting at the table looked up at him and smiled. Nick felt like hitting him right in the mouth. As he stood there, the dealer waited to see if he would place another bet.

Nick looked at the bills in his hand. It was all he had left in his wallet, but it would be a good win and would help him get back. He had lost four in a row, and he knew the numbers would save him on this fifth hand. He couldn't lose. He wondered how the cards were running, but he hadn't really been watching them for a few hands. He had focused so much on his bet. In the moment it took him to place the bet on the table, he tried to replay the cards in his head. He sat back down in the chair and laid the money out for the dealer.

"Ten thousand," the man counted out and slid the chips over to Nick. Nick looked up at the dealer's red, pockmarked face with disgust. He looked so self-righteous there standing behind the table in his pressed white shirt and bowtie. Nick took the chips and placed all of them out in front of him.

"The maximum bet on this table is five thousand, *monsieur*," said the dealer without looking up. Nick looked at him again. The manager was standing next to him watching Nick.

With a quick glance, Nick looked around the room and saw that the table opposite him had a maximum bet of twenty thousand francs. There were two other men playing there. As the table awaited his move, he pondered whether he might walk over to the other table and place his bet. The cards might be better there. He wanted to get it back. He was either going to win big or lose big. It was now a matter of pride. He decided to play the hand at this table. He was going to play this one hand. If he lost, he would walk away. If he won, he would walk away and take a break for a minute. He needed a drink. Either way, he would wind up several thousand down but would come back again to win it back. A cool drink would taste good right now. He was too warm in his suit.

Nick kept the full bet out there with a look up at the manager. He had known the man for years and looked up with a confident plea in his eyes to let him place it.

"Take it," the man said in French to the dealer. "Let him play if he wants." He gave a look to Nick and folded his arms with a smile. He knew Nick had lost a few hands in a row and was trying to help him out.

The dealer laid out a seven and a five for the man next to him and gave Nick a two and a nine. The dealer pulled a six for himself. Nick had the best hand on the table. There had been several low cards out, and now he could pull a high card and beat the dealer by making him bust. He knew he had a good hand and that the man next to him should not hit on a twelve. The dealer had sixteen, the worst possible hand.

The dealer made a motion to the man next to him, but essentially passed him over not expecting him to hit. Nick looked up at the dealer as he started to say he wanted to double, but the dealer's eyes unexpectedly went back to the other man at the table.

"I want a hit," said the man. Nick couldn't believe what he was saying. The man only had a bet of five hundred francs out there and had a decent hand with twelve against the dealer's sixteen. He gave a look to the man, questioning him with his eyes.

The man looked back at him with a dumb look on his face. "Twelve's a tricky one," he said. But he tapped the table for another card, and everyone standing around watching looked in disbelief. He obviously didn't see that the dealer showed a six and Nick showed eleven.

"Are you sure, *monsieur*?" asked the dealer.

The foolish man smiled and tapped the table again for the card.

"No…," Nick began, but it was too late. The entire table watched in disbelief as the dealer slowly pulled out a queen. The man went bust.

"Oh well," said the man with a stupid grin.

Nick's heart sank even lower when he saw the card he wanted being thrown away. The man had lost the hand, and it had been a card that would have given him twenty-one. There would have been no chance to lose his hand, but now he couldn't be sure. The man shook it off with a smile and set to counting his stack of chips.

Nick caught himself. He knew he still had eleven and that, against a sixteen, he should still have as much money on the table as possible.

"I want to double," said Nick. He knew there still might be another high card in there. He reached for his wallet.

Both the manager and the dealer looked at him and knew it was right to double with this hand.

"Um, I don't have any more money on me," said Nick, "…but I have to double." He looked up at the manager who he had known for years. "You know I'm good for it, Gabe." If he hadn't been drunk, he wouldn't have said it. He would have simply taken the hit.

The manager wrote something on his pad of paper and gave him a nod. "Let *Monsieur* Duncan double it," he said to the dealer.

The dealer nodded and pulled out twenty thousand francs in thousand-franc chips. He placed ten thousand on the table next to him and the other ten next to Nick's original bet. Then he waited for the manager's nod. Now all Nick needed was a ten or a face card.

He looked in disbelief at the twenty-thousand-franc bet he had there in front of him. It gave him a sinking feeling, not that the bet was high, but to know that he was not betting with his own money. He had broken a rule he always kept when he played. But he had broken a lot of rules tonight.

The dealer slid a card from the shoe and kept it face-down as he placed it over Nick's cards. A lot was riding on that one card. The money was insignificant. It was his pride that was at stake. He had let himself go. If he lost the money, he had more—it was just money—but he never wanted to be in this position where he was in debt to someone.

The dealer flipped over his own hidden card. It wasn't a ten, but it was an eight. He had fourteen and had to hit again. Nick wanted him to go bust. It would take away the sick feeling in his stomach. But the next card he pulled was a three.

"Seventeen!" Nick said aloud. His glance went around the table to the other people there, and he met each of their eyes for only a brief second. All he needed was a high card now in the card that sat face-down before him. A king, queen, jack, ten, nine, eight, or even a seven would give him a win. A six would push. He knew he had a good shot.

For a moment, he stopped breathing and waited for the dealer to flip his card. It was an eternity as the dealer's hand reached across the table and rested over the card for only a moment before turning it over.

It was a high card, all right. It was an ace. For half a moment, a rush of joy went through Nick's body before he caught himself and realized what that meant. He had doubled on an eleven and, with an ace, that gave him twelve to the dealer's seventeen. He had lost the hand.

But, even more than that, he had lost the part of himself that knew better than to do what he had just done.

Nick looked around the table. The dealer was fighting back an arrogant smile as he brought in the cards and took away the chips. The manager had a blank stare that showed no emotion.

Twenty thousand, Nick said to himself. Lost in one hand.

Then he thought about the rest that he had lost. He had set some vague limit in his mind when he had walked in, and he had gone over this many times over. He wasn't sure of the exact number in his daze, but it was many tens of thousands now.

Nick stood up from the table in disbelief. He was done playing. All the money in his wallet was gone, and he owed the Casino ten thousand on top of that. That was the worst part. That was something he had never wanted to do.

The manager looked over at him. "I'm sorry, *Monsieur* Duncan," he said.

"That's all right," said Nick with a loose smile. "Me, too." He told the manager Gabriel that he would send the money up the next morning when the banks opened on Monday. The manager smiled and knew he would. They knew Nick was good for the debt. The two shook hands with dejected smiles. As Nick walked away from the table, he went over it all again in his mind. He knew it would do no good now, but he couldn't let it all go. It had all gone so wrong so quickly.

"You lost a lot of money, Nick," he said under his breath as he took slow steps. "In less than ten minutes. That was stupid. Don't let that happen again. You shouldn't have let that happen."

The crowd still flowed through the Casino. Radiant people flashed all around him, but he did not see any of them.

"I'm not going to play for a while," he told himself as he walked toward the entrance. There was a deep, relentless throbbing in his head. He walked up to the elegant wooden bar that was surrounded by couples. A woman stood next to him and put her body close to his to get his attention right away. He knew this girl. Her name was Camilla, and she was a girl for hire. He could have her if he wanted her. In fact, he'd had her before, last summer. She spoke to him calmly, asking his name. He turned and smiled disingenuously. He spoke to her briefly among the buzz of the crowd, and she did not recognize him, and he did not ponder this too long. He wished her a good evening when she understood he wasn't interested and met the eyes of the bartender as she walked toward the *salle de jeux* from which he could still hear the clack of the chips.

Standing at the bar, surrounded by its swarm of dresses and tuxedoes, he ordered a martini. "Straight up, dry," he told the bartender. "Two olives." As he said this, he realized he didn't have any money to pay for the drink. It made him feel cheap. He hated himself right now.

"Hold that order," he told the bartender as he reached for his empty wallet. "I'll have to come back."

The bartender stepped in front of him. "I will get this one, *monsieur*," he said.

Nick looked up and recognized the man he had spoken to so sternly. The bartender was a short little white-haired Italian man that he had spoken with many times over the years. He regretted that he had spoken as he had to him. "Thanks, Marco, but I really…"

"*Monsieur* Duncan, you can buy me one another time," the man giggled quietly, and Nick caught himself and laughed inside.

"No, Marco. I couldn't," Nick began, but the bartender simply held up his hand.

Nick watched the man artfully make the drink by chilling the glass and rinsing it with vermouth, then stirring the gin with ice and pouring it over two olives on a long wooden skewer. He knew exactly how Nick liked his martinis. Nick was a regular fixture there over the years. He was glad that Marco remembered him. He was glad to have a cool drink.

"*Voila!*" said the man with an ecstatic grin. He slid the glass meticulously across the bar.

"Thank you," said Nick. "I'll have to owe you, Marco. I'll get you next time." He took a sip, and the drink felt good on his tongue. It nearly took away all the dismal sentiment he had from the evening so far.

"We haven't seen you yet this year, *Monsieur* Duncan," the man said to Nick after he had served someone else.

"I just got in a few days ago, Marco. This is the first time to the Casino. You know I'd come see you, Marco. Of course I would." Nick's supreme drunkenness had worn off, and he was suddenly enjoying himself a little.

"And how has luck been treating you tonight, *Monsieur* Duncan?

"Not so well," said Nick. "I had a bad run."

The man smiled gloomily. "This is no place to have bad luck," he said. "You have a bad run here and you could be in trouble!"

Nick knew he was right. He looked over the man in silence. He had always liked Marco. Marco, in his simplicity, always knew the right thing to say to make Nick think straight.

"How is your life, *Monsieur* Duncan? How are things going?" The man's smile had not left his face. It was contagious.

"You ask a lot of questions, don't you, Marco?" he laughed.

Marco laughed as well. "Just inquiring, *Monsieur* Duncan. You are one of my favorite customers. I always like to know that you are well."

Nick watched him as he served the other people. He was an amusing little man, full of enthusiasm.

"Who do you think will win the race next weekend?" asked Marco.

"I don't know," said Nick. He hadn't really thought about it. The Grand Prix was only a week away now, and there would be much excitement.

"My money is on the Englishman *Monsieur* Moss," said the bartender. "Mercedes has the fastest cars, and *Monsieur* Moss is the best driver. It is a very good bet."

"Good," Nick smiled. He had never been much into racing, but the Grand Prix was something he would enjoy. He had been here for the race in '52, but they had not held it the last two years. He was looking forward to seeing it again this year.

A few minutes passed, and another girl moved over next to Nick and glanced briefly at him but said nothing. She wore a long black dress and clutched her small glittering purse nervously as she looked around her. He didn't know her name and wondered if she were a hired girl as well. Perhaps she was new. He looked over at her and considered offering her a drink, but then decided against it, as he had no money. He just wanted to be done for the night.

After following Marco with his eyes as he attended to a few other customers, he tipped back the martini glass and sipped the last drop. As he stood up from the bar, he happened to look over to the blackjack tables, and he felt all the frustration and resentment swell back up inside of him. He had forgotten everything as he had sat and talked with the funny little man. "Don't lose it again," he said under his breath. "You can lose it all another day," he laughed to himself and felt better.

"Thank you," he called to Marco. "I owe you. Next time."

"It's nothing, *Monsieur* Duncan. *Di niente.* I will see you again soon?"

"Sure," said Nick. "I'll be back. You know I will." He reached between two men at the bar and shook the bartender's hand firmly.

Nick decided it was time to go. His evening had not turned out as he had planned, and it might only get worse if he kept on. It was certainly not getting better. As he made his way out of the Casino, he spotted a couple he recognized from earlier that day. The woman recognized him, too.

"Nick!" she called from far away.

He lifted his head and waved to her as they approached. *"Ciao, bellissima!"* he laughed and held up his hands in front of him with a smile. The martini he had drunk quickly, and he had again picked up the feeling with which he had entered the Casino that night.

"Nick, how are you?"

"Fine," he said. He kissed the woman on the cheek and shook the man's hand. It was Max and Christine with whom he had eaten lunch with Warren. "How was Cannes?" he asked.

"Crowded as always," said Max. "The whole coast is swarming with people already. So many new people. In the summer, when it really gets bad, we will have to find a new place to go!"

"It will be a little quieter after the race," assured Nick.

"Sure it will," said Christine, "but more and more people keep coming each year."

Nick spoke to them warmly for a few minutes and reiterated his invitation to the *Diamant* for drinks. He tried to speak coherently through the many drinks he'd had that night, which made his words seem slow. The couple said they would come over the next evening if they could, and he left them with handshakes and kisses. He didn't want to keep them long. He watched them go into the Casino excitedly and join the other handsome people. As he turned and walked out of the place, he bumped hard into someone's shoulder.

"Watch where you're going!" said a rough English voice. Nick immediately recognized it as Richard, the man from the Brecards' party, without having to look. He wasn't in the mood to deal with any of this right now.

"Sorry," he said flatly as he continued on.

"I didn't think they let crooks in here," said Richard contemptuously.

Nick looked hard at him but didn't feel like getting into it. Not tonight. He had other things on his mind. He continued on outside without a word. Richard called something after him as Nick was absorbed by the crowd, but he didn't stop to listen and stepped into a waiting black cab. But then he remembered he was out of cash and stepped back out. He wasn't used to being without cash.

"Sorry," he said. "No money."

The driver waved and waited there for another fare by the fountain where all the extravagant cars were parked in front of the Hôtel de Paris. Nick looked at his watch and did not believe the time. He tapped its face and shook it a few times, but it was working all right. His stomach hurt, and he wanted to get out of his suit. After the evening he'd had, the thought of the cool sheets in his bed called to him impatiently. He walked down the street between the Casino and the Hôtel and began his long gin-filled, irate walk down the steep hill to the harbor in the moonlight.

CHAPTER ELEVEN

Max and Christine arrived just after eight the next evening. Nick had almost forgotten they were coming until he was putting on his suit to go up to the Hôtel for a drink and saw the face of his watch that reminded him of the blurred events from the night before—after he had lost his money at the table. He had ridden up early that morning with a headache to the bank and then to the Casino to drop off the money with a manager there, and then he spent the rest of the day aboard the yacht avoiding drinking and trying to forget all that had happened. But now that he remembered his invitation to them he took off his jacket and decided he might go and see Benicio aboard the *Miradora* for a drink if they did not come. But, in fact, they did arrive just a few minutes later. When they appeared down on the dock, Nick was starting to read from a new book he had dug out that afternoon, up above in the cooler air of the higher deck. It was still fairly light out, and the remnants of the day were fading behind the high gray hills.

"Sorry we are late," said Christine.

"Late?" Nick laughed. "Not at all. I'm glad you could come."

"We spent the day at the beach and needed a shower and change," said Max.

"Of course," said Nick. He took Christine's hand and helped her aboard. Max came across the gangway with two chilled bottles of wine in his hands. "Who are those for?" asked Nick.

"They're for you," said Max, "or for us. I brought them if we wanted to open them."

"Thank you. We'll open one to start off with." Nick took the bottles and would put away the one he'd prepared above. "We'll have it up there."

"Up here?" asked Christine. She was standing at the foot of the steps that led to the second deck.

"Yes. Right up there."

The second deck of the *Diamant* was warmly lit, and there was a plate of olives and cheeses in the center of the table. Nick had been nibbling furtively on the food that Elena had hurriedly brought up while he was waiting there. There was also a half-empty glass of Scotch on the table. It was his first of the day and was meant to try and help his headache. Max saw the glass when he reached the top deck.

"We did not mean to keep you waiting, Nick," he said as he looked at his watch.

"Max," said Nick with a smile, "just relax and have a drink." He handed Max and Christine each a glass once he had uncorked the bottle and poured the wine. A piece of cork went in Nick's glass, and he fished it out with his finger. The three sat down at the table and toasted to each other's health, then Nick took the bottle and set it in ice on the table.

Nick had never really known Max or Christine. He had met them once or twice before at parties of some mutual friend perhaps, and it seems that they had been aboard once before, though he did not clearly remember. Then he had sat with them with Warren up at the Café for lunch. But beyond genial conversation he had never spoken with them at length. Most of the couples along the Riviera were just like these two—young and exceedingly friendly—and Nick often had new people aboard for drinks. It was always pleasant to get to know others. If they were not overly dull, as some often were, Nick usually found the people who came to the coast quite charming. To hear their stories and the places they'd traveled, where they were from and what life was like there, interested him greatly. Yet he found that people all over the world had comparable qualities no matter what their origin or culture. Genuinely good people here were no different from good people elsewhere. When Miriam had been here with him, when they had been a couple, Nick had mingled continuously with everyone along the coast. He felt like he knew everybody to some degree. But now, many of those friendships had faded, and in reality he could count on only one hand his real and true friends.

"It looks as though you went to the beach today as well, eh Nick?" asked Max. Nick laughed and shook his head no.

"Yes, he looks so dark!" said Christine.

"Oh, no," Nick smiled. "It's all from my time in Spain. I'm just getting settled in here. I haven't had much time to get any sun here yet."

"I wish I could get that dark," said Christine as she sipped from her glass. "I could never get that dark." Nick already liked Christine. He could tell she was simple, but he liked her. She smiled endlessly and always looked unnecessarily to her husband for affirmation, but she made Nick feel at ease.

"And you had an exciting night last night at the Casino?" asked Max.

"Of course," said Nick. "Warren and I were at a party before you saw me there. I left the party early so I could go and play a few hands."

"I'm sure you won a lot of money," smiled Christine.

Nick thought back on the night that he had tried to forget. "I just played a few hands. Didn't win anything, really."

He hated that he had lost money at the table. It wasn't the amount of the money that upset him, it was the way he'd lost it. He tried not to think about it, and how he had to take the money up with a note for Gabriel this morning.

"Marvelous!" said Christine. "Max always gives me a little money to play with. I always lose it, of course."

"What do you play?" asked Nick.

"Mostly roulette. I don't understand any other games. All I know is black and red and even and odd, and maybe I pick a lucky number now and then. When there are a lot of red numbers, I put it on black because black should come up next. I win a little, but then I always lose at the end. Max does not mind. It is only small money."

"I like roulette," said Nick. "But I always play cards. I guess it's all the same, really."

"Sure it is," said Max. "The casino ends up with the money in the end."

"And I like craps, too," continued Christine. "But I never know what I'm doing. I just do what Max tells me, and I win."

Max looked thoughtful as he lit up a cigarette and watched the smoke curl away from his face. He offered one to Nick and his wife, but they declined.

Christine looked over at Nick excitedly and jumped in her seat. "We ran into the Prince today!" she said. She nearly spilled her wine as she spoke.

Max looked over at her and smiled. He knew she had wanted to tell someone all afternoon. "Well," he said, "we got held up by a line of black limousines, anyway, on the way to the beach. We think it was Prince Rainier, but the windows are so dark, you know."

Nick nodded and tried to show Christine that he was interested in her incident, but he himself had been invited to dinners at the Palace several times.

"He is very handsome," said Christine. "He is looking for a wife so that he can have a son and keep the principality and not give it to France. If I were not married to Max, I would throw myself at him and become a princess! I would have many sons for him!"

"Oh," laughed Max, blowing out smoke with his laugh, "she's always talking about having babies. That's the last thing we need to keep us busy. I am going to get her a puppy; then she will see how much work it is!"

"Oh, Max, if I were a princess, I would have so many people to help me take care of them. But I don't want a baby yet. A puppy, though? That would be so wonderful!"

"Christine wants so badly to become a princess," Max went on. "She saw the Prince in passing once before, two years ago. She talks about him all the time now, I'm starting to get jealous! I don't have a drop of royal blood in me."

"No," said Christine, "I really couldn't bear the responsibility of being a princess. Too much work. Too many official duties and appearances. I'm happy where I am. And I am happy with Max."

"No, really, though?" asked Nick jokingly. "All the wonderful dinners and galas? Living in a palace? Traveling the world with your entourage? Having people bow to you? It's such a torturous life!" He laughed at himself. "You can't kid us, Christine. You'd love to be a princess! Any girl would."

She smiled as she reached for the bottle of wine. "Ok, well maybe you are right, Nick. No woman could ever turn that down if she had the chance."

Nick stood and took the bottle from her and poured each of their glasses full. Then he saw Max's cigarette case lying on the table and asked for one. His own case was down in his cabin.

"Of course," said Max. He lit Nick's cigarette for him.

Just then, Nick heard his name being called from somewhere. The three looked at each other around the table and wondered where it had come from. "Nicky!" the voice called again. It was a voice from the dock below. Nick stood up and looked down over the rail.

"Anyone up there?" shouted a man standing there with a girl by his side. Nick could tell by the voice that it was Warren.

"Where's the party, Warren?" shouted Nick down to his friend with a laugh.

"Up there with you, mate!" Warren started to come aboard and held the girl with one hand and a bottle of champagne in the other.

"*Salut*, Warren!" cried Christine, now standing at the rail. "Lovely of you to stop by."

"Oh, hello, Chris. Is Max up there with you?"

"Hello Warren," shouted Max. "Come up with us."

"I'll be right there."

"No!" called Nick. "You stay there, Warren, but send up the bottle and the girl!"

Warren came up to the deck with the girl, and Nick saw that it was neither of the girls from the party the night before up in the hills. He was glad for that. "I'm not interrupting anything, am I?" Warren asked as Nick slapped him on the back and he greeted Max and Christine who were leaning on the rail.

"No, not at all," said Max. "Come and have a drink with us."

"*Merci*," said Warren in his best French accent.

"Who is this?" Max said as he went over to greet the new girl and pour her a glass of wine.

"Everyone, this is Kate Bennett. Kate, this is everyone. Christine and Max…," he paused because he did not know their last name.

"…Gaudin," said Max as he took her hand.

"…and this is Nicky," continued Warren.

"Nick, really," said Nick. He always winced when Warren called him that.

"Nice to meet you," said Kate. "And does Nick have a last name?"

"Nope, just Nicky," said Warren as he helped Max fill some new glasses with wine and found a place in the ice for the champagne.

Nick looked at the girl. She was very pretty and immediately seemed more polished than the other girls he had seen Warren with so far. Her blonde hair was not dyed, and she had little need for makeup. She was closer to Warren's own age, maybe even older. Her thin dress was long and blue and meant for a party that night, and she was tall but slender. Her pearl necklace and bracelets, and the skin on her bare shoulders and arms, shone vibrantly in the light of the rising moon. Nick had sensed from her accent, or rather the lack of one, that she was American. But her voice was not crude like other American girls; it was gentle and charming. He was instantly fond of her.

"Where are you from, Kate?" asked Christine right away.

"New York," she answered after taking a sip of the wine.

"In the City?" asked Max. "We stayed in a hotel just off Broadway for a few months once. By the theaters, you know."

Nick had brought over some more chairs, and they all settled around the table. Warren was eating hungrily from the plate of food without looking up.

"No, afraid not," said Kate. "Poughkeepsie mostly."

"Where's that?" asked Christine. "On Long Island?"

"Just about two hours north of the City," said Kate. "It's really not bad if you take the train. Maybe two hours."

"She went to Vassar," added Warren between bites. His mouth was full and he didn't look up.

"Really?" asked Nick, turning to her.

"Yes, I just graduated. I'm here with my mother and father. They're taking a trip around the world, and I flew in to meet them in Europe for a while before I go back to New York."

When she said this, Nick saw that she really wasn't nearly as old as he had thought. Yet her youth did not show in the way she carried herself.

"Now you're on vacation," Warren added, wiping his face with his sleeve.

"I guess so. It's nice to take a little break after school."

"We met at lunch," said Warren. "I had to help her with her French."

Nick laughed to himself when Warren said this. Warren's French was atrocious.

"I had forgotten everything I learned freshman year. My Italian is far better than my French. I spent a summer in Rome."

Warren reached over and started opening the bottle of champagne. He untwisted the wire top and popped open the bottle, sending the cork flying somewhere over the rail and onto another boat. Everyone cheered. Nick watched Kate smile calmly and laugh to herself. Then Warren started pouring the overflowing bottle into everyone's glasses, whether or not they still had some wine in them.

"Thank you," said Christine as she took her first sip. "I don't even know if this is good champagne. You could give me bubbling grape juice and I wouldn't know the difference. Is this good, Max?"

Max took the bottle from Warren and looked it over meticulously, mostly for effect. He knew it was a cheap bottle, but he made a serious look and nodded his head.

"Good," said Christine. "I like champagne."

They all took a sip and then Warren filled all their glasses to the top.

Nick was feeling pretty good. He had wine in his hand and friends around him. "Who else have you met here?" he asked Kate. "Anyone interesting?"

"Just Warren. We arrived last night from Paris and I slept most of the morning before having lunch up in Monte-Carlo near the Casino."

"You'll never guess who I caught her with!" began Warren. He suddenly had an excited look on his face. He was waiting for someone to ask who. No one asked. Nick let him simmer in his attention for a moment, and then he finally spoke up.

"I saw her talking with Sir Richard!" said Warren. "I had to pull her away before she got into the wrong crowd."

"It's true," said Kate. "Warren walked up and started talking to me as if he'd been waiting for me. Then he pulled me right over to his table and we had lunch with his friends. I was only asking for directions."

"That's good," said Christine. "We don't like Richard either."

"What's the matter with him?" asked Kate. "He seemed like a nice enough guy. But everything I've heard since I've met him has been bad. Mostly from Warren."

"There's nothing wrong with him," said Nick. He didn't even want to talk about him.

"He's just a bit of a bully," said Warren as he took a sip. "Doesn't like Australians for one thing. Or Americans. I'm surprised he was talking to you. You should have seen the look he gave me, Nick!"

The bottle of champagne didn't last long with Warren pouring, and they moved onto the second bottle of wine. Nick could feel the drinks hitting him. He hadn't been able to eat much all day, so he was drinking again on an empty stomach.

"Sir Richard's got a hell of a lot of money," said Warren. "He doesn't like all the new people who keep showing up here. Thinks he owns the place. Thinks he's God damned Jesus Christ or something. But he's just a bum with a hell of a lot of money. That's all."

"Wow!" said Kate. "From what I've heard so far, I guess I won't talk to him again. But he seemed really nice to me." Nick saw that her glass was empty and filled it again. "Thank you, Nick."

"Welcome," he said with a nod.

"I think he has a grudge against everyone," said Max. "I've only met him a few times, but I've never liked talking to him."

"He's just English," said Warren, "and the English are just sore about everything."

Nick laughed at his friend. "Well put, Warren."

"Thank you."

"And what about you, Nick?" asked Christine. "I've heard you and Richard especially don't get along."

Nick didn't like the way the conversation was going. He never liked to talk about Richard, and he wanted to change the subject.

"Oh, I have no beef with him," he said. "He seems to have a problem with me. But you'll like most of the people here," he said to Kate. "Very nice people, generally."

"He doesn't like Nicky because Nicky here went to the big house!" When he heard the words, Nick wished that his friend hadn't said it. But he did. That was Warren.

"Is that right?" asked Kate. "You were in prison?"

Nick was silent for a moment. "Yep. I was."

"Oh, I'm sorry."

"Why?" said Nick. "Don't be sorry. I'm not ashamed of it. I just don't go around blabbing about it to everyone." He shook his head with a laugh at Warren.

"Why?" asked Christine. "What did you do?"

"Christine!" interrupted Max. "That is not very polite."

"Oh, it's all right, Max," said Nick. "I don't mind. Don't worry, I didn't kill anyone or anything. My good friend I worked with got in trouble with some business back in New York, and the Feds wanted me to testify against him. They didn't have a case otherwise, I knew. I refused, and so they locked me up for contempt. After a few months, they realized I wouldn't squeal on my friend, so they released me. I had some friends in the right places, I guess. Plus they had found some other evidence, and my friend made a deal and got just five years."

"I'm sorry to hear that," said Kate.

"Well, it's all right. I rather enjoyed it. Lots of time to read."

"You did nothing wrong then?"

"Nope," said Nick. "But it followed me here, and Richard found out somehow, and so he's got some grudge against me. Thinks I made my money doing some crooked business. I kind of like it though, having that attached to me."

"So why didn't you tell on your friend?" asked Christine. "If you did nothing wrong, you didn't have to go to prison for him. I would do anything in the world to stay out of prison!"

"He was my good friend," said Nick. "We went to college together. I'm not just going to rat him out. I didn't see he had done anything wrong anyway. It was all a misunderstanding."

"But why didn't you just tell them what they wanted to hear? You'd rather go to prison?" she asked, horrified.

"I wasn't going to testify against my friend."

"I'd be so ashamed!" said Christine with a gasp.

"That's enough, Christine!" said Max, looking sternly at her. He was upset at her being a bit rude.

"Why be ashamed?" said Nick after a pause. "I didn't do anything wrong."

"But you went to prison!" said Christine. "I'd be so ashamed!"

"Christine!" said Max again with another look. He took hold of her hand.

But she continued. "Of course I would have told on my friend!"

"Well," said Nick softly, almost under his breath, "I guess some of us have principles then, and some of us don't."

Max turned to Nick. "Be careful, Nick," he said. "Do not talk to my wife that way."

There was an awkward, silent pause. The conversation had turned very quickly.

"Oh, he's just drunk," said Warren with an uneasy laugh. "He doesn't mean it, Max, do ya, Nicky?"

"No," interrupted Nick. "I meant what I said. Even if I've had some wine, that doesn't mean I don't know what I'm talking about."

"Watch what you are saying to my wife," said Max again. He was on the edge of his seat. Nick saw this and was about to stand up.

"Nick's just drunk," said Warren to calm them down. "Here, Nick. I'll get you some water."

"No, Warren," said Nick. "I don't want any water. I'm not drunk."

Warren sat back down. "We're all drunk," he said to Max. "Let's just let it go. Kate, what do you...," he began.

"That does not mean he can act that way to her," persisted Max.

"Well," said Nick, "if she doesn't know what she's talking about, then she shouldn't criticize."

At that moment, Max stood up. Warren did the same to make sure Max kept to himself. "We do not have to stay here for this," said Max. "We do not have to listen to this."

Warren stepped in to calm him.

"Look…," began Nick.

"Nick…," said Warren with a raised hand to stop him from continuing.

"It's all right, Max," said Christine apologetically. "Maybe I should not have said it."

"No," said Max. "I think we will go. Come, Christine."

"But…"

"No. Let's go!"

Nick sat watching as the couple turned and walked down the stairs without looking back. There was a long silence as they heard the two leave and walk down the dock with Christine trailing her husband. Warren and Kate waited for Nick to say something. But then Warren was the first to speak.

"You shouldn't have acted that way, you know," he said. Both of them knew he didn't have to say it. "She didn't mean anything by it. You know that. You drank too much, Nicky."

"Yeah, that's what you think, isn't it, Warren?"

Warren paused for a moment. "It doesn't matter what I think, Nicky."

"Ah," said Nick, "always the diplomat. Never willing to offend, never willing to defend yourself."

"Never willing to get myself into trouble when I'm drinking…," Warren laughed apprehensively. He raised his glass and took a big sip. "Besides," he said, "I'm your friend, Nicky, remember? I'm on your side."

Nick sighed heavily. He sat in his chair and stared at the glass. A bead of wine ran down the side, and he watched it cling to his finger. "I know, Warren," he said. "I'm sorry."

"She didn't know what she was talking about," said Kate.

Nick nodded to her appreciatively. He had forgotten she was there.

"Max and Christine are good people," said Warren. "You just shouldn't have acted like that toward them."

"I'm sorry," said Nick. "You know I didn't mean to say that, Warren. It's just that..."

"I know, mate. I know."

The three of them sat silently as they heard Max start up the car and drive off.

"You should apologize the next time you see them," said Warren.

Nick wiped his forehead and took the last sip of his drink. "I will, Warren," he said. "You know I will."

Kate reached up and poured them all another glass of wine to finish the bottle. Nick looked at her and was glad she was there with them.

"I hate to see someone embarrass herself like that," she said when they had taken a sip. "And then her husband had to come and defend her, even though she was wrong."

Nick smiled at her. There was a long silence, and then no one spoke of it anymore.

"Nick, you got anymore champagne?" asked Warren when he had finished his glass.

"I'm sure I do somewhere. Hopefully there's some that's chilled."

"Champagne for three?" asked Kate. "That's supposed to be bad luck or something, isn't it?"

"Champagne is never bad anything!" said Warren. He was already up searching for a bottle under the bar.

Twenty minutes later, after they had only had half the bottle, Warren looked at his broken watch. Then he looked at Kate's and saw it was late. He and Kate were going off to a party at an apartment up above near the Palace and asked Nick if he wanted to join them.

"No thanks," he said. "I'll just have another drink and go to bed."

"You sure?" said Warren. "I don't want you stewing here on your own."

"Yeah, I think so. I just don't feel like going out."

Nick had another quick glass with them and then regretfully watched them leave. He stood at the rail and watched them walk down the dock and then waved good-bye to them just before they were out of sight. As he sat back at the table and picked at the remnants of food on the plate, he wished they had stayed. He didn't want to be alone.

Kate was a nice girl, he thought. She reminded him a lot of Miriam. He sat on the deck for a while longer until the rest of the bottle of champagne was gone and it started to get cool out. The finest sprinkle came down on him from a cloud above. Then, as he went down to his cabin and neared his bed, he smelled the perfume on his pillow and thought of Miriam, and he felt very much alone.

CHAPTER TWELVE

The ride along the coast in the coupe was a nice change for Nick. Warren was behind the wheel, and they were on their way to a wedding in Cannes for a couple Nick had never met. It was a fresh Sunday morning, and it was also the day of the race. There had been several days of preparations for the Grand Prix all around the city, as well as qualifying trials that Nick had been able to watch from his central position in the harbor. Nick hadn't wanted to go to the wedding, but Warren had been able to convince him that they could make the wedding and make it back to Monaco just after the start of the race. Nick had resisted, though, for several days. Once the *Diamant* was tied up in the harbor, he never liked to venture too far. It was his sole refuge. "Who the hell has their wedding on the same day as the Grand Prix?!" Nick had asked Warren seriously.

Nick had remained aboard the *Diamant* for much of the last few days, unwilling to venture out into society. He had only been back in Monaco a short time, but the people and the parties were already starting to wear on him. The evening with Max and Christine had soured him. Benicio had had him aboard the *Miradora* once for a pleasant evening drink, and that was the extent of his social ambitions. Warren had swung by the yacht to call on Nick several times, but he had been unable to pry Nick from the harbor. "A pickled seagull," he had called Nick, perched high on the second deck with a drink of gin in his hand.

Warren was being uncharacteristically quiet today. It was actually nice. The ride was cool, and there was a strong wind coming off the water and up over the cliffs. The water below was a deep blue with high, white caps that faded into the mist far from shore. The purr of the car's engine soothed Nick. Warren was driving his new car— a red coupe that he had bought off a friend, apparently. Nick hadn't believed him about the car when Warren had asked him for money. It was a few years old and the back right fender was dented, and Nick could tell the transmission was a little loose, but otherwise it was a very appealing car for a young man of ease.

But Nick's mind was also a bit troubled on the drive. It had been a week since Miriam had left for Rome, and there had been no word from her. If she had left the name of her hotel, Nick could have made a call. But as the days went on and he fidgeted alone aboard the yacht trying not to think of her, he decided it was best to let her be. She had only been back in his life a few days, and he did not want to suffocate her. She was her own woman now. And so he did not mention his concern to Warren. He just let it be.

Warren was driving fast, taking every bend in the road across the line along the high cliffs.

"What's the rush?" asked Nick, breaking the silence.

"Wedding starts at eleven thirty. We left late."

Nick looked at his watch. It was already past eleven. "No one gets to a wedding on time," he said calmly. "They won't start right away. They never do."

"I know," said Warren, "but we have to meet up with the girls and give them a ride to the church. I was supposed to pick them up half an hour ago."

"How much farther do we have?"

"Another fifteen minutes 'til we get into town, if the road stays like this."

Nick sat back into silence and watched the small coastal villages whisk by. The sun was beginning to break through the haze and warm his face. The red coupe was flying around the curves with the engine held at constant throttle. He knew better than to ask Warren to slow down.

"Whatever happened with that Kate girl?" Nick asked after a few minutes of quiet. "I haven't seen her since you brought her by that one night."

"Oh, Kate," said Warren with a shrug of his shoulders. "She's a nice girl. Still in town, I think. We've been out a few times. But I don't know if I'll see her again."

"Why not? I liked her."

Warren looked over at his friend with a laugh. "Then why don't *you* take her out?"

"I mean I liked her with you," said Nick. "I can tell she's smart. A little better than some of the other girls I've seen you with."

"Is that so? Well...I just can't stay with a girl too long. You know me, Nicky."

"That's just what I think. She's a nice girl." Nick left it at that and let Warren get back to the road.

Before long, Cannes came into and out of view around one of the sloping rock cliffs that ran down to the sea. The number of boats along the water multiplied as the city expanded before them and sloped down to the beaches. Nick kept an eye on the road and hoped there wouldn't be any cars or cyclists coming toward them. The coupe only had the two seats, and he wasn't sure how they would fit the girls in the car.

The wind was stronger today. It had picked up and was blowing the waves up onto the shore. Nick looked over at his friend whose hair was blowing back with the rush of wind that came over the windshield. He ran his hand through his own hair and felt how long it was and decided it might be time to get it cut. Elena always cut it for him.

"Where are we picking them up?" Nick asked. He could tell Warren was getting frustrated behind a sedan he wanted to pass.

"I know the place. It's on the way to the church."

Warren daringly passed the slower sedan on a short straightaway, just missing an oncoming car that was blaring its horn, and resumed his increased speed. Nick sat there and held on as his friend took the curves while they made their way into the city and towards where the church would be. Nick looked at his watch. It was more than twenty past.

"No wedding ever starts on time," Nick repeated, "especially French weddings." He was doing his best to reassure Warren. After a few more minutes, they were in the middle of the city. It being Sunday, the streets were filled with men and women on their way to do some shopping or out to see the town. Nick watched the people around him with interest, and before long he saw two girls standing alone on a corner waving frantically at them and knew it was them.

"This is the street," said Warren. He hadn't seen the girls right away.

"They're right there," Nick pointed.

Warren saw them immediately and cut across two lanes of traffic to the opposite side of the street and the oncoming lane. All Nick could do was hold on. The car screeched to a halt at the corner.

"Where were you?!" one of the girls shouted in French.

There was a pause where nobody moved or said anything.

"Well…," started Warren, "…get in!"

The girls just stared and looked at him.

"Where?" shouted the other girl.

Warren had no patience. Traffic was about to start moving his way. He didn't have time for this. "Get in, damn it!" he shouted. He said this in such a way that the girls could do nothing but jump into the car, and in a few moments Nick had the two girls sitting on top of him while Warren pulled out with grinding gears and did a screeching turn in the middle of the street with traffic rushing toward him.

The ride through the streets of Cannes was even more harrowing than the ride along the coast. Warren swerved in and out of traffic into the oncoming lane, nearly ran up on the sidewalk near a flower market, and had to swerve forcefully to avoid hitting a couple in a crosswalk. Again, Nick knew not to ask him to slow down.

"I want to change my blouse before it starts!" shouted one of the girls in French. Nick was translating for Warren. "We just came from shopping and I found something I liked better."

There was no reaction from Warren who was still intent on driving.

"There's no time to stop," said Nick calmly over the groan of the engine. Then Warren spoke, annoyed.

"We're going to get there just when the wedding's starting. We only have three minutes, and the church is still five minutes away." Warren had used some of the money Nick lent him to get his watch spring replaced.

Nick translated this for the girls.

"But I want to change!" the girl persisted.

"Then change right here, damn it!" Warren shouted.

Nick didn't know if Warren were serious, but when he saw the girl pull the shirt out of her bag and move a little toward the back so that she was between the two seats, he knew she thought he was.

"Ne regardez pas!" said the girl. "Don't look!"

Nick shook his head laughing in disbelief and turned to face forward. Warren had come to a stop at an intersection and was waiting for the light to change so he could make his turn. He was anxiously banging his hands on the steering wheel and revving the engine in neutral. There were people all around the car staring and pointing at the fiasco.

The light turned green, and Warren ground at the gear trying to get it into first.

"I can't see. Is anyone coming from that side?" he shouted.

Nick looked around to see if they were clear.

"Don't look!" the girl cried out with her shirt halfway over her head. Only her bra covered her.

Nick was stunned for a moment. Then the girl screamed at him again and he yelled to Warren, "Just go!"

Warren recklessly threw the car into gear with a crunch of the transmission and put the gas to the floor. The car screeched and lurched forward, sending the other girl toppling backward over Nick toward the trunk. She was almost thrown out of the car. Another car that had been coming toward them blared its horn at the moving spectacle. Warren shifted with a lurch and floored the pedal in second gear while laying on his own horn. Nick looked over at him and laughed. Warren was stoic, but Nick had a huge smile on his face.

"Don't forget your tie," said Nick. Warren didn't respond or look over at him. He was concentrating on driving.

"What?" shouted Warren over the two girls screaming, one back in Nick's lap and the other crammed between the two seats.

"Don't forget your tie," Nick repeated.

"I'll get it on the way in," said Warren. He didn't look over.

Warren took a corner sharply at speed. Nick saw the turn coming and reached around him to hold the girls in. Nevertheless, there was a shriek and a groan from both of them as Warren turned the wheel hard.

"It's right up there!" said Warren. Nick looked at his watch. It was eleven thirty-five.

The four of them, piled on top of one another in the tiny red roadster, arrived in a screech of smoking tires at the church as the bells were ringing loudly out across the town. The wedding was already beginning. At the same time that Warren pulled up in his little car, three or four other cars pulled up in a similar fashion. Nick saw that everyone was running into the church.

"See?" said Nick with a grin. "No wedding ever starts on time."

Warren looked back up at the two girls who were now fully dressed and trying to scramble out of the car. Their hair was in disarray, and they looked as if someone had simply thrown their clothes at them. He was laughing hysterically.

One of the girls tripped over Nick and fell out of the car on her way out. Nick reached down to help her. "Come on!" the girl shouted as she jumped up rubbing her knee. In another instant, they were already running ahead.

Nick casually climbed out of the car, which was parked with one tire up on the sidewalk. If he missed the wedding, he didn't care. He didn't even know these people.

"Nice job," he told his friend with a slap on his back. Warren just smiled and ran his hand back through his wild hair.

"Come on!" the girls shouted again from up ahead.

As Nick hurried his pace toward the door, he could hardly hear her over the ringing of the enormous bells high above. He passed a woman who was struggling her large feet into tall, thin boots as she was trying to walk. He just shook his head again in disbelief at the wild things women did to themselves. The woman's husband was trying to hurry her along. Another woman ahead of them was rushing to get her children out of a car and up the stairs to the church. As she did this, one of her boys wriggled his tie free and threw it flatly to the ground. At the same instant, she smacked him forcefully on the cheek and picked up the tie as she dragged him crying, screaming into the church. It looked as if the entire affair of the wedding had been thrown together last minute.

Nick reached up to fix his own tie. At the same time, he remembered Warren.

"You left your tie in the car," he said.

Warren reached up to his neck and felt that it was missing. "It's all right," he said. "I don't care."

The two girls were waiting on the stairs as a group of men dressed in tight morning suits were waiting for them to close the two large wooden doors of the church. Nick and Warren caught up with them and went inside as the organ began to play. The ceremony was just starting.

It was later that afternoon at the reception that Nick was first able to notice the two girls they had picked up. They were both very young, but pretty. There had been no time to really perceive them until the wedding was finished. The church that day had been crowded, and the four of them had been made to stand in the back with the other latecomers. A few minutes into the procession, Nick slipped back outside alone onto the steps for a cigarette. He hated weddings.

The church was a tall brown and gray stone building that was surprisingly plain. It didn't look like a church at all, except for the simple spire above the bell tower. Nick studied the stones in the façade and saw that they were worn and brittle. A fine layer of crumbs and dust lay at the base of the building, and he ran his finger along the mortar and watched the grit fall away.

Across the street from the church was a fountain that was not flowing. Nick sat there on its stone wall for a half hour burning through a pack of cigarettes. When he got bored of that, he threw francs from his pocket into the fountain and wondered if they worked the same as pennies back home. After he had thrown all his coins, he idly realized he hadn't made a single wish and then forgot the whole mess altogether. A woman walked by with her dog that smelled at Nick's feet. He said hello to her and she nodded at him. She was the only one to pass by the entire time he sat there except for a small flock of pigeons that landed near him and fought over a cigarette butt when he threw it at them, until he kicked them away. A few minutes later, the bells above him began to sound loudly over the town, and the large wooden doors of the church flew open and poured forth a restless crowd.

The reception was at a hall a few blocks away, and Nick found Warren and the girls and walked there while flowery black sedans ferried the wedding party through the mob.

"Did you understand everything?" asked Warren. He hadn't noticed that Nick had missed the whole thing. Nick just grunted with a nod.

Sitting at the table with the girls, Nick saw that one of them had been crying through the entire ceremony. Her face was red and puffy, and he hoped he wouldn't have to entertain her while Warren occupied himself with the other girl. He had been left alone at the table with the two girls while Warren was away talking with someone he knew. Nick wondered to himself where Warren found so many of these girls. What was it about him? He could hardly remember a time when his friend was with the same girl more than once. The girl who had been crying had short hair and was very pretty, but in a plump sort of way. The other girl who had changed her shirt in the car was smaller and thinner. When he looked at their faces, he thought they might be sisters, but he wasn't sure. But he could tell by their clothes and their jewelry that their families had some money.

"Where did you meet Warren?" he asked the thinner girl across from him in order to break an uncomfortable silence. She seemed a bit more friendly than the other one who was staring at the table, and there was no music or drinks yet to occupy him.

"We met a few weeks ago here in Cannes," she said. "I don't really know him that well, but he said he was coming back for a wedding, and it turned out to be the wedding of one of my friends. I like weddings."

Nick looked over at the other girl who had not looked up at all. It didn't seem like she wanted to talk.

"We met on the beach," the girl continued. "Warren makes me laugh."

Nick could tell the girl was very interested in his friend, just like all the girls were. As for the other girl, she didn't seem to be interested in anything. He watched her as she moved her eyes indifferently about the room, not looking at anything. Then she brought her eyes back to the table and stared blankly at a folded napkin without speaking.

"Natalie," Nick said. That was the girl's name. He was trying to make conversation. "Do you know Warren, too?"

She looked up at him with blank eyes. He could tell she was either bored or pondering what he had said as if she didn't understand. He asked her again in French.

"*Non,*" she answered bluntly.

Nick waited for more, but the girl said nothing else. Satisfied with his attempt, he sat back in his chair and sipped from a glass of cheap red wine that had just arrived.

The two girls were quiet across the table. The thinner girl looked around the room waving to people she knew and ignored Nick. Nick really didn't mind this, so he sat there quietly and wondered if he knew anyone there himself. He had scanned the crowd as they left the church steps, but he had not been able to pick anyone out. An older couple sat at their table but did not speak to them. They only talked between themselves and said hello to those who passed.

Nick looked at the plump girl who had fallen on the ground when they had first arrived. Her knee had been scraped, and there was a red tint to her skin. She had taken a handkerchief and dabbed at it, and it was now spotted with dried blood.

"I'll get some soda water to wash that out," he said with a tone of fatherly concern. Then he wondered jokingly if he might be old enough to be her father.

The girl looked down at her knee blankly, then at the handkerchief in her hand.

"No, thank you," she said politely but without emotion.

"You might get a scar from that," Nick laughed. It really wasn't serious enough to scar, but he felt like trying to make conversation.

"Do you really think so?" the girl asked with a sudden look of worry. It was the first reaction he'd seen from her.

"Maybe. Maybe not."

"I don't want a scar!" she said. She looked as if she were about to cry. Nick could tell she really was worried.

"Well," he said to comfort her, "I don't think it's that bad. In a few weeks, you'll never notice it."

The girl continued to stare at her knee inquisitively, moving it around in the light. Again, silence fell over the table and Nick turned his attention to the party where music had begun and waiters were rushing about. Presently, Warren returned with an open bottle of wine and filled all the glasses on the table.

"What did I miss?" he asked with a slap on Nick's shoulder. "Are you taking care of my girls?"

Nick smiled at this but said nothing. Both girls seemed to become captivated when Warren arrived. Their eyes came back to the table, and they looked up at him with great interest.

"Who were you talking with over there?" Nick asked. He thought he recognized the man but did not remember his name.

"Just a friend from somewhere."

Nick expected more of a response, but none came. Warren looked over at the two girls and smiled at them. They put down their glasses and smiled back at him.

"Do I know him?" asked Nick.

"Maybe. He said he had a car he wants me to look at. Says he can get me a good price on it. Mercedes, he says. His brother's car."

Nick nodded and took a sip from his glass. Then he looked over at his friend. "Hey, I though you just got a car," he said. "That one we came in."

Warren smiled his big grin at him. "It's not what you have, Nicky. It's what you'll have next!"

Nick shook his head with a laugh and let Warren turn back to the party and the two girls sitting eagerly before him. He was clearly distracted. The music was getting loud, and the reception was going now. Nick just nodded and sat back with his glass. Then he told himself he wasn't going to drink too much, and he set the glass back on the table. He looked at his watch and knew he wanted to get back to Monaco where the race had already started. He turned to his friend.

Warren was feeling the music. He had quickly downed his glass and had filled it again. He had filled the girls' drinks, too.

"Let's all go dance," he said to Nick and the girls.

"Really?" said Nick. "We should get going soon."

"Aw, come on, Nicky. Just a few songs. I can tell these girls want to dance."

Nick looked over at the girls who were already out of their chairs. It was as if Warren had commanded them, and they willfully obeyed. They were both waiting for Warren to join them.

"All right," said Nick. "Just for a bit."

Nick hauled himself heavily out of the chair and they all made their way to the center of the dance floor and caught the beat with the rest of the couples and moved easily with the crowd. The girl Nick was dancing with kept her mesmerized eyes fixed on Warren and the other girl, and at the same time was unnaturally conscious of the movements of her own body. Nick saw that she was staring over at Warren.

"Something wrong?" he asked simply.

The girl turned away from Warren and looked up solemnly at Nick.

"No," she said. "I didn't mean to…"

"That's all right," interrupted Nick with a laugh. "I just thought you might be a little distracted."

The girl smiled with a stare that went past Nick.

"I think you like my friend there," he said. "I think you've got a little thing for him."

The girl blushed, almost imperceptibly. She was very timid. "I do think he's very handsome," she said, "but Audrey likes him."

At the same time she finished speaking, the music stopped abruptly, and the dance floor cleared for the bride and groom. Nick and the girl stepped to the side and stood together silently. An older man, who seemed to be the bride's father but didn't look at all like her, said something in broken French with an Italian accent, and everyone applauded the new couple. A few moments later, Warren led Nick and the girls back to their table far from the dance floor.

"What do you say we get out of here?" said Nick when the girls had stepped away.

"What do you mean, mate?" asked Warren.

"What do I mean?! I mean I want to get back and see the race!"

Warren thought to himself for a moment and then spoke. "I want to get with this girl," he said.

"What do you mean?" asked Nick.

"I want to get with her. You know. I don't want to go back yet. Just give me a little bit."

Nick shook his head at his friend. "Where?" he said.

"Where what?"

"Where are you going to take her?"

"Oh," Warren paused for a moment, "anywhere'll do."

"Like where? You have to get a hotel. That'll…"

"Not at all," interrupted Warren. "There's got to be someplace around here. Any spare room is all right."

"Oh," said Nick, feeling irritated, "is that where you went the other night? To a closet or something?"

"Where?" asked Warren.

"At that party up in the hills. Did you take that girl to the God damned coat closet?"

"No, of course not. We went in the bathroom."

"Jesus, Warren!" yelled Nick. "Have a little class!"

"Oh, I intend to," laughed Warren.

Nick was not laughing. Instead, he just felt uneasy.

Warren reached over and poured a glass. "Have a drink, Nicky," he said. "Have a drink with me."

Nick took the glass from him and set it back on the table. "How old is she, Warren? Sixteen?"

"I don't know," Warren wavered.

"Damn it!" said Nick. "How old is she?"

"I don't know, Nick. Yeah, maybe."

"For Christ's sake, give her a few years then," he said sternly. "She's not going anywhere. Just give her a year to grow up a little."

Warren said nothing and just looked up blankly at his friend. Nick was also silent. The girls had come back and sat at the table talking.

"I consider myself a man of action," said Warren calmly with a smile. "I like to get my way."

"Well," said Nick impatiently, "I'm not waiting for you."

Warren thought for a second, then spoke. "Why don't you take the car back, Nicky?" he said. "You'll like driving it. I think I'm going to stay for a bit and come back on the train or something." He spoke so the girls could hear. "Why don't you take Natalie home, and I'll swing by the harbor tomorrow and pick up the car?"

"You're going to miss the race," said Nick despondently.

"That's all right. I'm having fun here."

Nick made a glance over at Natalie whose face took on the sudden look of disappointment. Audrey had the opposite look on her face. "Is that all right with you?" he asked Natalie. He knew she must be upset. "Wouldn't you rather stay instead?"

"That's fine," she resigned herself.

"You sure you want to leave so early?"

"Yes, that's fine."

"All right," said Nick. "Where do you live?"

"Close to Nice."

Warren threw Nick the keys from his pocket and a moment later was gone with the girl and the bottle of wine. Nick was left alone with the girl whose face now turned to a look of dejection.

"All right. Let's go," he said with a forced brightness, trying to cheer her up. But the girl looked up at him without a smile and followed him out silently.

By the time they were out of Cannes along the high road that ran along the sea, they had endured ten minutes of silence. Nick glanced over at the girl and decided to get her mind off all of it.

"Are you hungry?" he asked over the groan of the engine up a steep hill. He said this to make conversation, not that he wasn't enjoying the silence.

The girl placed her hand over her stomach as if that were how she could tell. "No," she said, "I'm not hungry." They had just had a little food at the reception.

The sun was warm in the sky above them. The wind from the ocean had slowed, and Nick was warm there in the convertible. He held his hand out over the door and felt the wind.

"Did you know the couple in the wedding?" he asked.

The girl was silent and he looked over at her. Maybe he'd missed her response.

"Are they in love, you think?" he said.

Again there was no response.

"Did you grow up here?" he asked in order to keep the conversation going, but before he could finish his sentence, she cut him off.

"It's not fair!" she exclaimed.

Nick wasn't really surprised at the girl's outburst and looked over at her. "What isn't fair?" he asked calmly.

"The way she always gets the boys I want…the way she always gets everything she wants!" She said this as if they had jumped right into the middle of a long conversation.

"Your sister?" asked Nick, knowing that was who she meant. "Audrey?"

"*Moi, moi, moi*, I get what I want, *moi, moi, moi!*" the girl went on without listening to him. "And I'm the good friend who just sits back and takes it."

There was a long silence. Nick was waiting for her to continue. "Wait, I thought you were sisters," he said. "You look like sisters."

"…and what does that get me?" she continued, more to herself than to him.

"I don't know," said Nick. "What does that get you?"

The girl looked at him for the first time.

"Nothing!" she exclaimed. "Stop the car!"

"What?"

"Stop the car!"

The girl grabbed for the wheel, and Nick quickly pulled over toward a bend at the top of a high hill where there was just enough room to pull off without going into the rail. A cloud of dust swirled up around them.

"What's wrong?" he asked, but before he knew it the girl was out of the car scrambling around to his side.

"I want to drive," she said.

"What?"

"I want to drive!"

Nick left the car running in neutral and sat there for a moment in his seat before cautiously opening the door. The girl was already climbing in behind the wheel on top of him.

"I'm not sure…," Nick began, but the girl quickly took off her shoes and jumped in the seat and shut the door behind her. Nick raced around to the other side so he wouldn't get left behind. He looked at her with astonishment.

The girl turned the key and there was a grinding sound from the engine that was already running.

"How old are you, anyways?" Nick asked.

The girl did not look at him. "I know how to drive!" She said this with a wave of her hand as if brushing him aside. She threw the car into gear with a grind of the transmission and, with an immense jerk and a skid of the tires in the gravel, she swung the car back onto the road. A car that was coming from behind them honked its horn as she crossed over the center line, then it swerved back in front of them and went on. The girl raced the engine in first gear before slamming it into second.

"Take it easy," said Nick. "This isn't my car."

The girl looked at him and seemed annoyed but a little more calm. She eased the car into third a little more smoothly.

"Thank you," he said. "That's better."

Nick sat back and was silent. The girl was speeding along pretty fast, but controlled. He looked over at her a few minutes later and saw that she was more composed. In the wind, her light brown hair flowed back around her face so that she seemed prettier now than before at the table or on the dance floor. She seemed more grown up as well.

"I don't think he likes her that much," he said finally.

The girl said nothing and did not look over at him. She wiped her already puffy face.

"I think you're very pretty," he said, trying to reassure her.

She paid him no attention.

Nick reached over and took the shoes from her lap. "Why did you take your shoes off?"

She said nothing and looked forward to the road.

"Why'd you take your shoes off?"

"I can't drive with my shoes," she said finally.

Nick set them down on the floor beside him and settled into his seat for the ride, trying to relax. The girl didn't speak for fifteen minutes or so, and he sat back and just hoped that she would stay on the road as they sped along the high cliffs. He knew the road, and they would be coming up to Nice in a few minutes. He watched as the green hills and tall poplars rushed by, town after town, village after village. There were few cars on the road, and the hills curved and rose and fell within his view with the water flashing by far below. The simple beauty of life here in the small towns along the coast delighted him.

He listened to the whine of the engine up the hills. They were coming up to the city a little ways beyond, and her driving had eased noticeably. She had stopped speeding so much. Nick looked over after a few minutes and saw that she had been crying again. He hadn't noticed this while he was watching the road, but now her eyes were smeared and her cheeks were even redder.

"You might want to clean up your face," laughed Nick, hoping to make her smile.

The girl looked up in the rearview mirror and saw the makeup that she had put back on after the ceremony smeared around her eyes. She didn't speak, but she wiped her eyes with the back of her hand. Before they had reached the dense center of Nice the girl slowed quickly and pulled up to the entrance to a long gravel driveway just off the road. She turned off the car and took out the handkerchief that she'd had back at the wedding to wipe her eyes. Nick could tell she was still steaming, despite the drive and the long silence.

Nick got out of the car and went around to take her place. He opened the door for her.

"We won't tell Warren about this, will we?" he asked to amuse himself. "About you stealing his car?"

The girl just sat there at the wheel. She didn't look at him and didn't get up.

"You're a very pretty girl," said Nick. "Prettier than Audrey. At least I think so."

He watched her for a minute in silence. She wiped her eyes again and then sat motionless with her hands on the wheel. Then, all of a sudden, the girl stood up out of the car and turned to him. She paused for a moment before him, and Nick had no idea what she was doing. Then, in a flash, she buried her face deep into his chest and wrapped her arms tight around him. Unsure of what to do, he simply froze. He raised his eyebrows. It looked like she was hugging him. Slowly, he lowered his arms to put them around her and to comfort her. But before he could do so, she had slipped away and was off running up the long driveway and was gone.

Nick stood there for a minute and finally shook his head with a confused laugh. "She'll be all right," he said aloud. "Young little girls and little broken hearts." Slowly, he got back into the car and turned the key. Several miles down the road, too late to turn back, he looked over and saw that the girl had forgotten her shoes.

CHAPTER THIRTEEN

Nick enjoyed the silence on the drive back into Monaco. The girl wasn't there, and Warren wasn't there, and he didn't allow himself to think about either of them. He just let it all go. The groan of the engine and the sound of the wind were all that filled his thoughts for some time. It had been a while since he had driven a car. He had not owned one for several years now, but it all came back to him easily once he was out of first gear and on the road. His watch showed that it was getting on toward late afternoon. He remembered the race and that he might still catch the end of it. It had started just over two hours ago and he had missed most of it already. This thought increased his speed a bit.

But as he approached the city the streets became clogged. Everything was blocked off for the race. And when he finally entered Monaco against the flood of cars on the road, the sun was behind him to the west, and he knew that the horns of all the yachts in the harbor, and all the cars in the streets, had sounded the finish and had celebrated the winner. He had missed the whole damn thing.

"Damn it!" he said under his breath. "Damn it, Warren!" He shook his head and tapped the steering wheel irritably with his fist. Nick, though not very enthusiastically, had been looking forward to the race for some time. He had made it a point to leave Spain to be here in time for the race. And now he had missed it. All thanks to Warren. He continued to curse as he drove.

The streets leading down to the harbor were packed with the departing crowd. Roads were still blocked for the track and would be for another day or two. A group of boys walked along the racetrack kicking along the chunks of rubber from the tires. Race programs and confetti blew all around him. Held at a stop in the middle of a packed intersection under a green light, he called to a man walking in the street.

"Who won?" Nick asked.

The man looked long at him with a wincing, sunburned face. "The Frenchman Trintignant," he said with a raise of his fist and continued on. Nick could not tell if the man were thrilled or disappointed by the victory.

Regardless, the city would be alive that night, even more so than usual, as people from all along the coast had descended upon this tiny place for the race.

Nick was genuinely sore about missing everything. It was a Ferrari team that had won, and he was glad for that, but he had also missed seeing Moss and Castellotti and Fangio and all the other good drivers. He had seen them in practice and qualifying laps the last few days, but that just wasn't the same as the race.

He drove on slowly through the crowd, unable to get down to the harbor through the track barriers on every street he tried. He ground along tediously in first gear, jerking ahead and then stopping. There were no parking spaces along the sidewalks, and he had no idea where Warren might have parked the coupe. Perhaps at his hotel, he thought. He found his way up from the harbor toward Monte-Carlo, but the streets suddenly burst with even more people and cars. There would be no way to get close to any of the hotels or the Casino. Instead, he cut down an empty back street and up toward the French hills above him.

Nearly an hour later the coupe was wedged into a small space just big enough in the hills above the beaches of Larvotto, well away from the harbor. The racetrack had not extended this far up, but the roads still were blocked off around much of town. Nick threw his suit jacket over his shoulder and started walking. He was thoroughly hot and frustrated, and all he wanted to do was to get back to the boat for a cool drink. The shadows were growing longer, and the sun was starting to fade, but it gave the place a glow of anticipation for the evening ahead. Nick, however, wanted little to do with it. He was a bit sick of everyone for the moment, and he had a long walk ahead of him through the traffic and the crowds before he would reach the harbor.

Along the beaches, young groups in bathing suits were ending their last few minutes of sun after the race, packing up for the evening. Nick looked at the girls and thought of Warren. Nick knew he could have had any of those girls anytime he wanted, just like Warren could. There was nothing stopping him. In fact, he thought, with the race today, there were a dozen places he could go right now, a dozen parties he had been invited to, where he could go and have any girl he wanted. Even if he stumbled into a party he had not been invited to somewhere, he would be welcomed just the same. No one would turn him away. And whether it was in a spare bedroom, or even the bathroom, he could do just as Warren did, with any number of women. It was not difficult. But that was simply not his way. Whether or not there was any truth to it, Nick felt that he maintained a certain level of integrity in his dealings with women. There had been lapses, of course, but he considered himself decent on the whole. He was upset at Warren for what had happened today.

From where he walked along the beach, there were two ways to go to get back to the harbor—up by the Casino, or down below along the water. Nick chose to avoid the Casino and much of the crowd high above. There would be many parties that evening celebrating the race in Monte-Carlo, and the Casino itself would be the center of attention. Reporters would follow the winner Maurice Trintignant and the other racers like Moss and Castellotti from place to place as girls swarmed them and people cheered. No driver could be disappointed, as long as he had a good showing. Though the excitement called to everyone, even a bit to Nick now as he approached, he knew he would be more content in the shelter and calm of his yacht.

Walking through the crowd below the Casino, nearing the harbor along the track that was still blocked to cars but open to pedestrians, he was stuck behind two men who were talking in English about the race.

"Is this where Ascari flipped the Lancia into the water?" one man asked.

"No," said the other. "It was further ahead, at the chicane." The man pointed ahead a little ways, past some of the yachts that were now at his side. Nick overheard them and looked to where the chicane was. "Right into the water," the man said.

Nick was only a step behind them. "Is he all right?" he asked. "I missed the race."

The two Englishmen turned in step. "Yes," the man laughed, "I think so. They pulled the car out of the water with a crane, and Ascari went out of the race, of course. They took him to the hospital, but I think he's all right."

"Thanks," said Nick, and he waved to them as he passed and hurried ahead.

The crowd along the track was thick there as people made their way around the harbor admiring all the yachts and taking pictures. But in another half hour, dripping sweat, Nick was back safely aboard the *Diamant* with a fresh bottle of Ricard open before him on the table and a glass full of ice. He was glad to be back and out of the crowd.

"Did you have a nice time at the wedding, Mister Duncan?" asked Elena in her Spanish accent as she served him a small plate of food.

Nick rolled his eyes with a frustrated laugh.

"Yes?" she said. "I see."

Nick sat there enjoying his food and listening to the sounds around him. The crowd had seemed to come to life again now that the sun had set, and there was excitement all around. Many of the yachts along the docks had music blaring and people laughing. He enjoyed hearing all of it, but he was glad to hear it from the comfort of his own deck. The only person in the world he wanted to see right now was Miriam.

With that thought, he rose from the table to find the captain. He wanted to know if there had been any word of her since he had gone to Cannes. He had forgotten to ask Elena. Nick stood and then reached back and filled his glass with fresh pastis and water. Then he went forward toward the bridge.

The captain was at the bridge, sitting in his white uniform, running through a checklist of some sort. He immediately rose to his feet when he heard Nick's knock.

"Yes, Mister Duncan?" said Burke. "What can I do for you, sir?"

"Hey, Burke," said Nick.

"Good evening, sir," he nodded.

"Burke, any news about Miriam?"

The captain seemed to think for a moment. "No, Mister Duncan. Not that I have heard. I can ask the crew if they have heard anything of her. I asked them this morning, but they had not."

"No," said Nick. "That's all right. I just thought…," he trailed off.

After a few moments, the captain spoke up. "How long has it been, sir, that she's been gone?"

"It's been a week," said Nick, "since she took the cab to the station. I thought she would have been back by now. Unless…"

Burke waited for him to speak. "Unless what, sir?" he finally asked.

"Oh, I was just thinking. Maybe after the wedding she caught a flight or something back up to Paris. She did say she was filming the movie up there."

"Yes, sir," the captain nodded solemnly. He watched as Nick thought things through, but he didn't want to interject his own thoughts.

"I thought she might have at least called the Hôtel and left a message for me or something."

The captain shrugged his shoulders. "I can go up to the Hôtel and check for you, sir. It's no trouble at all."

"Well," said Nick. "Thanks, but I'll run up there myself in the morning and check in. Once things calm down a bit from the race, you know."

"Sir," said Burke, "it's no trouble. I can go right now, if you'd like. No trouble at all."

Nick didn't like the fact that he felt so anxious right now. He had resolved not to let Miriam occupy his mind so much over the last few days. She was her own person now, with her own life and her own commitments. She did not owe it to him to call and leave a message, or to return at all for that matter. She was probably enjoying herself in Rome right now. She had said the wedding was that of a family friend. Perhaps her family was taking up all of her time. There was no reason to interfere, or even to worry for that matter. Nick waved away the thoughts with a wave of his hand. He took a sip from his glass to hide his uneasiness. But, inside of him, he was about to bust with worry.

"No, it's all right," said Nick with a troubled laugh. "It's all right, Burke. I'll go and check myself in the morning. Don't worry about it."

"You're sure, Mister Duncan?" asked the captain.

"Yes, of course." He turned to leave.

"Well, sir," said Burke, "just let me know if you need anything else, then."

"Will do, Burke."

"Anything at all, sir."

Nick nodded and thanked him and left the bridge.

It was a warm evening, but it was beginning to cool slightly with the wind coming off the sea. Nick had been out in the sun for much of the day, and the heat and sweat had left him desiring a shower. After finishing the drink in his hand at the table, he went below for a shower and change. But, even though there were several small parties aboard the yachts along the dock to which he would surely be welcomed, he decided that he would not dress for a party. He was enjoying himself alone on deck just fine. If only his mind had not been so occupied with Miriam.

When he emerged from his cool shower, he changed into a light suit in his cabin. Even though he was not going to another party, he liked to dress nicely so that even sipping his cocktail alone on deck he would feel like he was part of the energy that night. It was the Grand Prix after all. He had missed the race, and he was upset by that, but he was not going to let that ruin anything for him.

As he finished combing his hair, there was a light knock on his cabin door.

"Mister Duncan?" called a muffled voice. It was the captain.

Nick's heart jumped a bit when he opened the door. Perhaps there was some news of Miriam. He took a breath to relax himself. "Yes, Burke," said Nick as he opened the door. "Have you heard something?"

"Oh, no, sir. I'm sorry. Nothing about Miss Banks."

"That's all right," said Nick. "What is it?"

Oh," said the captain, "your friend Mister Prado is up on deck. He arrived several minutes ago, but I did not want to disturb you."

"Oh, all right," said Nick. "Thank you."

The captain continued. "I called for Elena, and she is fixing him a drink and offering him something to eat."

"Thank you," said Nick. "Please tell him I'll be right up."

"Yes, sir."

When Nick emerged on deck, Benicio was sitting at the table with a glass, smoking a cigarette."

"Ah, good evening, Benicio," laughed Nick. He was genuinely happy to see the man. He enjoyed speaking with him.

Benicio rose. "Oh, good evening, Nick Duncan," he smiled. "It is a wonderful evening tonight, isn't it?"

"Oh, don't get up," said Nick. "Stay right there and be comfortable." They shook hands.

"Thank you," said Benicio. "I hope you do not mind. I do not want to intrude or anything. Do not let me hold you up if you are going out for the evening. You look like you are dressed for excitement."

"No," said Nick. "Of course not. I was just going to have a drink or two on deck. I'm not going anywhere. Things will be a bit too hectic for me up by the Casino. Can I offer you anything to eat or drink?"

Benicio raised his glass. "No, thank you. Your lady Elena had asked me. I am just having some Ricard here. I saw the bottle." He picked up the bottle and turned it over in his hand. "I hope you do not mind."

"If there's anything else you want...wine, whisky, or I can mix you something..."

"Oh no," said Benicio, "this is quite fine."

Nick sat down and poured himself a drink. Then he lit himself a cigarette.

"I thought you would have had a party tonight," said Nick. "For the race. No party tonight?"

"Oh," the man laughed. "I have too many parties. No one wants to spend their evenings with an old man like me." He waved his hand in front of his face at the idea.

"I enjoy them," said Nick. "Of course I do. Best parties in town."

"Well, thank you. No, I just came by to say hello to you. I did not see you during the race. Did you watch it up in town?"

Nick laughed. "No, Benicio. I missed the race altogether."

"No!" the man exclaimed. "It was such a fantastic race. You missed a magnificent time!"

"It's all right," said Nick. "I got called away for the day. Maybe next year, if they hold it again next year."

"Yes, I am sure you will be here next year as well. You have been here many years now."

Nick nodded.

The two smiled and sipped their drinks in silence for a few minutes, enjoying the sounds of the evening and the music and people laughing in the distance.

"And," said Benicio, interrupting the silence, "and Miss Miriam, where is she these days? Is she down below getting ready?"

"Rome," Nick said flatly. "She's at a wedding in Rome. She left a week ago. I'm not sure when she'll be back."

"I like Miss Miriam," said Benicio. "She is one of my favorite girls, you know. She is so beautiful now. She was always beautiful, of course, but she is truly becoming a beautiful woman now. And we knew her when she was so young, eh?"

"Thank you," said Nick. He believed that he'd had something to do with how she had grown up and the woman she had become. He did take a little credit.

"It is so good to see you two together again. She was not here last year, and someone told me that you were not together anymore. I was very sorry to hear that."

"Me, too," said Nick. "But it's not clear we're together just now. She just arrived out of the blue last week. She stayed for a few days, and now she's in Rome. I wouldn't say that we're together again. Not a couple, anyway."

"Oh," said Benicio. "I hope that things work out. You two are both so happy when you are together. I saw it the night on my boat. You two are very good together."

"Thank you," said Nick.

Benicio spoke no more of Miriam. They sat again in contented silence.

"Well," said Benicio, "I do not mean to intrude. I only came to say hello. I did not mean to invite myself. I do not want to keep a young man like yourself from enjoying the evening. It calls to you."

"No, of course not," said Nick. "You're never intruding. You're welcome anytime, even if I'm not here. Stay a bit longer if you'd like."

Benicio rose to get up, but Nick enjoyed having him there and wanted him to stay. It was far better than being alone with his thoughts.

Nick, in a crafty move, reached out with the bottle and filled Benicio's glass with a good portion of Ricard before he could get up. "Just stay for another drink," he smiled. "No need to rush off so soon."

Benicio laughed at him. "Well," he said, "one more if you insist, and then I will leave you for the evening. An old man needs his rest. And a young man needs to enjoy himself."

The two remained on deck and talked for a while longer. Benicio told him several highlights from the race that day, and about how the French and Italians had dominated the standings. He also told him a few stories of other Formula One races he had been to. He didn't follow racing very much, but he liked to tell stories of the races he'd seen.

They talked about Brazil and about how Benicio missed Rio so much. He only flew there every year or so now that he stayed aboard the *Miradora* for much of the year. He didn't like to fly, and getting the boat back and forth took many weeks on the ocean, out of sight of land.

Nick had never been to South America, but he enjoyed hearing about new places. He wondered to himself if the *Diamant* might ever make the trip back across the Atlantic to the Americas again. But the Mediterranean was his home now, and there was nothing calling him back there anyway. Everything he wanted was here.

It was much later in the evening when Nick found himself alone again on the deck. Benicio had gone back to the *Miradora*, and Nick remained on deck smoking his cigarettes. He was sad to be alone. It had been nice talking to Benicio, and he had not wanted him to leave. But Benicio insisted that Nick did not need to entertain an old man when he could be out on the town. Yet Nick was just happy sitting there in the coolness of the evening with his good friend.

When it was time to go below, he was feeling very good from the pastis, and he was happy and had forgotten the frustration of missing the race, and about Warren with his girls at the wedding, and about the coupe parked far on the other side of town. As he washed his face before bed, the idea crept into his mind that, since he was almost fully dressed, he might in fact head up toward the Casino for a quick drink, or perhaps down to one of the yachts further along the dock where there was a boisterous party going on. What would be the harm? There was a tall glass of Scotch next to him—his "mouthwash" he called it, as one of these usually followed him to bed. He was feeling pretty good after the few sips he had taken.

The call of the night had not gone away completely as he had expected it to.

But as he dried his face with a towel, he heard another knock at his cabin door. Nick checked his watch on the nightstand. It was late. It was nearly midnight. But he could tell it was the captain again by his muffled voice.

"Yes, Burke," said Nick, a little confused as he opened the door. The captain never called on him this late.

"Sir," he paused. "Mister Duncan, I did not mean to disturb you…"

"No, Burke, that's all right. What is it?"

"Well," said Burke, "Elena was setting out the evening papers for you for tomorrow morning, and…"

"Yes," said Nick anxiously. "What is it?"

"Well, sir, Elena saw something that concerned her. I wanted to bring it to your attention right away."

"Yes?" Nick was confused. But he was also growing more apprehensive.

"It's about Miss Stockton," Burke began. "I mean it's about Miss Banks, sir."

Nick's ears perked up. "Yes? What is it? What's happened?"

The captain was holding the newspaper in his hand. He raised the folded page up for Nick to see. "I think you should read this, sir."

Nick took the paper in his hands and scanned it over. It was one of the French papers. There was the headline about the winner of the race. He scanned lower, and a headline caught his eye. There was a small picture of

Miriam just below the fold. Translated, the headline read: "Actress Miriam Banks Missing From Her Own Wedding."

Nick was absent of thought. He just stood silently for a long while. The captain looked at him but said nothing. Finally, after a long minute, Nick spoke. "But...but she went to Rome," he said softly, confusedly as he shook his head. He glanced down over the article again. It was a short article, and there was no information other than that of her disappearance and the expected date and location of the wedding. The Italian authorities were investigating.

The captain stood there awaiting any instruction from Nick. He said nothing.

Nick folded the paper methodically in his hand. He looked up at the captain with a blank stare. "She...she went to a wedding in Rome," was all he said to him.

CHAPTER FOURTEEN

Nick lay awake before dawn, unable to sleep. He hadn't been able to sleep at all that night, despite finishing his glass of Scotch, as well as a second one. In the blue darkness, he was left only with his own thoughts. The boat swayed beneath him. Photographs, hung in frames on a wall across the cabin, puzzled him as he tried to make them out in the absent light. When a person sees the same object every day, he never really looks at it. And in his trance-like state he tried to remember who was in them and where they'd been taken. From the window shone lines of dull light that swung leisurely back and forth around the room with the movement of the boat. After an hour, he wearily rose and put on some clothes and went above deck into the cool air. It was still very early, and the harbor was silent. Even though he could not see the horizon, he knew that the sun had not yet broken through into the sky. The high cliffs over Monaco were not yet awake—no movement from the city, no cars, no people in the streets. The harbor was calm except for the sway of the boats in their moorings and a lone gull that called out over the glassy water. The sound traveled alone to his ears as everything else was still. A moment later, a ray of soft light broke against the hills and flashed in the sky above, and Nick knew a long day had begun.

The dawn turned quickly from the grayish blue to a deep orange along the horizon. Nick sat quietly in a cold chair and watched the day come alive. He felt a small drop of water on his arm, and he looked down at the deck and saw a few droplets that had speckled the dry wood.

"It's starting to rain," he said absently to himself for no reason at all.

He grabbed some papers that had been left for him on the table and went below.

Around eight o'clock that morning the first of the reporters came to question him, and the crew of the *Diamant* was brought back on duty by the captain to keep the reporters and photographers away while Nick stayed below. In his cabin, he read the morning paper, and he saw his own picture there with Miriam. He could not tell where or when the photograph had been taken or how they had obtained it. The article stated that the actress had last been seen with him and, to be sure, mentioned that Nick had spent time in prison back in the States. He decided not to let it all bother him—there was nothing more he knew, and nothing he could do. In any event, he had plans to meet Warren for lunch, if Warren still remembered. Around noon, after some police had been called to drive the reporters away, he made his way up to a restaurant near the Hôtel Hermitage in a cab. As he walked in, the restaurant immediately went silent.

"You're a bit of a celebrity, Nicky!" laughed Warren loudly for everyone to hear. Warren was leaning back in his chair with a cigarette between his lips. Nick looked down and saw with immense surprise that Kate was with him. He remembered how pleasant she'd been that night aboard the *Diamant* with Max and Christine. She looked at him with a soft smile. For some reason, he felt more comfortable with Kate there.

As he sat there looking at the menu, he felt the dozens of pairs of eyes fixed upon him as if the people in the restaurant expected him to do something—to burst out at them perhaps. The room was unnervingly quiet. Beyond the clang of silverware and the occasional murmur, there was only silence. The groups at the tables surrounding him attempted to listen in on their conversation. Nick said nothing and looked at Warren who returned his silence with an uneasy smile. It was impossible not to feel the tense air around them.

There was indeed a buzz around Monaco that day concerning Miriam's disappearance. It was well known that she had been with Nick, as everyone had seen them together the night of Benicio's party aboard the *Miradora*. That was what was known of her. What was not known was anything about her since, except that she had stayed with Nick aboard the *Diamant*. And so the eyes of the town were apprehensively upon him. It was only a few minutes into the lunch when Nick couldn't take it any longer.

"This is all very awkward," he said to Warren and Kate. "My being here is ruining lunch for you." He made a move to get up and leave.

"Don't be silly, Nick," said Kate. "All these people are just nosy!" She said this last part loudly so that the people around them heard her clearly. At that moment, the pairs of eyes that had been fixed on them simultaneously diverted their attention downward to their plates. Nick and Warren almost broke into laughter. Nick now felt even better that Kate had come.

"Yeah, Nicky," said Warren. "Just sit down and relax. We're treating you to lunch."

He relaxed again in his chair and took a drink from his glass. The gin and tonic felt cool in his mouth. He felt the low murmur of the room rise again as people turned back to their own conversations. It was apparent that he wasn't going to put on any kind of show for them.

"You haven't heard any news from her since she left?" asked Kate quietly. She had never actually met Miriam, but she knew all about the story from the papers, and of course from Warren.

"No," said Nick softly. He didn't want to talk about it, but he felt the two deserved a response, especially Warren. "She said she was going to Rome. That's all I know."

"I think the whole thing is intriguing," whispered Kate. "It sounds like she ran away from the wedding because she didn't want to marry the guy. And just like that without telling anyone! Warren says she's still in love with you. I believe it."

"I just hope nothing's happened to her," said Nick.

"Oh," said Warren, "I'm sure she's fine. She could always take care of herself. You know that better than anyone else, Nicky."

Nick sat there and listened but felt uneasy. It was all too much for him right now. "I don't like it," he said. "It's got my mind so wrapped up, I can't think straight."

"But she obviously came to Monaco to see you, Nick," said Kate. "She left the shooting of her film in Paris to come here and see you. That's what I gather."

"It's pretty clear she didn't want to marry that director fella," laughed Warren. "Don't know why she never told us anything though."

"She didn't know what to do, so she came to see you, Nick."

Nick looked at Kate and knew she might be right. "I guess so," he said, but he didn't want to think about it anymore. He sat back in his chair and finally picked up the menu again. He stared at it blankly for a few minutes before realizing he didn't know what he wanted. He really didn't care, and he wasn't that hungry. A look around the table showed that Warren and Kate were ready to order. Nick looked at Kate and smiled. She had cut her hair an inch shorter from the last time he'd seen her. It was straighter, too, and he felt it had lightened a little in the sun. Her skin was darker, as well. So was Warren's. He watched Warren glance up at the girl and saw the way he looked at her. Maybe he had listened to what Nick had said.

The waitress came for their order, and in another few minutes their food was served.

"What's your plan when everyone leaves the coast?" asked Warren at a more normal volume.

There was no response from Nick. He was ruminating over a bite of salad on the end of his fork.

"Nicky?" asked Warren again.

"Oh, I'm sorry," said Nick. "I thought you were talking to Kate." He put his fork down on his plate with the bite of food still on it. "I haven't even thought about it. Maybe head down to Corsica or something. Maybe head back to Spain. Don't even know, really."

The waitress came by and filled their water glasses. Nick hadn't touched his.

"And what about you, Warren?" Nick asked.

"Well, Kate here's invited me to come visit her in New York when she goes back. I might take a few weeks there."

He thought for a moment. "Why don't you come for a bit, too, mate? You could show me around your old stomping grounds."

"Oh," said Nick, "I've got no plans to head back to the States. I'll just bounce around here for a bit, I guess."

"Is that the way you do it?" laughed Kate. "Just bounce around with no plan?"

"I guess so," said Nick. "I don't like to know where I'll end up. I just start heading in one direction, and I end up wherever I end up. Burke…I mean, my captain puts up with me."

"Must be nice," said Kate.

"It is, sort of."

"You seem so relaxed about everything."

"I assure you," laughed Nick, "it's all just a façade."

Warren ordered another round of drinks as the table was cleared. Nick had pushed away his untouched plate.

"Will you stay in Monaco for a while, Nick?" asked Warren. "Until the season's over at least? Or will you leave before the summer crew arrives?"

"Well, I just got here. But with this whole mess about Miriam, I don't know if I want to stay."

Nick watched Kate light a cigarette, lean back in her chair, and cross her legs. He saw that she had very nice legs. Her short flowered dress showed off her tanned skin. Nick watched Warren look at her, too.

"My father's leaving in about a week for New York," she said. "On business. He's supposed to be retired now, but he can't stop working. It was his own firm. He's leaving my mother in Europe for a few days until he can rejoin her and continue on eastward. I'm supposed to go back around the same time, but of course I think you know I'd rather stay here."

"Of course," said Nick. "Why wouldn't you?"

Just at that moment, shouting and yelling were heard out on the street in front of the restaurant. Everyone looked toward the door and watched as a swarm of photographers burst in and began flashing pictures of Nick and the people around him. The restaurant staff rushed in, but they could not keep them all back.

"Damn it!" shouted Nick. As the three of them tried to stand, he looked over at Warren who was laughing and posing for the cameras.

"Right here, gentlemen!" laughed Warren. He turned and stood between them and Nick. "This is a better angle for me!"

Kate grabbed Nick's hand and pulled him away. "Come on!" she shouted.

Stunned, Nick followed her through the mob of cameras toward the door. She swung her arm and pushed the men out of the way. Nick ran over several photographers and knocked one of the flashing cameras to the floor.

On the sidewalk outside, a small crowd had gathered for the spectacle.

"You all right?" Nick shouted.

"Just fine," Kate replied. She was rubbing her wrist where there was a small cut but no blood. She winced when Nick reached up to look at it. "Just go, Nick," she said. "I'll stay here with Warren."

"You sure?" Nick looked back toward the door to see Warren there blocking the men from coming out. Bulbs flashed all around him as he laughed wildly.

"Of course," said Kate. "Look, there's a cab across the street." She pointed, and Nick saw that a woman was getting out of a cab. "Run and catch it."

"Thank you!" said Nick.

Kate smiled and waved to him.

"I'm sorry!" he shouted back as he crossed the street to the cab. "You and Warren come by the boat when you can. I'm sorry, Kate!"

Nick returned straight to the *Diamant*. It was the only safe place for him. But instead of being up on the deck where he wanted to be, he was confined to the interior of the yacht, where no cameras could follow him. Elena had insisted on serving him something to eat in his cabin when the captain had repeated to her the story from the restaurant. Nick was not at all hungry, but he promised Elena he would eat at least half of what was on the plate after some convincing.

An hour later, while Nick was staring at the lines of a book below, the captain came down to speak with him.

"Any news?" asked Nick.

"No, sir. I'm sorry. But two men are here to see you, Mr. Duncan."

"Reporters, Burke?" asked Nick.

"No, sir. Detectives, I think. French officials. Should I send them down?"

"I'll come up. Let them aboard."

"Yes, sir."

"*Monsieur* Duncan?" said the man as Nick reached the deck, putting on a suit jacket.

"Yes." He could tell immediately they were not reporters. They were wearing identical cheap suits and carried notepads. They both still had their hats on. He offered them a drink.

"*Non, merci,*" said the man in charge, so Nick poured himself one.

"We are from the Monaco principality police," said the younger man. He held out his identification.

"I guessed so much."

"This is Detective Joliet, and I am Sergeant Barré." The man beside him made a slight bow.

"What can I do for you two fine gentlemen?" He said these words sarcastically.

"We're here to make an inquiry. We've come to ask you about Miss Banks."

"Clearly."

The man in charge, Detective Joliet, cleared his throat and seemed to wear his tie too tight. "Do you know of her whereabouts, *Monsieur* Duncan?"

Nick was prepared for this. He responded with an annoyed tone. "All I know is that she showed up and stayed with me for a few days and then left a few days ago for Rome. She said she was going to a wedding there. We used to be…friends."

The younger man was writing things down on his pad of paper.

"And which day was that?"

"Which day what?"

"The day she left."

"Oh…," he thought for a moment, "last Saturday, I suppose. No, Sunday. In the morning. She took a taxi to the train station."

"And so she is no longer with you?"

"Of course not."

"And so you do not know where she went?"

"She told me she went to Rome. My guess is she's in Rome somewhere. That's where the wedding was supposed to be, wasn't it? From the papers?"

The younger man was scribbling furiously to write everything down. Nick sat down and sipped from his drink, but the other two remained standing.

"And so can you tell me where she is now?"

"Of course not," answered Nick, annoyed. "She went to Rome on the train, and that's all I know. I saw her off with her suitcases."

"And you are engaged to her? She is your fiancée?"

"Not anymore. That was years ago. Two years ago. She broke it off."

"Then why is she with you now, *Monsieur* Duncan?"

"Look," sighed Nick, "I don't know. I didn't ask her why she came. I had her stay here instead of getting a room at a hotel. She just showed up here."

"And so you do not know where she is now?"

"No," said Nick. "I told you she went to Rome. That's all I know."

The conversation continued in such an inane manner that only left Nick more and more frustrated. The detective asked if they could search the boat, just to see if Miriam were hiding below. Nick sent Burke around with the sergeant to make sure he kept his hands to himself while Nick stayed above. The sergeant rejoined them a few minutes later.

"And you have a criminal history, *Monsieur* Duncan, is that correct?" asked the detective.

"Sure," said Nick. "I went to the big house. Enjoyed every minute of it." He wasn't ashamed of it. He lit a cigarette and offered one to each of them. The deputy reached out, thought about it, and then refused. He went back to writing his notes.

"So, then you know how serious all of this is?"

"I guess so. Am I under arrest?"

The man looked down toward his poorly polished shoes. "No, *Monsieur* Duncan, but you are surely a person of interest in her disappearance. Do you have any plans to leave Monaco?"

"Not at the moment. I haven't seen enough of the fine beaches. Weather's supposed to be nice next week." His sarcasm had no effect on the two men.

"Yes, the beaches are quite nice," said the detective.

Nick nodded.

"Then you will not mind turning over your passport to us?"

Nick thought for a moment. "Of course not," he said. "I don't plan on running away, if that's what you're getting at."

"We thank you for your cooperation, *Monsieur* Duncan."

"I'll get it below." Nick put out his cigarette in the ashtray and went below. At his desk in his cabin, he considered giving them an expired passport of his, but he thought better of it. That might only invite more trouble. He returned a minute later. The deputy was picking up the bottle of gin from the table and turning it over in his hand.

"*Merci*," said the detective. "We will return this to you once everything is cleared up."

"Take your time. I'm not going anywhere."

"We intend not to take very long," said the man. "We are very efficient in our work. We are already speaking with the detectives in Rome." He turned to leave but then turned back. "I will leave you a card with my number. Please call me if you remember any detail of importance or if you hear from Miss Banks. And," he added, "you might assume that you are being watched, *Monsieur* Duncan. So there is no use in trying to slip away." The man slapped Nick's passport against his hand and placed it in his breast pocket.

"Naturally," said Nick. He took the card without looking at it and tossed it on the table.

The two detectives left, and Nick watched them walk back up the dock through several reporters to their sedan and followed them with his eyes until they drove out of sight. He sat back down at the table and lit another cigarette and had a laugh to himself about the two men.

Nick only left the *Diamant* the next day for a quiet drink aboard a sailing yacht of another acquaintance that was tied up further down the dock. He had spent another long, torturous night of little sleep alone in his cabin, filled with worry and irritation. Benicio had invited him along that evening, and Nick did not want to be rude by refusing. They shared a few drinks together with the other yacht owner and his wife, and they all stayed late into the evening talking about their travels. Nick was glad that no one brought up Miriam and all that had come out in the papers over the last few days. Benicio didn't even ask him about Miriam. Nick, of course, had thought about her all day, wondering about her, and he was glad to get out for a bit and speak with other people. It was good to get out of his own head. He had decided to stay in the harbor altogether to avoid everyone in town and the reporters. He knew he was safer there.

It was late, and a few other parties were ending or moving on, and so several young couples straggled by him on their way up to the city. At the end of the dock toward the street, they had to pass through the line of policemen keeping the remaining photographers at bay. Nick had requested that of the detective, for the privacy of all the yacht owners. He smiled and waved to the couples as they passed him. Then he waved down to the photographers in the distance, with several flashes in reply. He made his way back to the *Diamant* and, with some effort, to the deck above. But once there, he wanted only to be in his cabin and for another day of worry to end. His cool sheets called to him, and he was very tired.

Once down below, he noticed from a few feet away that his cabin door was slightly open and that a light was on inside. He looked at his watch and thought it strange that the captain or one of the crew was in his room at this hour. Perhaps the light had been left on by Elena when she had made the bed or left him towels. Still, he was cautious on entering, as he thought he heard a noise inside. The door was slightly open, and the light glared out in a long beam to where he stood in the passageway. He stopped for a second and listened. The feel of the drinks he'd had quickly wore off, and a slight sense of fear passed over him. Someone was in his cabin, and no one, not even Burke or Elena, should be in there at night.

At first, he hesitated to open the door. It might be a reporter who had snuck aboard. There had been several in the last day who had tried to sneak aboard adjacent yachts for a closer look. He put his eye up to the door and looked inside. It might be the detectives going through his things.

Or it might be Warren who had come back looking for his keys to the coupe. Nick had forgotten to give them to him at lunch the day before, though he'd had them in his pocket. A figure moved around the room as if searching for something. Nick kept most of his money locked up, so there was nothing to steal. He peered in but couldn't see who it was. So he pushed the door open slightly to get a better look and, as he did this, he heard the soft hum of a woman's voice.

"Excuse me…," he began.

The woman turned around. Nick froze for a moment in confusion. He looked and saw a girl with short blonde hair that he did not recognize. Then, as he squinted in the dull light, he recognized her face. He was speechless to see it was Miriam standing there before him.

"Oh, hi, Nick!" she said with a wide, cheery smile.

Nick just stood there and said nothing.

Miriam looked back at him and reached up and touched her hair. "I cut it short," she said. "Do you like it?"

CHAPTER FIFTEEN

Nick stood there looking at Miriam in silence. One of her suitcases sat open on his bed behind her, and her clothes lay about, half of them folded in an open drawer and half of them strewn on the bed. In that still moment they looked at each other and neither of them knew how to begin. Their silence might have told them what the other wanted to say. Finally, Nick spoke.

"Miriam…," he began.

"Don't be mad, Nick."

He caught his words and looked to the floor. Miriam turned quietly to finish putting away her things but did not move. Nick walked over to the bed and sat down cautiously next to her.

"Do you like my hair?" she asked him with a forced smile. She turned her head from side to side for him to see.

"How was the wedding, Miriam?"

The smile left her face and she was silent, standing motionless with a wrinkled blouse in her hands. "Nick…I can't…"

At that moment, he saw the tears well up in her eyes, and as he did so his anger died away as he saw that she stood there before him now, and she was real, not just in his mind. She was back. She had really come back to him.

"Nick, I…," she began. Then she was silent again.

They looked at each other and past each other at the same time; their silence said everything. Nick sat on the bed for a few long moments looking at her and then put out his hand. She took it and held it to her.

"Let's not do this," he said, putting his other hand to hers. He went up to her and kissed her gently. She kissed him back and put her arms around his neck and held him tightly.

"I'm sorry, Nick. I didn't mean to…"

"I know."

"…but I didn't…"

"I know, Miriam," he said softly. "It doesn't matter. None of it matters."

She stood there with tears on her cheeks, and all he could do was feel sad for her and at the same time grateful that she was standing there before him.

"You're all right?" he asked.

"Uh huh," she said between sobs.

"It's late. We can talk tomorrow."

"All right. Please don't be mad at me."

"Of course not," he smiled. "I'm just glad you're here and that you're all right. I was worried." He kissed away a tear on her cheek and sat back down on the bed and watched her for a minute. He watched as she put away her things in secure silence.

"I hope you don't mind me taking over your drawer," she smiled with a half-smile. "I'm only taking up a little bit."

Nick nodded without speaking. He loved to watch her. He watched her face and her eyes without letting her know he was watching them. He loved the little expressions as she folded her clothes and sorted things from her suitcase, moving things and then moving them again. Each movement of her lips and her brow told him what she was thinking without words. She was fascinating, this fantastic little creature who stood before him now.

"I don't want to take up much space," she said. "I know how you like your space."

Nick laughed to himself. It was funny how she had a way of saying things. No time had passed at all. They had never really been apart these two years. It was as if she had never left for Rome a week ago, as if she had never left him at all.

After a long while of watching her, he stood up from the bed and spoke. "Finish unpacking," he said, "and we'll sort everything out tomorrow. I'll leave you alone for a bit. I'm going to go up to have one last cigarette. You can join me in a minute if you want."

"No, I'm so tired, Nick. I'm just going to go to sleep."

"Sure you don't want a drink or something? What about something to eat? Elena can make something."

She thought for a moment. "No," she said, "I'm fine. Thank you though."

"Of course. Anything." He smoothed out the bed where he had sat.

"Look, I'm sorry, Nick," she said seriously as she turned to him. The smile he had watched for the last few minutes had left her face, and he would have done anything to see it back there again. "I didn't know what else to do."

"That's all right," he said. "Let's talk about it tomorrow. It's already late."

"All right." She sniffed and turned back to the clothes before her.

"I'll just be up there for a few minutes. I promise I won't be long," he said and turned to go. As he did so, he stopped in front of a vase on his desk. "What's this?" he asked as he reached down and touched some flowers he hadn't seen before.

"Oh," said Miriam, "I had Burke buy some flowers for the boat tonight while you were gone. It was so dreary in here. He has such good taste, doesn't he?"

"Hmm," Nick nodded. "So he knows you're here then?"

Riviera

"Of course. I had Elena put out different sheets and pillows as well," she said, running her hand over the bed. "These are softer than the ones you had on. How long have you had those anyway?"

Nick looked at the bed and hadn't noticed the new sheets. "Ha!" he laughed. "They'll do anything you ask, won't they?"

"Of course!" said Miriam. "Burke loves me!"

"Of course they do. Everyone loves you. If I don't watch out, you and my crew are going to run away together."

Miriam smiled at him. She blew him a kiss and he turned with a laugh and left her to go back up to the deck for some air.

The night had cooled considerably and was quieter than when he had come aboard. The Casino was going to close soon, but the parties that had sprung forth from its doors would keep lively corners of the city awake until dawn. A low whistle of air blew through the masts and shrouds and resounded in the harbor as the wind had picked up from the east and swirled around the city. Nick felt the *Diamant* sway under him with the low waves coming from the sea as he lit a cigarette and threw the match into the water. The boat bumped lazily against her taught lines.

So, Nick thought to himself, Miriam had come back to him. She had been running away, and now she was running back to him. He didn't quite know how to put his mind around it, particularly because the drinks from that

261

evening on the sailing yacht still clouded his thoughts. He always knew she'd come back to him, over these two years. The cigarette ash grew long as he stared out over the city until the wind finally caught it and threw it to the deck in a gray and orange flash whose movement caught Nick's eye and brought him back to the moment. He looked at the end and watched the cinders glow red and crawl toward his fingers in the wind. A long restrained draw warmed his lungs, giving him strength against the night air. He flicked the cigarette into the water and listened as the orange glow hissed out and floated lifelessly at the surface.

A few minutes passed with him standing there thinking. His mind drifted, focusing on nothing at all. Then, in the distance, Nick heard voices from a group of people before they hit the dock and knew immediately two or three who were among them. Their voices told him they had been drinking and were on their way from one party to another. He looked at his watch and saw that it was nearly one o'clock in the morning now. He hoped they would pass by and land on another yacht, so he pulled away from the edge and sat down quietly in a chair where they could not see him.

"Nick!" a voice he recognized called out as the sound of the footsteps approached. It was Warren, but he didn't even want to see Warren right now. Instead of answering, he sat at the table silently, wishing he had not turned on the deck lights when he had come up. He waited to see if they would move on.

"Nicky, you there, mate?!" Warren called out again.

Nick knew Warren had seen him. He stood up reluctantly and moved to the edge and waved hello.

"Where were you, mate?" shouted Warren. "You weren't at the Casino or anywhere." Warren was standing there with a bottle in his hand while the group continued on without him.

"No," said Nick quietly. "It's not good for me to be out right now. You saw the reporters. I'm trying to avoid as much attention as possible."

"Nick's scared to come out!" one of the other men in the group called back to the boat with a heavy laugh that followed from the crowd. Nick wasn't sure he recognized who it was.

"See," said Warren, "you've got to come out to defend yourself against such accusations like that." They both laughed, Nick uneasily.

Nick hesitated. He could tell that Warren wanted to go on and join the group, but Nick wanted to be alone and to go back down to Miriam. "I'd better not," he said finally. "I just don't think it's best right now."

"Suit yourself, mate. We're just going to have a drink down the way. Come join us if you want."

"All right. Thanks. I probably shouldn't though. The detectives are coming by tomorrow," he lied. He hated to lie to his friend, even little lies. "But have fun. I wish I could go. Have fun without me."

"We will!" said Warren. "You know we will." He turned and called to the group before him that was already boarding a yacht further down the way.

Nick stayed on the deck and listened as the voices faded away until music started from a record player and filled the harbor with a low, scratchy, distant melody that sounded as if it came from another time altogether. He was miserable to see Warren go without him. He wished he could tell him that Miriam had come back, but he thought it better to wait until things were all sorted out. He wished none of this had happened about the wedding and that he could go downstairs and get Miriam so they could join Warren and the others for a few drinks in peace. Instead, he sat on the deck a while longer and felt the cool night air come over him. The record player and cries of laughter resounded softly in the distance.

In the deep blue darkness, Nick felt his way back to his cabin, down the steps and through the long, narrow hall. Past the half-open door he could see the lights were off in his room and could hear that Miriam was already sleeping from her slow, heavy breaths. He paused for a moment and listened to her at the door. Then, he opened the door with slow creaks and moved over to sit on the bed.

She was wonderful. Even her breaths were wonderful, he thought. The soft sound among the silence mesmerized him where he sat, laying his hand gently on her warm body, feeling it rise and fall. He closed his eyes and smiled that she had come back to him. He wanted nothing more than to be lying next to her, feeling her soft skin against his. Yet, not knowing what strain she had been through these last few days, another part of him wanted to let her sleep there. There was no telling what had gone through her mind. She was so fragile there, and he dared not disturb her for fear that she might break.

He hesitated, sitting motionless listening to her, listening to the soft breaths, each breath more delicate than the last. Then, quietly, he rose and walked to the door in the darkness. He looked back at her for a moment, then he closed the door until it clicked and felt his way back up to the deck from where the blue light of the night crawled down into the cabin.

It was just a short walk along the dock before Nick came upon the party where he could hear Warren and the others laughing and talking wildly. It was the only yacht still lit, and there was music playing from the record player that had been set in the middle of the floor. Four or five couples sat around the player or danced with glasses in their hands. Nick didn't recognize the yacht, and he was sure he didn't know the owner. He walked over the gangway and up the stairs to the top deck and emerged before the group that he could tell had finished off several bottles during the course of the evening. When he stepped out before them, he was instantly welcomed by the small crowd with a drunken roar and applause that surprised even themselves. He was there only because Warren was there, and because he wanted to let Miriam rest.

"Nick, glad you came," said Warren who thrust a drink in his hand.

Nick made his way around the group and shook hands with the men and kissed the women on the cheeks. Most of the girls were Italian, and he spoke his simple Italian to them. *"Buona sera!"* Those who were seated did not get up. One of the girls sitting in someone's lap grabbed him drunkenly and held onto his hand. He laughed and said thank you and eventually got his hand back. He recognized almost everyone there at least faintly and felt more at ease. Only two people asked him where Miriam might be, and he said with an uneasy laugh that he wished he knew. He found his way into a teak chair and made himself comfortable listening to the music and watching two of the couples dance sloppily to the music. The single jazz record came to an end a few minutes later and someone set it to play again and turned the dial louder. When he had nearly finished his drink, a bottle was passed and he found his glass filled again without any effort. He resolved that he'd take it slow.

Nick had not wanted to leave the *Diamant* with Miriam there, but he wanted to let her sleep without disturbing her. He knew he would not be able to sleep, himself, with her lying next to him because of all the things on his mind. And now that she was back, much of his worry had been lifted. What was the harm in having a drink with Warren and some friends? And yet, his mind was surely on Miriam lying there in his bed. He would not stay long.

At that moment, a girl emerged from below. It was a girl Nick recognized. He smiled when he saw that it was Kate. They waved to each other and she came over to him.

"Hello, Kate," he said.

"Hi, Nick," she said as she leaned down toward him.

Warren rushed over from where he was sitting and gave Nick a slap on the back. "You remember Kate, don't ya, Nicky? She's a real dolly doll."

"Of course I do, Warren. We all had lunch together just the other day, remember?" Nick could tell Warren was drunk. Nick and Kate greeted each other with kisses on the cheek.

"Real doll," repeated Warren and grabbed her and gave her a sloppy kiss on the cheek. Kate and Nick laughed at how drunk Warren was. She smiled at Nick and saw that he was alone. He expected her to ask if he had heard from Miriam, but she did not, and he was glad that she said nothing of it. Warren pulled Kate away and danced drunkenly with her near the record player, and everyone laughed and clapped at them in time with the music, their bodies moving spasmodically.

Nick sat back in his chair with a profound sigh and watched everyone with contentment. Then, after someone poured a drink in his already full glass, he thought of Miriam and wished he were back with her. Or, even better, that she were there with him now and that none of this mess had ever happened. He wondered why he had come out and left her at all.

"I can just stay for one drink," said Nick when Warren passed dancing by with a bottle of whisky he had found somewhere.

Warren smiled at his friend. "Then we'll make sure your glass is never empty." He raised the bottle and poured whisky in it until Nick's glass overflowed and spilled on the deck. Kate, who was attached to Warren by his hand that also held half a lit cigarette, laughed wildly. It was fun to see Warren drunk like this, Nick thought; and Kate, too. It was fun to see them happy. He smiled and handed her the glass of whatever concoction had been created, and she drank seriously from it before handing it back to him.

"No more for me," he said to Warren. "I've had too much tonight already."

"That's the problem with wine," said Warren. "It hits you before you know it."

"This isn't wine," Kate shouted over the music, "it's whisky!"

Warren looked at the bottle confused, then continued around the circle in his feral dance. Nick took a sip from the awful drink in the glass and watched the couple move around the deck.

It was quite a while later, perhaps an hour, and Nick shook his head with a smile. He had unintentionally let the time slip by on him. When he laughed, he felt the burn of the sips of whisky in his breath. "Whose boat is this anyway?" He looked around and no one answered. The two couples sitting on the floor had fallen asleep and lay sprawled on the deck with their drinks lying next to them. Splinters from a broken glass lay at the heeled feet of one of the girls whose dress had fallen over her shoulder and whose left breast lay bare. Another couple was up dancing sloppily over the record player, their bodies seemingly unaware of the music that flowed from it. A lone girl sitting in a chair across from him spoke aloud incessantly in Italian to no one, gesturing wildly into the air.

"...*sia fatta la tua volontà come in cielo così in terra dacci oggi il nostro...*"

She might have been singing, but her words did not match the music on the record.

"...*ma liberaci dal male...,*" she kept repeating as she laughed. "...*ma liberaci dal male...*"

Nick wanted to ask his question again, about whose boat it was, but he knew that no one knew the answer.

Watching Warren lead Kate adoringly, bouncing around the deck from couple to couple, Nick laughed and slipped a cigarette from his pocket to his lips and reached for his lighter, but Warren, on his next turn around the record player, bent down for Nick to light the cigarette from his own lighter while Kate climbed onto Nick's lap and hung around his neck laughing. In the brief moment that their eyes met before Warren pulled her away to fill another couple's glasses, there was a supreme understanding between them that she was completely drunk and that it was all right to be so and just to let everything go. Nick smiled to himself and tasted the cigarette, and for just an instant he thought of nothing at all except the moment that was being played out eternally before him—the relentless pursuit of ultimate pleasure. It lasted only a moment, but he felt it inside of him and all around him in the music and the people and in the air that surrounded them. And in that moment he concluded that he could indeed be happy. He now had everything he searched for, everything all at once, and he dared not blink and let it cease to exist.

Another half hour passed in a kaleidoscopic whirl before Nick suddenly found the music had died with the record player still spinning a rhythmic static beat from its lone speaker. He waited for some time for someone to play it again, but no one did, and he saw that he and another couple were the only ones awake while Warren and Kate lay asleep on a seat across from him. He had no idea where the time had gone. In that moment, the feeling of complete isolation overtook him, and he wished that he had never left Miriam behind. He hadn't meant to stay so long. He had only meant to come and say hello to everyone. Heavily, he picked himself up and blinked hard several times and made his way clumsily down the stairs and back down the dock to where the *Diamant* sat quietly in her slip. He climbed aboard and saw a figure on the deck look at him, and he nodded and knew it was Burke, and something told him that Burke knew that Nick had seen Miriam and that Burke was glad Miriam had returned as well. But he could also tell that the captain knew he was exceedingly drunk, and that he knew why.

Back down below, he opened the door to his cabin as slowly as he could. The light was off, and the girl lay on the bed in surreal blue darkness and he tried to make out her outline as he heard her breathing. It took a few moments for his eyes to adjust. He closed them tightly for a second or two and then could make out her shape again when he looked toward the bed.

She was asleep. He didn't want to wake her, but he walked over next to the bed and watched her as she lay on her side, curled tightly around the blanket. There was nothing like her in the world. Her soft cheeks and handsome face begged to be touched. Though it had been nice to see Warren and Kate, he wished now that he had not left her. Reaching over her, he brought his lips to the side of her mouth and felt them make the lightest touch against hers.

"Good night, Miriam," he whispered so that only he could hear.

"Nick?" said Miriam softly as she stretched her body.

"What is it?" he asked, still whispering.

"Come lie next to me."

He reached down to the bed and looked at her. "I still have my clothes on," he said.

"I don't care. I want you to lie next to me. I'm cold."

"All right."

Nick clumsily slipped off his shoes next to the bed and sat next to her. His eyes had almost fully adjusted to the darkness now, though everything seemed to move around him, and he could see her body stretched out before him beneath the thin sheets. In a moment, she had moved to the side, and he lay down next to her, bringing the covers over both of them.

"Better," she said. She leaned over and put her arm over his chest and kissed him on the cheek. "Who were you talking to up there?" she asked in her half-sleep, her eyes still closed.

"No one," he replied.

"Oh." She pulled the sheet up tightly over her. "Your breath smells like smoke," she smiled.

"I'm sorry," said Nick. He knew it smelled a bit of whisky as well.

"No, I like it."

"Good. I'm glad."

The two lay silently, and Nick looked up at the ceiling as time passed immeasurably. The sounds came from the harbor, and Nick listened carefully to see if he could hear the sounds of anyone from the party. Instead, he heard Miriam's breathing slow and listened to her heart. He moved his body against hers and felt their breaths rise and fall together. He could feel her heartbeat through his entire body, concentrating on the rhythm and on the darkness above him until his eyes fell closed and he felt his body sink deeply into the bed. Miriam reached up once more and kissed him lazily on the cheek in her sleep, her warm lips bringing him a few steps back to into reality. She settled back with her face against his shoulder. Half asleep, Nick leaned over with his eyes still closed and felt his lips brush against hers. He paused for a moment in the darkness, then lay back and felt the swirling night come over him.

CHAPTER SIXTEEN

Nick stood in the morning sun, mindlessly drinking from a cup of black coffee that hurt his stomach more than it helped. But each time he pushed it away from him, his beating headache forced him to take it up again. He had not thought that he had drunk so much last night. Miriam had come back to him. She was still sleeping down below. He thought about this without really thinking about it and stared blankly out at the water in the harbor and at the boats going by beyond and wondered at everything that had gone through her mind when she had first boarded the train in Paris to come here. After a few minutes, he brushed these thoughts aside with a wave of his hand since none of it mattered and the only matter of importance was that she was there now and that she was his again. After another cup of coffee brought by Elena, who knew it was a rough morning for him and would scold him later for it, he went below and found Miriam just waking up. He sat carefully on the edge of the bed and paused for a moment to see why she looked so serious.

"How did you know about the wedding?" she asked, still half asleep with the side of her head deep against the pillow.

"It was in the papers, Miriam. Every newspaper in Italy and France. In the American papers, too. The whole coast is talking about it."

"Oh," she sighed. "I didn't know." She turned over with a frown and propped her head up to see Nick better.

"I can't go anywhere without a half dozen reporters and these two idiot detectives following me around. Nothing but trouble." This he had meant with a laugh but felt that he had scolded her instead and wished it had come out differently.

"I'm sorry, Nick. I didn't mean to drag you into all of this."

"Eh, I don't care," he smiled, brushing his hand over her skin. "It is what it is. All that matters is that you're all right."

Nick thought for a moment. "How did you make it past the photographers onto the dock?" he asked. "How did you get to the boat?"

Miriam looked at him, confused. "I just walked right by yesterday evening." She said. "There was a couple walking, and I just walked right by with them. Nobody said anything to me. Not even with the suitcases. I changed my hair, remember? No one recognized me at all."

Nick laughed to himself.

"I just didn't know what to do, Nick," continued Miriam. "That's why I came to you in the first place, when I first got here."

"We were all so worried about you. Warren and Elena and everybody. You know how much they care about you. Everyone was so worried when we saw the papers. Maybe something had happened…"

Miriam sat up and brushed her hands over her face, catching the light coming through the window with bright flashes as it passed over her. "I don't know why I left to go to Rome anyway. When I got to the train station there, I knew I couldn't go through with it. I just checked into a hotel for a few days with a different name until I knew it was over. I kept thinking I might go through with it, but I just knew I couldn't. The only thing I could do then was come back here."

"And no one noticed you coming back?"

"I guess not. I cut my hair at the hotel and had the maid help dye it for me." She reached over and put on a large pair of dark sunglasses. "Now I look like every other girl on the coast."

Nick smiled at this. He ran his hand through her short hair and she smiled. It reminded him of how she had kept it shorter years before.

"What about the film?" he asked. "Didn't you have your hair long for the film?"

The smile she wore faded quickly and she turned and buried her face back in the pillow. She didn't say anything for a few minutes.

Nick moved his hand from her hair down to her back and held it there a while. After a few long moments, wanting to changes the subject, he spoke. "I'm going upstairs to have breakfast, kid. Do you want to come up?"

She shook her head no in the pillow without a word.

"Do you want me to bring something down for you? You know you can have anything you want."

She paused for a moment, then shook her head no again.

Nick ran his hand along her back and up to her neck. "Do you want me to come back later then?"

She hesitated a moment and then pulled her head away from the pillow and tossed the sunglasses onto the bed, showing a puffy face that told she had been crying. "Yeah," she said as her body jerked with sobs, "I don't want to talk about anything right now."

"You sure?" He wiped her wet cheek.

"Yes."

"All right," he said. "I'll come back after eating something. You'll feel better then?"

"Uh huh."

"You don't mind if I leave you?"

"No, it's all right."

He reached down and kissed her on the forehead. All he wanted to do was to make it better for her, but he knew there was nothing he could do just then. "You sure you don't want me to bring you anything?"

She shook her head no and lay slowly back into the pillow as if her body would break with any degree of force.

"You still like pancakes, don't you?" he said from the door with a forced smile that she struggled to return, as if that would make it all right. He took that as a sign that she would feel better in a bit after being alone and closed the door softly behind him.

Up on deck he struggled down breakfast against his stomach that wanted nothing to do with it and poured himself a drink to make his headache go away. It took two strong glasses of gin and tonic before he started to feel better, and he poured himself a third for posterity before making his way down the dock to see if Warren and Kate were still on the commandeered yacht from the night before. For the first time that morning he noticed the sounds of the city reaching him, and he heard them more strongly than he ever had before—the hum of a city alive. He wondered what time it was and thought it must be at least eight or nine, but he looked and saw that he didn't have his watch on. He walked casually down the dock, past the yacht from the night before, to the end of the dock, and then walked back to make sure no one was watching him, then he slipped aboard the yacht and climbed the stairs up to the top deck where the party had taken place.

Surprised, he found no one aboard and decided that they must have all crawled away when the sun had come up. It was hot and bright now. The sky was clear and blue. Nick surveyed the damage. He saw the record player sitting in the middle of the floor still turning its beat, and he followed the cord to an outlet behind a table and unplugged it. Then he found a single black stiletto lying underneath a chair. For no reason at all, he stacked the record player, the shoe, and the glasses against a wall and kicked the broken glass into a pile. Then he thought better of it and tossed the pieces of broken glass overboard into the water using the cover from the record. Black and red makeup smeared the cushions where one of the girls had slept. Her blurred face was imprinted there. He knew nothing he could do would get it out but would only smudge it more and make it worse. After a few minutes, he looked around feeling proud that he had tidied things up a bit and sipped the last of the gin from his cool glass in the sun before finding his way back along the dock to the *Diamant*.

He went along the lower deck and walked the length of the side of the yacht to the bow and stood there leaning sluggishly against the rail with the Casino and all of Monte-Carlo hazy before him the in the brightness of the day. Cars ran up the high sloping avenue that led up there past the Hôtel Hermitage and the Hôtel de Paris, by the Casino and around to all the shops that poured shiny little objects from their doors. He turned and looked back at the *Diamant* and thought about the crew and knew that

Burke had told them that Miriam was aboard and not to say anything to anyone, especially to the reporters or the detectives. Burke was good like that. Nick then raised his eyes and looked up to the bridge and saw a figure standing there and knew it was Burke and waved to him and moved to walk up to talk to him.

"Good morning, Mister Duncan," the captain said with a wide smile when Nick had reached the bridge. Nick shook his hand sturdily and could not hold back a smile himself. Burke did that to him. He waited for the captain to say something, but the man only stood attentively.

"G'morning, Burke," said Nick.

Burke nodded, still with a smile.

"Miriam's back from Rome."

"Oh, yes, sir. She had me bring her flowers for the room last night."

"Oh yeah, I forgot. Flowers." Nick's mind was not really all there yet and he was still trying to gather his thoughts from the night before.

"I hope you don't mind, sir. I also hope you don't mind I didn't say anything to you about Miss Banks. She said she wanted to surprise you. She insisted."

"No, of course not. Thank you."

The captain nodded again.

Nick stood for a moment and did not say anything. His headache lingered incessantly, and the gin had not fully hit him yet to take it away. He knew it would last all day, and he thought about getting himself another drink when he was done speaking with the captain, but he knew he shouldn't.

"What would you like the crew to do, Mister Duncan?"

"What's that?"

"The crew, sir. Should I keep them aboard?"

"Oh, yes. Just tell them to keep the reporters and the detectives and anyone else away and don't let anyone know Miriam's here." Nick knew when he said this that Burke had already given those instructions.

"Yes, sir."

"You already let them know she's here?"

"Yes, sir. I didn't want them coming across her and then telling the police. Of course, they would come to me first, but I didn't want to take a chance."

Nick nodded solemnly in agreement.

"Anything else, Mister Duncan?"

He thought. "Nothing for now, Burke." Then he turned to walk back downstairs. "Oh," he said, "maybe best to keep Miriam aboard if you can, until we get things sorted out. She probably shouldn't leave the boat."

The captain nodded that he understood, and Nick again went below.

Burke was always on top of things—always had a way of anticipating what Nick was thinking. He had been the captain of the *Diamant* ever since Nick had had her built, and even now he continued to surprise Nick. But beyond this, after all these years, Nick knew very little of the man— nothing except that he went by his last name and that he delighted in the very occasional sip of Scotch whenever Nick could convince him of it.

Down in the cabin, Nick found Miriam lying in bed from where she had not moved. Her tears had dried and she smiled at him without speaking in the sun that shone through the curtains. Nick climbed in the bed to sit next to her, and she laid her head against his thigh. He reached over and ran his hand through her hair as before. He did this silently and waited for her to be the first to speak. A small, white down feather from a pillow lay on the bed next to his knee, and he blew it softly so that Miriam did not hear and watched it fly up and float down to the floor below. A few minutes passed and Miriam finally spoke.

"I didn't love him, you know."

"I know," said Nick.

"I never did."

"Miriam," he said with a pause, "you don't have to say any of this. I understand everything."

She lay silent for a minute, thinking. "I didn't want to marry him. It just seemed like the right thing to do at the time. He's one of the biggest directors, you know." She stopped when she heard how ridiculous she sounded. "I tried to break it off, but he wouldn't let me. He said I would never work in Hollywood again." She looked up at him and he knew she felt ashamed. "I'm sorry, Nick. I'm sorry I dragged you into all of this."

"Don't be sorry. It's not your fault."

"But it *is* my fault," she said. "Of course it's my fault."

Nick shook his head without speaking, and she saw that he did not want to see it that way.

"I'm glad I came to you, though," she continued. "I didn't know where else to go, but I just had a feeling you'd be here. And then you were here, and it was all like it used to be. You and Warren, and Benicio, and…and everybody. It made me so happy again."

Nick nodded. "I don't know how you knew I'd be here. I had just gotten in the day before." He said this more to himself than to her.

"I came to you because I needed you, Nick. You were the only one I could go to. And when I saw you here, I knew it was right, and I just couldn't go through with it. It wasn't what I wanted. I know that now. I had forgotten all about this world, and about you."

There was a long period of silence between them where no one spoke. Their minds were both taking in all that had happened.

"Well, what do you want me to do, Miriam?" Nick said finally.

She thought for a moment and then stared out before her. "I want to go away," she said. "I want to go away from all of it."

Nick could see her tears coming back and reached out his hand to touch her. She turned to him.

"I want to spend my time with you. I know that now. Above anything else, I want to be with you, Nick."

After all that had happened, and after she had run away and come back to him, he had told himself he would be firm and would not give into her so easily as he had always done in the past. He had meant to scold her a little for her recklessness and her selfishness, for bringing forth all the feelings he had laid to rest long ago; but now he could not bring himself to be so rigid. Here she was, right there before him. Not just for a moment, but wanting to remain, to be a part of his life again. Here was the chance to have everything back that he had ever wanted. And no matter how hard he tried to hold it back, not to let it happen, a hint of a smile crept across his face, and he could tell by the look in her eyes that she saw it and loved him for it. In that moment, all of the thoughts that had been building and churning in his mind ever since he had first seen her standing there on the dock in the sun with her suitcase came rushing forth in one uncontrollable surge.

"Then let's go away," he said, "if that's what you want. Let's get away from all of this."

Her face brightened up. "Do you mean it?"

"I mean it. We'll go and leave all this director wedding mess behind."

"Yes? Where will we go?"

"I don't know," he said. "Spain maybe, for a little while anyway. Or some little Greek island no one's ever heard of. Somewhere away from everybody. Until this all blows over."

Miriam moved herself over to him and wrapped her arms around him. She pressed her wet face against his.

Nick held her tight and kissed her softly. This was what he wanted. He knew it was real. He knew he finally had her.

"And whatever happens, Miriam," he said then with a more serious tone, "you've got to promise to do exactly what I say."

"Of course, Nick. Whatever you want."

He thought for a moment. "I only say that because the police and the reporters would never leave us alone."

"I will. I'll do exactly what you tell me. I promise."

"All right," he said. He looked down at her and knew she believed in him. He was forming the plan in his mind as he said it. "You can't leave the boat until we've gone. Does anyone know you're here?"

"No. When I came aboard last night it was almost dark. No one recognized me on the train either."

"Good. The reporters would never let us get away if they knew you were here. They'd follow us to Spain or wherever we go. You have to stay out of sight. I'll keep telling them I don't know anything." Then he thought for a few moments. "We'll leave tonight, head for Barcelona or Ibiza or Valencia. It's not much time, but Burke can get everything ready right away."

"Oh, I love Spain," she laughed. "It will be like how it used to be."

Nick smiled and ran his hand through her short hair, and for a moment they both remembered their time there, both the good and the bad.

"I know," she said, "but it will be even better this time."

Nick's thoughts turned to the detectives and his passport. "I just have to tell the police detectives you're safe and get my passport so we can leave."

"Oh, do you have to tell anyone, Nick? I just want to go away." By now she was sitting up facing him with an excited look.

"I do," he said, "or they'll keep looking for you and they're sure to follow me until they find you. If I leave Monaco, they'll arrest me the first port we stop into. You have to stay completely out of sight until we go. I've told the crew not to say anything and to stay near the boat to keep everyone away." Though Nick was trying to put together a reasonable plan, he knew he shared her excitement, and he tried to keep it under control or at least give that impression. "We'll have to stay away from the cities for at least a few weeks, until the press dies down. I know a place where they won't find us if we don't want them to." He turned to her. "You'll have to send a message to your family telling them you're all right. The Colonel's probably on his way over here already, if he's seen the news. I'm certain he has. You'll have to call him as soon as we arrive in Spain."

"Aw, do I have to?" She flopped back down on the bed next to him.

Nick looked at her and laughed. "Of course you do, so they'll not come looking for you. I don't want your father getting the police involved any more than they have been."

"All right," said Miriam, "I'll do what you say."

"And I'm sure that Detective Joliet character will take care of the press once we've gone. God knows he's dying to get his name in the papers. You don't have to worry much. Just stay out of sight on the boat and we won't draw any attention. We'll leave tonight when it's dark, and I'll take care of everything."

"Oh, thank you, Nick," she said. "Thank you so much. You know I love you." She wrapped her arms around him and kissed him again. Her warm lips felt good against his skin.

"I know." He smiled and ran his hand through her hair.

She was right, he knew. It would be exactly as it had been, before she had left him years ago and before he had thrown himself into the crowds and the parties that they had known together but made him feel more alone than ever without her. He pictured her now, arms and legs bronzed from the sun, her hair lightened from the summers on the sea, the bridge of the *Diamant* and the high rocky hills of the Spanish coast behind her. There were afternoons diving from the boat, Rioja wine and salted fish and olives at cafés in coastal villages he had never even heard of, that no one had ever heard of, the taste of the sea between them as he kissed her, and all the while the sun shining from the water over her as if the oceans had been created solely for that reason. And he would do anything for her. He would show her everything, protect her from the world, and she would love him for it and prove it to him more every day, more than he could ever know.

Because she was just a child. A fragile little creature lying there before him that relied on him, needed him. And without him she would perish, and without her he would do the same. It all played itself out before him in an instant. He saw it there as his fingertips felt her skin, and all that had been in his daydreams and now was real again.

"Miriam," he said as he looked down at her.

"Yes?" She smiled simply as he knew only she could smile. No matter how hard he tried, he could not help but smile back.

"You know, I really do like your hair better this way."

CHAPTER SEVENTEEN

Nick knew that if he stayed away from the Hôtel and the Casino that he might avoid being recognized by friends, as well as the photographers that were always hunting him now. But the detective he must see—there was no way around that. One of the crew went down to the end of the dock at the base of the harbor and saw that the photographers were gone, for now. Only a single policeman rested lazily in his patrol car. A cab was called, and Nick went down the dock quickly and got in.

The town late that morning was languid as warm spring mornings on the Riviera go. It was not as alive as it had been earlier. A lone man on a bike passed him and waved to him as he crossed the quay and left the safety of the harbor. Monte-Carlo, sitting quiet on her hilltop, showed stark contrast from the bursting radiance she had heaved forth the night before. All the world, it seemed, lay hungover from last evening, and at the same time slumbering in anticipation of the night that yet could be.

He inquired at the police station for the detective after the short cab ride up, but the dull woman in the office there said in broken English that he was away in Nice and that he would be back around noon. Nick nodded and thanked her for her time and took note of the hour on the clock behind her. He left the office less assured than he had set out. Unable to find a cab back without going to the Casino or to one of the hotels, he started to walk down, shying away as he passed the few people in the street that the city had thrust forth into activity. On the way back to the harbor, he happened into Warren, still dressed from the night before, as he passed a café where serious waiters dashed about preparing for the coming lunch crowds.

"*Ciao*, Nicky!" Warren called before Nick had seen him.

Nick waved cautiously and pulled him around a corner away from passing cars, out of sight from passersby.

"What's the deal, mate?" asked Warren. Nick could see the makeup stains on his white, half-buttoned shirt and creased suit, and his red, sleepless eyes. He was still exceedingly drunk from the night before and moved bulkily against Nick's grip.

"Sorry," he said anxiously, "there might be reporters around."

"No worries. I heard about a big fire in Nice last night. I'm sure they're all over there. I've been hearing about it from everybody this morning."

"Oh," said Nick.

"It started in town and spread up into the hills. Someone told me they brought in seaplanes to drop water on it. To save the houses, you know."

Nick nodded. He relaxed a bit and leaned against the stone wall of a jewelry store and pulled out a pair of cigarettes. "Where're ya coming from?" he asked.

"Ha!" laughed Warren loudly, taking his cigarette and lighting it from Nick's flame. A man passing hurriedly by paused for an instant looking at them before continuing in silence against the stares of Warren and Nick. "Just dropped Kate off at her place. Some old lady gave me a pretty bad look at the door. I think it was the mother."

Nick smiled and drew from his cigarette. "Not the best impression?"

"But they've got a great view of the racetrack. Balcony and everything. Perfect shot down on the chicane. We should've watched the race from there."

"We didn't even get to see the race," Nick reminded him. "That wedding in Cannes, remember?"

Warren nodded blankly as if he hadn't understood the words Nick had said.

"Oh yeah," said Warren, "what about my car?"

Nick felt his pockets and remembered the keys back on board. "Been meaning to get the keys back to you," he said. "I left it parked somewhere over by the beaches after the race. You don't have an extra set of keys do you?" Nick knew there was no reason in asking this. "Well, I should've brought you the keys the other day at lunch anyway. Sorry about that."

"No worries," said Warren. "I'll get it soon enough."

Nick sat back leaning against the wall, feeling a little guilty about the keys. He was usually good about these things.

"Say," said Warren after some silence," "You heard anything about Miriam?"

Nick looked at Warren. He realized only then that he had seen him and Kate the night before on the yacht. "No, nothing." He avoided Warren's eyes when he said this. He knew they would be on their way to Spain before tomorrow. They wouldn't tell Warren anything before they left.

"I heard she was spotted in Milan. They've got the police looking for her there."

"Oh?"

It's a shame" said Warren. She's got herself in a mess somehow, and you're the one who's catching everything for it."

Nick nodded and thought about how he would call Warren when they arrived in Spain in four or five days, if they traveled through the night as well. Or maybe he'd have a note sent up to his hotel. He was still formulating the plan in his head. They would want Warren to take the train and meet them in Barcelona the following week perhaps, for a few days maybe, since it would be tough to get him away from Monaco later on with the summer season coming up. But Warren would want to see Miriam, of course. Nick wanted to tell him everything now, but he knew Warren couldn't keep his mouth shut, especially when he was drinking.

"Oh, Nick, I forgot something," said Warren as he reached for his wallet and took out a stack of French bills. "I said I'd pay you back." He counted half the stack methodically and then handed the entire fistful to Nick.

"Thanks." Nick took the cigarette he was holding between two fingers and threw it out onto the street.

"With interest," said Warren with a wink. "Count it, it's all there."

Nick didn't count the money but folded it and put it in his pocket. "I believe you."

"You can count it if you want."

"It's all right, Warren." He laughed to himself and wondered from whom Warren had gotten the money. He only found later when he took out the bills in his cabin that Warren was three hundred francs short, but he knew he would never tell him so.

Back aboard the *Diamant*, Nick found Miriam, still dressed from bed, sitting at his desk with her face in her hands.

When he entered, she looked up and showed the tears in her eyes. His heart sank.

"What happened?" he asked.

At first she said nothing. She threw her face back into her hands and couldn't speak for the sobbing. He closed the door and put his arms around her and felt her whole body tremble as she sobbed.

"What is it?"

The girl turned to him and buried her face in his shoulder. She said something but he could not understand.

"What, Miriam?"

She pulled her face away. "I have to give up the movies!" she burst out between sobs.

Nick smiled and then held it back. He stroked her hair until the sobbing subsided. "Only for a little while, I'm sure. You're not going to be thrown out of Hollywood just because of this."

She was silent.

"There have been far worse scandals, Miriam." He held her until her convulsing slowed.

"But he said I'd never work in movies again!" Tears burst forth once more, and Nick's smile left his face as he tried to reason with her.

"You're a star, Miriam. One of the biggest. You can act here in Europe. They love you here. Or in London. There are tons of American actors in England. Tons of studios, too."

"It's not the same!"

Nick held her tight and coaxed her to the bed where she could lie down, but her crying continued. He sat on the bed next to her and looked over her body shaking as she sobbed. There was no way to know what to say.

"Once you're out, you're out," she continued. "That's the way it is. Once you're out, there's no way back in."

"That's pretty cruel," said Nick. "I'm sure you'll be fine."

"No. It's all over for me now. I'll never star in another film again."

Nick bent down to her with a sigh and reached his hand up to her face and stroked her between sobs. "Well, what do you want, Miriam? I'll do anything you say."

She looked at him and closed her eyes and leaned into him. She moaned something that he could not hear.

"What?" he asked.

"But I want to be with you," she said with a whimper.

Nick sighed again and held her for a minute longer. He lay her back down on the pillow and looked over her bare shoulders and arms as she stared vacantly up at the ceiling, over her face and sad eyes that did not look at him. He felt as though all life had gone out of her, all energy had been used up, all passion expended. At that moment, he understood the gravity of what he had ventured. She would no longer be a film star, loved by the entire world. That was the reason she had left him in the first place. He committed there to himself that he would be everything for her, so selfless and thrilling for her that she would never once think about this past life of hers—this life of the films. It would be his only aspiration, and he knew that it would be realized as soon as they arrived on the Spanish coast. She would soon forget everything, and life would be new again, unbounded and absolute. It was all he could offer her, and he would compel himself to that end and to that end alone. He had to make her forget about Hollywood.

"Why don't you rest a little more?" he said.

She looked at him but did not move and said nothing.

"Why don't you eat something? A little breakfast maybe. I'll have Elena bring down something for you."

She raised her eyes back to the ceiling and nodded in agreement.

"You'll feel better once you've eaten something."

Nick pulled a cool sheet from the side of the bed and brought it over her body. He reached up and combed back her blonde hair that had fallen over her forehead and felt her warm skin, flushed from crying. Immense sadness ran through him for her, and all he wanted was to take it all away. And at that same moment a hint of a smile crossed her lips as his fingers touched her, and he felt the same smile rise up within him and he leaned over her and kissed her forehead. Maybe everything would be all right.

Nick found Elena reading in her room when he knocked. She stood and nodded seriously when he asked her to prepare something and take it down for Miriam, and he apologized for interrupting her while she read because he had seen the smile on her face from the book she was reading when he had entered.

He went up to the deck into the full force of the day and sat heavily in the chair with the sun all around him, tossing notions around in his head. He stared blankly until the strength of the sun hurt his eyes, and he inattentively reached down for sunglasses that were not on the table or anywhere around him. This brought reality back to him and he thought for a while on what he was to do about Miriam. If he could only get away from here and to the coast of Spain. Then she would forget everything about the films. Or maybe he was rushing things and it was better to stay and give everything some time. Maybe he was to blame for that. He thought this and knew it was probably true. There was nothing to do but let the girl decide. He loved her. He knew he did. But as he had loved her before, so had he lost her for holding her too tightly. The past told him he could not keep her there as his cageling.

And so he sat and settled with himself that he would only do what she wished, go only if she wanted to go, and stay if she wanted to stay. He might have to let her go completely again to make her happy. He knew that now. Let someone else have her. Let California have her once again. The notion cut through him like a knife in his heart. But it was all up to her—she was in control. She had come back into his life for a reason, and he was content that way, leaving things to her, because it was only in being with her that he was happy. But he could not have that if it made her unhappy, because he knew he would lose her again. Maybe the last few days were all he would get.

He put these exhausting thoughts out of his mind and began to sense all the things around him. The day was hot and he felt a bead of sweat run down his cheek to his jaw. He licked his lips and tasted it there, too. And around him the world had come alive once again. Cars on the hilly streets raced their engines in ascent, the sound resounding in the harbor as it had early that morning. Footsteps and voices went by on the dock below, but he was out of sight, and no one called to him. An empty glass lay on the table from a drink he'd had that morning, and he looked around him and lacked the energy to get up and fill it.

His decision of indecision had relieved him of the burden he had felt upon him since the moment Miriam had returned the night before. She had come back to him, and he just wanted to take pleasure in the simplicity of that fact. Why did he have to push everything beyond that? There was that part of him that could never just let things be. He shook his head and laughed at himself and breathed heavily against the warmth of the air around him.

Miriam, when he found her in his room below, was sitting up in the bed with a magazine propped against her knees. When he closed the door behind him he smiled at her and sat next to her in the bed. Her face showed that the sadness had left her.

"Did you have something to eat?"
"Uh huh."

"Was it good?" Nick saw the empty plate sitting on his desk.

"Yes. I had an omelette and some pancakes. Elena always used to know what I like."

"Good. And you feel better?"

"Uh huh. Thank you."

Nick reached out and ran his hands over her bare legs. He adored her skin, and if he could just touch her every day for the rest of his life, he knew he could be happy.

"Miriam," he began with a sigh, "I just want you to know that…"

"I was looking in this magazine," she interrupted as she picked it back up. "There's a little village just beyond Barcelona we could live in if we wanted to. I don't think anybody would bother us there."

Nick laughed at her beaming smile and let go anything he was planning to say. Every troubling thought left him with her words. "Oh yeah?"

"Yep. It's called La Mora. I was reading about the beach they have there. Only a few hundred people live in the village." She pointed to a tiny map in the magazine and a picture of a statue in the town below it. "Can we go there first?" she asked.

Nick smiled and slid down in the bed to lay his head in the girl's lap. She felt cool against his warm skin and he sighed heavily in contented resignation. "Of course," he said. "Anything you want." He watched her eyes pensively, gratefully as she turned excitedly through the magazine.

She spoke, but he did not listen to the words she said. He read everything he wanted to see in her face. She wanted to run away with him after all. Suddenly, she looked down at him with an expression of surprise. "What?" he said. "What is it?"

She reached down and held his face in her hands. "What's this?" she asked.

"What?"

"On the side of your cheek?" She ran her fingers over his skin. "What happened?"

"The scar, you mean?" He could feel her fingers running along it.

"Yeah."

"I've always had this."

"No," said Miriam. "You didn't have it in that picture." She pointed across the room to one of the photographs hanging on the wall.

Nick looked over at it and saw from a distance that it was a picture of him and Miriam from a few years before. He had forgotten the picture was there. In the light, he could see the other photographs as well. He didn't recognize the faces of the friends in them right away, but he could tell even from there where each of them had been taken.

"Oh," he said.

"What happened?"

Nick smiled up at her. "You just noticed it? It happened a few years ago swimming off Marseilles. You don't remember?"

"I remember you cut yourself. I didn't know it left such a scar."

"With Warren, remember? Elena had to put in two stitches. You never noticed it?"

Miriam didn't answer him. She just smiled and ran her fingers along his skin and felt it there. She passed her fingers over the scar, back and forth, making his skin tingle where she touched it. "I just love it!" she laughed. "It makes you look so…so rough!"

CHAPTER EIGHTEEN

The cab took Nick back up to the police station to meet with the detective just after noon, but as the car pulled to a stop there he asked the driver to go another block further and turn the corner. He had seen the crowd and photographers as the cab had approached along the street, and they were the last people he wanted to endure right now.

"*Ici?*" the man asked. "Here?"

"Go around the block again," Nick motioned.

The man did as he asked and looped back around toward the station.

"*Arrêtez ici,*" Nick said. "Stop here." They were still a half block away from the station, but Nick had the man pull to the opposite side of the street and put the car in park with the meter running. From there, Nick could see the photographers and watched them for a minute to study the situation. There were men with cameras and others on scooters in a frantic swarm. But he could see that instead of coming toward him they were following someone else. They hadn't even seen him. Amongst them he saw the object of their interest—a young brunette he recognized as an Italian singer who he had last seen up near the Casino several nights before, with a fat man he did not recognize in a dark suit and glasses. The man was pushing his way through the crowd for her, but she was loving the attention, stopping to pose every few steps.

Nick breathed heavily and sat back in the cab until the crowd had gone out of sight with her around a corner. He watched for a few more minutes, then had the driver pull up to the station and handed him a few extra bills to wait there until he came out, just in case he had to get away quickly.

"The meter is still ticking," the chubby driver said rudely.

"Yes. I know."

Nick went through the heavy red doors of the station, but the woman, who he could tell from her face when he'd entered seemed annoyed with him now, said that the detective had gone to eat lunch and asked him to come back in an hour. Nick looked at his watch and saw that it was nearly one o'clock.

"He's a busy man," he said sarcastically to the woman in French.

"*Oui*," she said blankly.

"Where did he go to eat?"

The woman looked at him sternly. "It is not good to disturb a man while he is eating," she replied impolitely. "It affects the digestion."

Nick nodded his head in agreement, then thought about asking her about his passport. The passport was really all he needed. He could write a message to the detective about Miriam and leave it with her. He was already getting tired of playing this game. But, he thought better of it. He was certain the detective had the passport on him or had it locked away somewhere. He thanked her dryly once again and turned to depart.

As he left the station, he stepped out into a street filled with people going from shop to shop—women burdened by shopping bags from various stores, men trailing them obediently or waiting anxiously for them in black sedans and red coupes. All things he had not noticed when he had first arrived because he'd been watching the photographers. He walked toward the waiting cab, but a man passing in the street stopped and looked at him. Nick stopped and looked back at him reflexively. As he recognized him, he wished he hadn't stopped. It was Richard.

Nick nodded at the man without saying anything. He waited for Richard to say something terse to him as he always did, but the man said nothing. He just stared at Nick who he had just seen come out of the police station. Nick waited for a comment, but the man just stood and stared at him, watching his eyes without moving.

Nick turned his eyes away and said nothing and climbed into the waiting cab whose engine was still running. When the driver had gone a block down the street, Nick turned around and saw Richard still standing there in front of the station watching them drive away. Nick shook his head slowly as the driver turned the corner.

When he arrived back at the harbor, he went below in the *Diamant* to find Miriam. He had made the cab driver stop at a flower shop so he could buy something more for the room, and he had taken longer than he'd wanted to. He opened the door to his cabin slowly, expecting to find her there reading as he had left her, but when he had pushed the door open he saw that she was not there. He listened closely, but she was not in the shower and was not moving about. He went up to the kitchen to see if she had gone to find lunch, but he did not find her there either. Nor was she up on the deck in the sun.

"Burke," said Nick to the captain when he had found him up near the bridge, "where did Miriam go?"

"Is she not below, sir? I just saw her there several minutes ago."

"No."

"Strange, sir. I just saw her there not more than five minutes ago. She said she was going to lie down and take a nap."

"Well," said Nick, starting to get annoyed, "she isn't there. I told her to stay on board."

"Are you sure, Mister Duncan? Should I go down and look for her again? Maybe she's speaking with Elena in…"

"God damn it, Burke!" Nick shouted, "She's not there! I thought I told you to…"

The captain lowered his head. This made Nick pause.

Nick had a sinking feeling inside of him when he realized that she was not on board. "No, Burke," he said more agreeably. "I'm sorry. She probably just slipped away for a minute to call her father. I told her she would need to call him. I'm sure she'll be back soon."

"I had the crew keeping an eye on her, sir. I just saw her not more than five minutes ago myself." The man looked up gravely. "I'm sorry, Mr. Duncan. It's completely my fault."

Nick shook his head with an uneasy laugh. "It's not your fault, Burke. It's mine." He slapped the captain on the shoulder. "Don't worry. I'm sure she'll be back in a few minutes."

Nick went up to the top deck to wait for her to return and poured himself a drink to stay cool in the sun. He purposely made it weak because he did not want to be drunk right now. His headache was steady but endurable. The heat of the day had increased, and the port was even more alive with activity as the day passed. Larger yachts and little boats alike were heading out of the harbor for the afternoon to escape the heat. He thought to himself that Miriam might have gone for a minute to make a few calls from a phone booth nearby, or to talk to Benicio over at the *Miradora*, but he resisted the urge to leave the boat and go looking for her. He didn't want to seem too protective—too controlling, really. She could handle herself. He knew she wouldn't go far. She had promised him she wouldn't leave the boat.

His plan was that they would leave that night well after midnight when no one would see them slip out of the harbor. Once he had his passport in hand and had notified the detective that Miriam was all right, there would be no more trouble, except maybe from the press if the detective wanted to make a spectacle of it. He would probably demand to see Miriam for himself in exchange for Nick's passport. There might be a short interview with the sergeant taking notes. Burke had already been given his orders, and the boat would be loaded that evening once it was dark, and they would set out until they reached the quiet coast of Spain a few days from now. There was more than enough fuel to get there. The boat had been built with extra fuel tanks for long spans at sea. Everything was in order and going according to plan, except he didn't have his passport, and now he didn't have Miriam.

Looking to divert his attention until Miriam showed up, Nick sent one of the crew below for a stack of mail he had been avoiding in his cabin. He distractedly sifted through the letters and scanned them to separate them into the pile he would answer and the one he wouldn't.

There were letters from friends, both here in Europe and from back in the States. There was a message from his mother that he did not open but set aside for later. Then he came across his club's quarterly newsletter from New York and, in reality, read it with some interest. It was a club he had frequented while he was working at the investment firm there, and he still sent a check to the club's Staff Christmas Fund each December, even though he had not been there in many years. It was his small effort at charity. And it was his only connection back to New York.

A torturous hour passed and she still had not returned. Nick looked at his watch after he had had a couple of drinks and saw it was after two o'clock. He felt the alcohol hit him as he stood up and knew he shouldn't have drunk so much, not yet anyways, not until he had spoken with the detective. He knew he needed to go now and catch the detective after his lunch. He couldn't wait for Miriam any longer.

Just as Nick rose to leave, he looked down and saw a young couple approaching the *Diamant*.

"*Bonjour*, Nick!" cried Fabien. He was carrying a bottle of champagne in each of his hands. His wife Michelle waved up to Nick and carried with her a small leather bag. They were both dressed for a day on the water in shorts and sunglasses.

It was the Brecards. Nick's heart sank when he recognized them and remembered why they were there. He had invited them for an afternoon aboard the *Diamant* in order to see the coast and to stop at a hidden beach or two along the cliffs. Through a handful of short messages between the harbor and the Hôtel over the last week, they had settled on that particular day several days before, and the whole affair had completely slipped Nick's mind with all that was happening with Miriam. He had even forgotten to tell Burke and Elena to make preparations. He cursed to himself and shook his head in disappointment at his absentmindedness. He was letting things slip. But it was certain they had heard of Miriam's disappearance and his connection to her in the papers. Maybe they would understand.

"*Salut*, Michelle, Fabien," he called down solemnly. "I'll be right there." When he reached the lower deck, the couple had already climbed aboard. Nick felt uneasy that they were aboard.

"I brought some more of that champagne!" smiled Fabien as they shook hands firmly. "A bottle for each of us. We're almost done with the last case."

Nick shook his hand and then kissed Michelle hello. He tried not to show that he had already had several drinks up above. "It's great to see you," he said.

"I have not seen you since our party!" said Michelle. "I wanted to thank you for helping me." She said this genuinely, and he felt a little more relaxed with her. "Fabien said you were so wonderful to help me."

"Oh, of course," said Nick. "We were all very worried about you."

"I'm fine now," she said, smiling.

"Of course you are." But then, Nick knew he should get right to it. He could not have them there with Miriam back. Not even for a drink. He was just trying to avoid everyone right now. "Look," he said, "I'm sorry. I can't take you out on the boat today."

"Oh, no?" said Michelle. She looked quite saddened by this.

"I'm sure you've seen the papers," said Nick. "About Miriam Banks and everything?"

"Yes," said Michelle. "I saw your name in the papers."

"Well," said Nick, "I'm sort of involved because she had visited me before she went to Italy. The detective here sent a note down and said he wanted to speak with me. Some news from Rome," he said. He was making it all up as he went. "They think they may have found her staying at a hotel there, or at least someone matching her description. Sort of an emergency. I just found out this morning. I should have sent a note up to you. I'm very sorry." Nick knew he was fabricating everything, and he was hoping it all made sense. He hated to lie to his friends. But he felt it was necessary for the moment. He certainly could not have them aboard right now.

Fabien looked at him with understanding. Michelle was visibly disappointed and dropped her bag by her side.

"I'm very sorry," said Nick. "I really am."

"Ha!" laughed Fabien. "Next time, then," he said. "I'll take Michelle up to the pool, then, where she can get some sun. But," he lifted the champagne, "take these two bottles, Nick." He handed the bottles over. "Keep them cold and we'll have them soon. When we come next time. Maybe we can meet Miriam!" He laughed loudly. This last bit made Michelle smile.

"Of course," said Nick. "Thank you. Again, I'm very sorry. I should have sent a note. Michelle, I'm very sorry."

"It is all right," said Fabien. "It happens sometimes. Michelle will have fun up at the pool."

Nick nodded. He hated to send them away like this. "I will call you in a few days," he said, "to reschedule. I want to make it up to you. I promise I will. We'll go out and have a great day on the water."

"All right, Nick," said Michelle with an exaggerated frown, pretending to look more disappointed that she probably was. "I will hold you to your promise." She reached up and gave him kisses on each cheek.

Nick set the bottles down and shook Fabien's hand once again and walked them onto the dock. As he watched them go, he remembered something quickly and hurried after them.

"Wait, Michelle!" he shouted.

They turned and smiled back at him.

"I forgot to say congratulations to you both," he said when he had caught his breath. "For the baby. I heard the good news a few days ago. I'm very glad for you two."

"*Merci*," said Fabien.

"Yes. Fabien and I are so happy," beamed Michelle. She rubbed her tummy, but of course nothing was showing there yet. "I should not have been drinking that night. I did not know. I thought it was just the warm air."

"But everything's fine, then, with the baby?"

"Oh, yes," she said. "We had a visit to the doctor yesterday afternoon and everything is fine."

"Great. I'm glad to hear that."

"If it's a boy we want to name him Léon," said Fabien, "but Michelle wants it to be a girl."

"I want to name her Marie. I know it will be a girl."

"Yes, Marie," said Nick. "I hope so." He gave Michelle a hug and kissed her goodbye once again. Then he shook Fabien's hand and slapped him on the back. "Best to both of you," he said. "And to the baby."

"Thank you," they said.

"Again, I'm sorry about today…"

"Not at all," smiled Fabien. "Goodbye, Nick. *À bientôt.*"

Nick waved to them and went back to the boat to put the two bottles away where they would remain cold. He watched them walk down the length of the dock to their car and felt bad about what he had done. But there was nothing he could do. His first priority was Miriam. It always was. When they had driven away, Nick ran up the dock to the street to hail a cab with a familiar wave to the policeman sitting in the patrol car.

When he walked into the police station, before he could say anything, the woman told him the detective had just left for the Hôtel, and before she could say anything more, the door had shut and Nick was on his way there.

CHAPTER NINETEEN

Nick burst into the lobby of the Hôtel de Paris in a huff and found all eyes turned on him at once. The place was filled with people coming and going, many of whom he knew or had met at one time or another. He saw in blank faces that everyone recognized him, if not personally then from the papers. But no one came up and spoke to him. He cursed himself when he realized exactly where he was. In his rush, he wasn't being very careful. Slowly, everyone's eyes turned away, back to their previous conversations, and the murmur of the place rose again around him.

He looked around hastily but did not immediately see the detective. A short line of guests waited to check into or out of the hotel, but most of the people there were passing through with friends in the lobby or going to or from the bar. Nick found the concierge and inquired about the detective.

"No, *Monsieur* Duncan. I do not know about any detective," the man said.

"Short man...tacky suit," said Nick. "You didn't see anyone come in who looked like that?"

"*Non, monsieur.* I am sorry."

Nick thanked him and scanned the room again and found a deep leather chair in an unoccupied corner and placed himself there. From this spot, he could see the elevators and the front door and would know if the detective came or went. He observed the people passing before him and felt easier now that he went rather unnoticed in the corner.

Several minutes passed, and a young woman Nick recognized soon came out of the elevator landing; but instead of recoiling from her view, he half rose and waved to her before he could catch himself. It was Christine, Max's wife. Nick quickly fell back down into the chair and turned his face away, hoping she hadn't seen him. The night aboard his yacht where he had insulted her flashed in his mind. He would do anything to avoid talking to her right now. Any other day, he would have spoken with her and apologized, but not today. A few moments later, he turned back and watched her as she spoke with the concierge. Then, she turned and headed for the door. Nick looked around the room for her husband Max, but he was not there. He was glad for that.

He sat back in his chair and continued to scan the room for any sign of the detective. An older woman with an enormous pearl necklace carrying a small terrier walked over toward him and made him feel anxious when she sat in a chair across from him. He watched her for a moment and then looked away, avoiding her eyes. The dog looked uneasily at Nick and started a low growl. The woman set the dog in her lap and pulled out something from her purse and fed the dog from her hand. Nick watched her as she did this, seeing that the dog also wore a pearl collar, then looked away again when the woman looked up and met his eyes. She smiled at him, and he looked back and nodded in her direction. Then he looked away. The waiting was making him tense.

A few minutes later, Nick saw Max coming out of the elevator landing with another man. Max looked very serious, as he always did, and the two walked straight for the door. Again, Nick looked away and raised his hand a bit to hide his face, trying not to be too conspicuous. In doing so, his eyes met those of the woman again, and she smiled at him. The dog looked at Nick and growled again.

"He likes you," the woman said in French.

"What?" asked Nick. He wasn't sure if she were speaking to him.

"Charlie. I can tell he likes you." The woman smiled and petted her dog in her lap.

"Oh. Very nice," said Nick, but he felt even more uneasy at the attention and shifted in his chair.

"Are you waiting for someone?" asked the woman.

Nick sighed heavily and wanted to be left alone. "Yes," he said. "I'm waiting for someone shortly. I was supposed to meet him here."

Just at that moment, he saw the detective and his sidekick come out of an elevator and walk toward him through the crowd.

"There he is now." He stood and waved to the detective.

"Ah, *Monsieur* Duncan," said the man. "We were on our way down to see you."

"Great," said Nick sarcastically. "Hey look. Can we..."

At that moment, a man Nick did not recognize that had been walking with them rushed up to Nick with an arm cocked. Nick reflexively held out his hand and, grabbing the man firmly by the collar, held him at arm's distance. The detectives rushed to intercede.

"Is this the jackass who's hiding her?!" shouted the man.

Nick felt all the eyes in the Hôtel fall on him once more. There was a hushed pause in everything around him. Then, the man swung another arm out to hit Nick but could not reach him, his rage being much larger than his physical stature. Nick knew immediately that this must be the director that was engaged to Miriam. He held him away with his arm and turned to the detectives.

"*Monsieur* Winston!" the detective pleaded with his hands restraining the man's shoulders. "Please be *civil!*" He stressed the last word in his French accent.

The crowd in the lobby started to gather around them. A loud murmur surrounded them.

"This is Jim Winston, I take it?" asked Nick. "The director?" He had read the name in the papers and knew it was him from his picture.

"*Oui*," replied the detective as he reached up to pull the man away.

In the next moment, Nick, out of the corner of his eye, saw a flash of blonde hair enter through the Hôtel doors. Then he heard his name called with a scream. It was Miriam.

"Nick!" she shouted. She rushed toward him through the crowd and saw the man he was holding back. "James!"

Nick turned to her. At the same moment, the man in his grip pulled loose and put a fist to the base of Nick's jaw. Without thinking, Nick squared and struck the man in the face so that his whole body was thrown to the floor. The crowd that had swelled rushed back in alarm.

"Nick! No!" screamed Miriam.

The detectives watched without moving as the girl they had been looking for rushed up to the man that lay bleeding, holding his face on the ground.

"Oh, James!" she shouted.

Nick stood dumbfounded. He watched as Miriam rushed to console the man and kneeled down to him.

"Oh, James! James!" She turned and screamed to Nick. "Why did you hit him?"

Nick didn't say anything. He just stood there and shrugged his shoulders.

"Oh, James!" she cried. "Are you all right? They told me you were here." She was sobbing.

"But Miriam…," Nick began.

"Nick, don't!" cried the girl. "Just don't!"

"But…I didn't mean to…" In the next moment as he stared down to her, Nick found himself held back by the detectives and did not resist as he felt the cold metal handcuffs placed on his wrists. The old woman's little terrier had run up and was barking in high shrieks at his ankles. He just stared down at Miriam.

"Go away!" Miriam screamed to the crowd as she held her hand to the man's bleeding face. "Everyone just go away!"

"Miriam…," Nick began again.

"Go away!" she yelled directly at him. "Just go away, Nick."

"But…"

"Leave him alone! Just leave us alone!"

Nick looked at her vacantly. Instead of rushing to him, Miriam had rushed to this other man, this man she said she did not love. In that instant, Nick saw who she was— who she really was. She was not his.

"Let's go, *Monsieur* Duncan," said the detective, pulling Nick's arm. Nick pulled away absently, but was pushed away from Miriam through the crowd. He was still thrown by what had just happened before him. It had all happened in a flash. He looked back at Miriam who was bent over the bleeding man on the ground.

As the detective led him toward the Hôtel door through the crowd, there was more loud yelling from outside, and a moment later a group of photographers burst into the room. All of a sudden, everything was a blur of flashbulbs and shouting. Nick said nothing but looked back toward Miriam, whom he had now lost among the people standing around her. He was pulled through the doors and out to the street into a growing mass of bodies and flashing camera bulbs.

CHAPTER TWENTY

It is a misfortune to lose someone you love to the hands of fate. It is, however, an outright catastrophe to lose the one person you love most in the world when she turns herself against you. Nick knew that he had been tricked. Miriam had played him for it, and she had prevailed— gained something from all this, of which he was not quite certain. Maybe he would never know. Was it fame? She already had that. This had, if anything, given her that much more. Of course she wanted fame. She wanted the whole world to love her. But she wanted it on her own terms—no one else's. Certainly not Nick's. Maybe that was it all along.

Was it the pure enjoyment of using people to her own ends? Using Nick and everyone else as her little playthings?

Even Warren? Even her director? He thought that might be the case. Either way, she had done what she had done, and Nick had fallen right into it, completely and blindly. She hadn't grown up at all. Two years apart, and nothing had changed. If she had grown up, all the glamour and all the attention had taken it right back. She was a child, more so now than ever before, he was certain of it. He'd had her to himself, here, in Monaco, all over again. It was everything he'd wanted all at once. But it was spoiled now, and so was she. And what had it all come to?

Nick had a lot of time to think about these things alone in his cell. The detective had kept Nick at the station until that evening and then released him with his passport, as Miriam had returned and there was no reason to hold him once everything was cleared up. He had done nothing wrong except hit the other man, this Winston character, but the detective knew there was nothing else to be done. But there was the matter of paperwork that had to be filed and procedures that had to be followed. Authorities in Rome had to be called. As the detective said, it was "all quite necessary."

When it was all over, instead of returning to the *Diamant*, Nick left the station and walked a few blocks to find a seat at the bar of an empty Casino before the crowds came in for the night. This was where Warren found him hours later after hearing around town about the incident; and when he leaned on the bar next to him, he saw that Nick had already finished a half of a bottle of whisky.

"I heard about Miriam and this Winston fellow," said Warren.

Nick did not look up but acknowledged his friend's presence with an aggravated grunt.

"Too bad, mate. Wild time though, I'm sure of it." Warren slapped him on the shoulder and waved to the bartender to come over. "It's creating quite a stir, her being found and you being arrested and all."

Nick rolled a half empty glass between his fingers.

"Saw your picture in the paper. They've got you in handcuffs, of course. But you look fantastic! Real thug! We've got to get it framed."

After a few moments of silence, Nick tipped the glass back and emptied it.

"You're taking it well, I see."

"No more Miriam," said Nick, staring blankly at the glass in his hands. "Maybe this time it'll stick."

Warren lit a cigarette and offered one to Nick who didn't respond. He took the pack and shuffled the cigarettes around and placed it back in his breast pocket. The bartender came over with an ashtray and stood in front of them with his hands spread on the bar.

"Whatcha drinkin', Nicky?" Warren asked with a breath of smoke as he put himself in a stool next to him.

There was no answer.

"Whisky, I see. Marco, bring me a glass, too. I'll go the same way. Rub some whisky on it. Makes everything better, right?"

"Certainly." The man pulled out another glass from behind him and poured a drink from the bottle that sat before them. "But I think maybe *Monsieur* Duncan should not have any more."

Nick pushed the glass toward him. "Pour another one, Marco," he said rudely and knew he hadn't meant it that way. But he didn't have the energy to take it back.

"Of course, *Monsieur.*" The man reluctantly poured another drink and put the bottle below the bar, out of sight.

"Why don't you go sleep it off, Nick? You'll feel better tomorrow," said Warren.

"Just shut up and have a drink with me. I don't want to hear it."

They both lifted their glasses, and Nick downed all of his as Warren took a heavy sip himself.

"Strong stuff," said Warren. "Not nearly strong enough, but I like it."

The pair sat in silence for a few minutes as the first couples of the evening came into the Casino and went into the *salle de jeux* where the tables were waiting. Warren heard the dealers preparing the decks of cards and heard the clacking of the chips. It was a good sound. He turned to Nick a few times to speak, but he didn't know what to say. And so the silence remained.

"That's a nice one," Warren said finally. He was turned halfway in his stool watching the girls come in. "That's exactly what you need to take your mind off all this." He winked at one of the girls and waved to her as she passed.

She smiled. "I think her name's Vanessa. First time I've seen her this summer. Not the last, I can tell you."

"What happened to that girl Kate?" Nick grumbled. He didn't look up.

"Oh, yeah. Kate? Nice girl. Looks like her father had to go back early, so she left this afternoon with him back for New York. Hated to see her go. Always a shame to say goodbye to an impressive girl like that. Didn't bore me to death, for one thing. That's a first." Warren thought to himself for a moment. "I'll see her again," he said. "I'm sure I will."

Nick lifted his glass and finished the last few drops that had settled in it and reached for the bottle that wasn't there. "Marco!" he called.

The man came over and smiled at Nick. "Yes, *Monsieur* Duncan?"

Nick held out the glass and showed it to Marco as he turned it over in the air to prove it was empty. "Another, please, Marco."

The man looked at Warren and Warren nodded at him. "It's all right, Marco. I'll take care of him tonight."

The bartender poured another drink and left to serve other customers. The place was beginning to fill.

Warren continued to watch the girls walk by and all but forgot about Nick. Nick finished his glass in a few minutes and finally spoke.

"I'm getting the hell out of here," he said without looking at his friend.

"Where? Back to the boat?" Warren's attention was pulled from a girl in a glittering green dress he had seen walk in with another man. Her eyes had met his when she came through the hall, and he knew he would go up and talk to her the first chance he got.

"No. Out of here. Monaco. Away from the coast. I just got here and I'm sick of it."

Warren turned to him to say something and then went back to his glass and sighed.

"What?" said Nick. "What the hell is it? I know you want to say something. So say it."

Warren turned to him again and paused. "Don't get too damn cynical about this place just yet, Nicky," he said. "It's too early in the season. We've got a long way to go, mate. It's not even summer yet."

"Whatever," said Nick gruffly.

Warren turned back to the bar and turned his glass in his hands. Another minute passed, and then he burst out into laughter.

Nick, for the first time, turned to him. "What's so damn funny?"

"You!" he laughed and slapped Nick hard on the back. "You and your...your mood! I've never seen anyone so sensational. You'd think the world just ended, listening to you there sobbing over yourself! Jesus!"

"So what?"

"So what? So you lost one! Yeah it was Miriam. It hurts, I know. You lost her two years ago, too. But you just need to find a dozen more to fill the space. That's all it'll take. That's all it ever takes. Nick Duncan's never had any problem getting girls."

Nick smiled slowly at his friend through a haze of whisky. Then his face went serious. "It's not the same," he said. "It's Miriam."

"I know, I know. I'm sorry. I know you love her and everything. I respect that."

"*Loved* her," said Nick. "Past tense." He had already resigned himself to the whole thing, but he'd be sore for a long time.

Warren laughed again. "Oh," he said, "you'll be fine. There's no use feeling sorry for yourself. So what you going to do then? Go to Paris to find her? Go to Hollywood?"

"What the hell for?"

"I don't know. I don't know anything about this damned romance business. That's what they do in the movies anyway. Chase after the girl."

Nick grunted again. "Whatever."

Marco came by and slowly poured them each another glass.

"This'll put her over the top," said Nick.

"What?"

"This. This whole fiasco. The papers are going to eat it up." It was true. The American reporters had already called back to the States where producers were calling frantically to get Miriam under contract. "She can go to hell for all I care."

"Oh, don't say that. That's not what you want."

"Sure it is."

"No, no it's not. You just need some time. You just need someone else to take your mind off her." Warren nodded to two girls passing by and pointed them out to Nick. "Hello, ladies," he said. "You just need someone like her." The girls smiled at him and went in toward the tables.

Nick turned back to the bar and finished his glass. Warren was always right. This had all happened before. Two years ago, in fact. He hated him for being right. He tapped his fingernails against his glass, and it sounded like the chips in the Casino around him. All his movements were slow and methodical as though he were trying to prove to Warren and to himself that he wasn't drunk. "I know you're right," he said. "I just won't admit it yet." Nick reached to pour himself another drink, but Warren slid the bottle away just out of his reach. He could tell Nick was gone.

"Let's go back to the boat," said Warren. "I don't want you making a fool of me with all these pretty ladies around."

Nick clumsily raised his hand in protest, then blinked a few times and gave in. "All right," he said. "But I'm gonna open a bottle when we get there."

"Perfect!" shouted Warren. "We'll drink until we see fish!"

Nick smiled, then his face contorted. He didn't understand what that meant. But he stood to reach for his wallet.

"I'll get it, Nicky," said Warren.

"No. I'll get it." Nick thumbed through his wallet and tried to find some bills. Then he opened it and looked inside, and Warren saw that it was empty.

"Were you playing, Nick?" Warren asked sternly.

"No."

"Nicky?"

Marco walked over to them.

"Was he playing before I got here, Marco?" Warren asked.

Marco hesitated. "Umm…no, *Monsieur…*"

"Marco, tell me the truth."

"Yes," said Marco. "Yes, he was. But only for a minute."

"Nick," Warren turned back, "what were you playing?"

"Nothing."

"Come on, Nick. You weren't playing blackjack were you?"

Nick looked at him seriously. "No."

Then Marco spoke up. "It was baccarat, *Monsieur…*"

"Christ!" yelled Warren. "Baccarat, Nick? Jesus! How much did you lose?"

Nick paused. "Just fifty."

"Thousand?!" shouted Warren. A few people standing at the bar looked over at him. "You lost fifty thousand, Nick?"

"No," Nick said blankly. "One fifty."

"Christ, Nick!"

Marco had left them. Warren disappointedly reached in his pocket for enough money to leave on the bar. "Christ!" he said to himself over and over. "Christ, Nick!"

"*Grazie!*" the bartender called out to them with a wave as they stepped away.

Nick reached up to wave back and accidentally hit a man on the shoulder. "Sorry," he said with a rough voice. The man rolled his eyes and looked away.

Warren grabbed Nick's arm and led him through the crowd to the door. "Christ!" he kept saying to himself under his breath. "One fifty."

More people were coming into the Casino, and Warren wanted to get Nick out of there. The faces that passed by seemed to stare at Nick but were all a blur. Then, Warren stopped.

"Wait right here a minute, Nick," he said. "I have to say hello to someone. Don't move."

Before Nick could say anything, Warren was gone, and he was left standing against a wall near the entrance. The people stared at him as he stood there, and he nodded heavily at them with drooping eyes. But then, Nick looked up and saw someone he knew. But it wasn't Warren. It was Richard. Nick grinned.

"Hellooo, Sir Richard!" Nick called with a drunk, gleaming smile.

The man's eyes tightened on him. "Hell. I knew you were no good, Duncan," he said.

Before he knew what he was doing, Nick stepped forward and swung his fist at the man. Richard dodged it and, without seeing it coming, Richard's fist hit Nick in the face. There was a scream from the crowd and a loud clamor as everyone saw what was happening. Nick stumbled back against the wall and somehow kept himself from falling but knocked a large gilt-framed painting sideways. He got his balance back and stood square to Richard as he tasted blood in his mouth, with one hand on the wall holding him up. As Nick stepped forward again to hit him, there was a flash, and Warren came out of nowhere and hit Richard who went sprawling onto the floor. There were screams from the crowd as the Casino staff rushed in. Warren stood above Richard rubbing his hand. Nick, still leaning against the wall, slid down to the floor as he saw the man on the ground. The staff rushed over to Warren and grabbed him and held him back. Before Nick knew what was happening, he was being grabbed, too, and Warren and Nick found themselves thrown out of the Casino into the street where the evening crowd was coming in.

Nick landed on the sidewalk next to Warren and reached up to touch his lip that was already swelling and bleeding. When he touched where it was cut, he felt the sharp sting. His heart hammered with energy. He looked over and saw that Warren was laughing.

"What's so damned funny?" said Nick as he licked his lip with his tongue and spat blood. People were stepping over them to get into the Casino, laughing at them.

"I thought you knew how to fight!" said Warren, laughing. "You did a fine job holding that wall up, though!"

Nick stared blankly and then laughed to himself. The full force of the whisky was hitting him, and he felt himself about to be sick.

Warren stood up with the help of the crowd, and Nick found himself standing as well, without any effort. Two or three men had grabbed him and had helped him up.

"Let's get you back to the boat," said Warren. "You're gonna be nothing but trouble here." He stopped a cab that had just let a couple out and helped Nick in before getting in himself. Nick held Warren outside with his arm.

"I'll go alone," he said, pushing Warren out of the cab.

"No, Nicky."

"Yes." He pushed him out of the cab again. "I'll be fine. You go have your fun." Nick just wanted to be alone.

"You sure, mate?"

"Of course. Go!" Nick pushed him away again forcefully.

"All right." Warren gave the driver instructions to take Nick down to the harbor and see that he got aboard the *Diamant*. He slipped the man a large handful of small bills, and the cab was off with a rough jerk. Instantly, the sound of the crowd was gone, and Nick found himself alone in the cold back seat.

The cab made it a few blocks from the crowd before Nick shouted for him to stop.

"Let me out!" he said.

The driver said no and started to explain.

"Let me out!" said Nick. "I'm gonna be sick!"

The driver stopped immediately and pushed Nick out of the cab by reaching from the driver's seat. Nick stumbled onto the sidewalk, and the cab drove away in a rush.

When he regained his footing, the feeling that he was going to be sick passed for the moment. He breathed deeply several times and felt the world spinning around him. There was something cold on his warm face. It was sprinkling. He looked up in amazement as if he didn't understand what it was. He shook his head and felt the small drops of rain between his fingers.

Unsure of exactly where he was, he could see the harbor lit up between the buildings as he looked out over the narrow streets that cut back down to the sea. The road sloped downward, and he followed the slope because he knew somewhere in his mind it led to the water. As he turned to walk, he stepped through a couple he didn't know was there, and the woman shrieked and he turned to apologize, but they had hurried off through the starting rain. He stumbled on down the road where he thought he should go. A few blurry blocks later, he saw a car in front of him that he recognized.

"Warren's car!" he said aloud. It was a red coupe that was parked just a few blocks away from the Casino. Nick stared at it for a moment, confused. Then, he felt in his pockets and felt the keys he had meant to give back to Warren. He looked up at the rain falling. "Better to drive," he convinced himself. "Don't wanna get wet."

He approached the car and saw that the top was put up. He didn't remember doing that. He put the key into the door and turned it. Nothing happened.

"Come on!" he shouted.

He tried the key again and shook it around. It still didn't open.

"Damn!" he said. He stood there for another minute, perplexed. He bent down and put his face to the window to look in, as if that would help. "Damn!" he said again. He ran his fingers along the top of the window but couldn't get his fingers inside. He didn't realize it, but this wasn't Warren's car at all.

Giving up, he kicked the car as hard as he could. In the same moment, the car's brake released and the coupe rolled backward, coming to a hard rest against the sedan parked behind it with a crunch. Nick just looked at the car and stared vacantly without a word.

He stepped back onto the sidewalk and heard a party through some doors and walked into a bright building he didn't recognize. When he stepped inside, a man near the door saw him drunk and bleeding and pushed him back out and shut the door on him. There was another shriek, and before he knew it he lay on the street outside under the feet of a passing group. He still heard the voices inside the party, and he rose and tried to make his way back again through the door. But this time, two men dragged him outside and left him lying in front of an apartment building across the street. They threatened to call the police.

Nick stood up after a minute and brushed himself off and walked down the block, but there was no clue where he was going. He couldn't see the harbor anymore. The low orange glow of the street lamps was all that told him where he was. He recognized nothing. The buildings, the street names, everything was a blur. As he made his way further from the Casino, there was no one else on the street. No cars. He heard his own footsteps ringing loudly in his head. They were the only sound he knew.

As he went on, he heard a couple walking behind him, but he did not turn around. He couldn't understand what they were saying, but he could tell they were talking excitedly, especially the girl. They were walking faster than him because he could hear their footsteps coming closer; and then, when they were right behind him, he stepped into the road to let them pass. A car swerved and blew its horn. "Hey!" yelled the driver. Nick threw his hand up at the car and turned to watch the couple pass. He was certain he recognized the girl, and he made a motion to speak, but the words did not come. A few steps later, the pair crossed the street and was gone. Nick was alone again with only his footsteps and the lowering haze of the warm night.

A few minutes passed and he knew he was closer to the harbor because he felt that he had descended. But the need to be sick rose up inside of him and he stopped and knelt hard on the ground. He stared at the pavement before him, concentrating, eyes watering for a long time, but nothing came. He sat back on the ground against a wall and waited. His eyes blinked and he squeezed them tight. Before him, a fat black and white cat jumped into the street and scurried along. Another lone soul in the night. Nick lifted his fingers in the shape of a gun and pointed at the cat. He followed it with his eyes and pulled the trigger with the soft sound of a gunshot. "Bang!" he said. Immediately, the cat bolted away. "Got the bastard!" he said under his breath. He sat for a few minutes and beat his head slowly against the wall, humming something he did not know. But the humming felt good, and the soft beat of his head against the wall felt good, too. When a car passed, he comprehended what he was doing and laughed at himself as he struggled to rise. He turned for a quick second and thought he saw a figure behind him, but saw nothing when he looked that way. The low glow of the streetlights were playing tricks with him. He listened to see if he heard footsteps, but the pounding in his head drowned out everything else.

The light rain had ceased for the moment, and he looked up and thought he recognized the apartment building before him. He tried the front door, but it was locked. He could hear the sounds of music above and wanted to go up. He tried the door again more forcefully, but it did not open. A uniformed man inside came to the glass door and waved him away.

"I'm a guest!" Nick shouted above the night air. "I want to come in!"

The man shook his head and waved him away.

"I want to go up!" he pleaded again.

"Non!" said the man behind the door. The sound was muffled by the thick glass.

"Eh!" Nick resigned himself. He pointed at the man through the glass and squinted his eyes, then stumbled away.

It was a half hour later when he found his way to the dock through the tangled streets. The soft rain had come again, and Nick's head and suit were soaked. When he felt a droplet roll down his neck, he ran his hand through his hair. The dock seemed so long, and when he started walking, he didn't see the *Diamant*. All the boats looked alike. But then he recognized her and climbed carefully aboard the gangway and up the stairs. Up on the top deck, he found a chair at the table and a half bottle of wine already open in the ice box at the bar. He sat in the chair and turned the bottle over in his hand for an imperceptible length of time. Then, he brought the bottle to his lips and started to drink, but the smell of the wine brought something up inside him. He dropped the bottle with a smash and fell to the floor. In a moment, he was on his knees convulsing, heaving, shuddering, as if all the world loathed him, even the air he breathed. The whisky had finally done it to him. He couldn't hold back.

Several minutes later, after it was all over, Nick lay on the deck staring vacuously up at the stars. The night was clear except for the occasional passing wisp of a cloud, and when it passed overhead, it reflected the glow of the city, and a light sprinkle fell over him. His eyes blinked involuntarily and he coughed every now and then when his muscles tightened. But he opened his eyes and looked up at the lights above. They were stunning, pure, the stars were, against the black night. The sky was so clear. He had never looked at them the way he did now. His head thudded with the beat of his heart; his whole body ached. In his mouth he tasted blood, whisky, and bile. But he closed his eyes and opened them again and it all left him. As he stared out, the world and the sky and the stars above swirled around him so that no matter how hard he tried he could not make them stand still. Some time passed, he knew not how long, and there finally came an instant when he could focus on the stars no longer. He closed his eyes and felt the pounding in his head and let the night take him into its grasp.

CHAPTER TWENTY-ONE

I t was a Thursday afternoon. Nick sat alone on the deck of the *Diamant* in the cool breeze that came from the sea. The wind had died down, and the rain that had awakened him early that morning had moved in off the coast and had settled far over the French hills behind him. His head reeled from the drinks the night before. When he had awakened, he had found himself not aboard the *Diamant* but on another yacht one dock over. His torn clothes reeked of smoke, and his mouth tasted of whisky, vomit, and blood. An empty feeling had spread throughout his whole body while the blur of the night before played itself over in his mind, but he managed to get himself up in the bright sun and make his way to the *Diamant* where the bed and a cool shower brought him back. Elena threw away the suit and, when Burke saw him, he asked Nick no questions—not about Miriam, not about why they had not departed for Spain as planned.

Nick took a sip of a strong gin and tonic. It hurt his stomach and repulsed his senses, but he knew it was the only thing that would ease the pounding in his head. He had already had two. He might be sick again, but he knew he had to do it. If anything, he would feel better afterward. As he took the sip he thought to himself that he might lay off the drinking for a while, maybe until summer arrived, but only after he had had enough to feel better from last night. His lip was cut and swollen from the hit he had taken from Richard, but he knew Richard was hurt just as bad. Warren had laid into him pretty good. Just one punch. Nick laughed at the thought of this. He and Warren would have a good laugh over the whole thing.

Earlier that morning he'd had Elena send the rest of Miriam's things up to the Hôtel. If she had already left, they would surely forward her bags on to Paris and send him a bill. A thought crossed his mind in passing that he might go to the Hôtel himself, but he thought it best to leave things alone. As the day progressed, he knew it was best to do so.

"Nick Duncan!" came a familiar voice from down below. It was a man's voice, but he knew it wasn't Warren. That morning, as he had found his way back to the boat, he had passed Benicio on the dock and had nodded to him with a hello but without saying anything. Then, after he had walked on, he turned back and waved to him and called out to invite him for a drink later on. Like Burke, Benicio had seen the condition Nick was in from the night before but had said nothing. Nick was glad of it.

"Come on up!" called Nick. He was relieved not to be alone anymore.

Benicio climbed the stairs and found a seat across the table from Nick. Nick poured them each a tall gin and tonic. "Thank you," he said and took a sip.

"Is that all right?" asked Nick. "It's just what I've been drinking."

"Yes, of course, Nick."

They both sat for a moment in quiet and felt the warmth of the day over them.

"So tell me," said Benicio, breaking the silence, "how is Miss Miriam? I did not see her since my party more than a week ago."

"She's fine," said Nick. Then he thought for a moment. "I think she's happy now."

"Where is she? I wanted to ask her something. Is she below?"

Nick smiled at the man. "No. She's on her way back to Paris, I suppose. To finish filming."

"Oh, she's gone already?"

"I'm sure she is, by now."

"That's too bad," Benicio said. "I saw she was in the paper. I could not read the article—my French is no good."

Nick laughed. He knew his friend was playing inno-cent for Nick's sake and that he had read everything in the papers and knew of Miriam's return. He watched the man looking at his drink, rubbing his thin white beard over his tanned skin, darkened by dozens of summers on the Mediterranean now, and wondered if he had it in himself to look so dignified one day.

"I met a nice young lady myself," said Benicio, chang-ing the subject. Then he laughed. "I say young, but I'm sure she could be your mother. Young to me, I guess."

"Oh, yeah?" asked Nick. "So you found your lady then?"

Benicio looked at him, confused. "What do you mean?"

"Your lady. The one you said you were looking for the other night."

"Oh!" said Benicio, remembering. "I'm sure I had too much to drink that night. I was just feeling sad. But I feel better now. There is so much of life to enjoy."

Nick nodded. He took a sip from his glass and winced when the drink stung his lip. He could tell Benicio saw him do it but did not bring attention to it.

"We have a wonderful trip ahead of us," continued Benicio. "I'm taking her to Belgium with me to see the Formula One race in a few days."

Nick smiled and nodded at him. He was pleased to see his friend so happy.

"I am going for Juan Manuel Fangio. You know him? The Argentine driver?"

"No," said Nick, "I don't think so. Oh yeah, maybe."

"He was at my party on the boat. He introduced me to this young lady the other day after the race. Her name is Sophia."

"Very nice," said Nick. "And you like her?"

"Ah, very much so. We are going to watch the race and visit some friends of mine in Brussels. We are leaving on the train tonight to spend a few weeks there, and to see the race."

"Well," said Nick, "I may not be here when you get back."

"No?" Benicio shrugged. "Why is that?"

"Well," he said, "I just need to get away from this place for a bit, that's all."

"But you just got here several days ago. Certainly you are enjoying yourself?"

"I know," said Nick. "I am."

The man nodded and said nothing. Something told Nick he understood. Nick leaned forward and poured them each another drink. Then they both sat there in silence, admiring the brilliance of the day, despite Nick's pain. Benicio finished only half of his drink, then he got up to leave.

"I hate to go," he said, "but I have to go pack. I have not been on a train in a very long time!" He laughed energetically.

Nick rose and shook his strong hand. "Oh, it's just like riding a bike. You'll do fine."

"Yes. I hope to see you very soon, my friend," said Benicio. "If you do go, I hope you are not gone very long.

There is no better place to be this time of year! The summer is not far away."

"Thank you," said Nick. "I hope to see you soon, too."

Benicio shook his hand firmly and smiled widely at him. Nick could tell his friend was very pleased.

He went back and topped off his drink. He searched at the bar and found some more ice and another bottle of tonic water. As Benicio went down the stairs and onto the dock, Nick heard him speak with someone, and a minute later a young woman with long dark hair appeared on the deck before him. He sat there for a moment looking at her.

"Hello, Nicholas," said the girl in a deep French accent.

As he saw her in the light, he could barely recognize her. He did not recognize her face right away. A flash in his mind told him it was Miriam and that she was playing some sort of trick on him. Then, all of a sudden, his mind flashed with other images that seemed now so long in the past. It was Aurelia. He was speechless when he saw it was her. She looked even more striking standing there than when he had seen her at the Brecards' party when he had first arrived.

"I hope you do not mind that I came up" said the girl. "That nice man said you were here and you would want me to come up."

"Oh, of course," Nick smiled as he shifted in his chair and rose to greet her. "I don't mind at all. Welcome."

She was pretty there in the sun, wearing a short summer dress that showed her long, slender legs and the lightly tanned skin of her shoulders and arms. She took off her glasses and pulled her deep auburn hair to the side and kissed him on the cheek. "I'm sorry I didn't send a note first. I just returned this morning."

"Really?" said Nick. "I'm glad you came." He offered her a seat.

"I said I would see you when I returned from the trip with my father."

"Yes," said Nick, thinking of when he had last seen her. "That was ages ago."

"I know. Not too long, I hope. I only planned to be away for a few days. I had to stay in Geneva much longer than I wanted. My father insisted."

Nick shook his head and looked at her. She almost didn't seem real.

"What did I miss while I was gone?" she asked him. "Anything exciting here? Any good parties?"

"No, nothing really." He rose and offered her a drink.

"Please," she said. "I'd love one. I am starting my holiday again now."

Nick got up and looked at the bottle of gin that was nearly empty. He searched around the bar and found an unopened bottle of champagne that was still cold on ice. One of Fabien's. "Is champagne all right? I don't see much else."

"That's perfect," she said. "I love champagne. I love it very much."

He popped the cork in his hand and poured them each a glass. As he did so, he looked at her. He couldn't explain it, but there was something assured about her that he did not see in himself.

While the bubbles settled, he took out a cigarette and offered her one, and she raised her hand to decline his and then pulled out a silver cigarette case of her own. He lit hers, and as he did so he decided it was too hot in the day for a cigarette for himself. He put it back in its case and set it on the table beside him. Then he topped off the glasses from the bottle and reached up to take a sip.

"Not yet!" she said with a smile. "You must toast to something. It is bad luck!"

"Oh," smiled Nick, "what should we toast to?"

"Um," she said, looking around her, "how about to the *Diamant?* It is such a very nice place to have for your home."

"How 'bout to you?" said Nick, "and to your holiday."

"And to you as well then," she said with a raise of her glass.

They clanged their glasses together and took a sip. She smiled, but as Nick took a sip he winced from the pain in his lip. He moved the glass to the other side of his mouth and took another sip.

"Oh, what happened?" she asked. She pulled herself close and reached over and put her fingers to where his lip was split.

Nick glanced over her face and smiled. She looked and smelled so charming there, and he adored the feel of her fingers on his skin. He felt her brush his rough whiskers, and he remembered that he had not shaved in several days. "Oh, it's nothing," he said. "Just a cut."

Nick sat there and pondered this splendid girl before him. He was pleased she had come. He had not expected her and had forgotten about her completely with all that had happened. It was all so long ago. She sat there before him and played with the twisted wire top from the champagne bottle and smiled. The longer he looked at her, the more quickly the last week faded from his mind. Something changed within him. His disgust for the world diminished slightly. There was a new spark of brightness again.

"How long are you in town now?" he asked as he watched her pick up the champagne cork and turn it over in her fingers.

"Oh, I'm done traveling for a while. I want to spend the summer here if I can."

"You don't plan on running away like last time?"

"Oh, no. I hope not. I want to relax here and just sit on the beach and become dark like you. You look so amazing."

Nick leaned back in his chair. "So, if I'll be here in Monaco, I might see more of you then?"

The girl smiled at him and looked for a long time in his eyes. "I hope so. I thought about you while I was gone. I could not wait to come back to see you again."

Nick nodded and smiled at her. He poured their glasses full once more with champagne.

"You know," he said, "there's a party tonight up at the Hôtel."

"For Isabella and Alessandro Bianco?" the girl asked.

"Yes," said Nick. "You know about it?"

"Of course. The Contessa is one of my best friends."

Nick nodded. "I had them both on the boat once last summer. We spent the day off the coast swimming. Just a short trip. Just for the day."

"They are very nice people. Very pleasant. I have not seen them in so long, but I have known them for all my life." Aurelia took another breath from her cigarette.

Nick smiled at her. He watched the thin smoke rise from her lips and felt the drinks from that afternoon start to work on his headache again. "I'd love for you to go with me," he said. "I won't know anyone there besides you." He winked at the girl. "Would you like to be my date?" He raised his glass up to his lips and felt the bubbles tingle as he took another sip.

"Yes, Nicholas," she said eagerly, "I would like that very much. We will have such a wonderful time!"

The girl smiled and raised the glass of champagne to her lips. Nick looked at her there with the sun behind her so that the hint of smoke that rose in a thin white line from her cigarette before curling away in the wind formed a light haze around her. And, in that single moment, more than ever before, the hills of Monaco took on a greater magnificence than he had ever perceived. It was not just a solitary moment in time that would simply come and go that he truly wanted. No, it was something much more than that. It was what he sought endlessly each night, every time he touched a glass to his lips, every time he lighted a cigarette, and every time he opened a bottle of champagne, only to be left holding emptiness. The true splendor of this place, where the bright, lavish world met the limitless sea, showed itself fully there before him now, not in its own brilliance, but as a backdrop—a perfect canvas upon which to paint the fantastic pleasures of life.